Cock & Bull

LAURA BARNARD

This book is dedicated to my Grandma Breda and all of the Irish family I inherited from her, especially my cousin Nicola Cassells, who helped me with so much research.

CHAPTER ONE

'You've been left your great aunt's Cock and Bull.'

I look at my younger sister Ella. She seems just as confused as me as she stares back at the solicitor with her head tipped to one side, lips pursed.

She left us cock and bull. So nothing? No that can't be right, solicitors are normally posh, not people to use Cockney rhyming slang.

'Sorry?' I ask, blinking far too much. 'So... nothing?'

It would make sense. We never even knew Great Aunt Breda until we were called to attend her will reading. According to Dad, the only thing he's heard about her was that she had loads of cats.

In a way I'm relieved.

Me and Ella have half been expecting to be told we've inherited *them*. I've always been more of a dog person.

The reader smirks. 'No, I'm afraid you've misunderstood. You have inherited the Cock and Bull public house in Ballykielty, Ireland.'

Public house? Ireland?

'You mean like a pub?' Ella shrieks, her hand over her mouth in over-played shock. She starts bouncing up and down in her seat. *Chill out drama queen.* 'Are you seriously telling me we just inherited a fucking pub?'

I cringe. Why did she have to swear in front of this guy? The reader leans back in his chair, barely concealing his horror as he twiddles nervously with his spectacles. 'Yes. That's correct.'

We've inherited a pub? How bloody awesome is that? Not that we have time to run one. God, I barely have time to straighten my hair these days, let alone take on a business. But we can sell it! Me and Ella have been talking about buying a flat together for years, but with me surviving on temp jobs and her being a flighty fairy, it's never been realistic. Still, I've managed to scrimp and save a decent amount, not that it would get us anything in or around London. With the sale of an unexpected pub, we might actually be able to get a deposit together now. This is amazing news!

'Wow.' I gasp out loud as endless opportunities rush through my head.

Ella looks to me, her dark brown eyes bright with excitement. *Calm down Lassie.*

'We're obviously selling it,' I tell her and then turn back to the reader to ask, 'Has it been valued by a local estate agent yet?'

I'm already wondering how much it might be worth. If its anything like the house prices here, we're gonna be loaded.

He clears his throat, adjusting himself in his seat. 'Well...'

'Well?' Ella chirps. 'Well what? Spit it out boyo.'

I roll my eyes. Who says boyo?

He avoids meeting our gaze, his neck reddening. 'I'm afraid that your great aunt tried to sell it, but to no avail.'

What the hell is wrong with it?

'To no avail?' Ella gasps. 'What does that mean?'

God, she's dumb. If she wasn't my little sister I don't know if I'd put up with it. Sometimes it feels like there's more than a two year age gap between us.

'It means it won't sell,' I snap, my tone sharp. I turn back to the solicitor. 'How long has it been up for sale?'

He grimaces. 'Three years.'

I spit out my badly made cup of tea. 'Three bloody years? How awful are we talking here?'

Surely if it were in any way decent, a property developer would have snapped it up? Three years? Really?

He looks through some papers. 'Its turnover has been pretty dire previous to this. If I'm honest it looks like your great aunt simply gave up, closed up the doors, and put it up for sale. I'm guessing due to her old age.'

That sounds sad. She must have been so depressed right before she died. And with having no family, apart from us, the poor cow must have been desperate for company. I feel ridiculously mournful for the family member I've never met, who must have withered away slowly, day by day, by herself.

'So if we can't sell it, what can we do?' Ella asks, glancing around, her attention span already maxed to the limit.

'It's up to you.' He looks to me, obviously realising I'm the decision maker. 'You could simply leave it to rot, but I personally think that would be such a waste.'

'Surely *someone* will want to buy it?' I ask. I'm nothing if not optimistic.

He frowns, leaning over his desk, pressing his fingers

together. 'With the state it's in I doubt it. But you do of course have the option of trying to turn it around yourself. It could help the sale.'

'Run a pub?' Ella shrieks, fist punching the air. 'Fuck yeah!'

I roll my eyes at her. *Stop swearing in front of the solicitor,* I warn her with a glare, and then turn back to him. 'Where in Ireland is it anyway?'

'A town called Ballykielty.'

Bloody Ballykielty. I have no idea where that is. It's not enough to be in a different country, but it also has to be some little town with no doubt nothing going on. It's not like we can just up and leave everything to try and turn it around. I mean, I have a job. Well, yes, it's a pretty shitty basic temping job, but it's still a job.

At least I don't have to worry about leaving a relationship. Just last week I caught my boyfriend Garry in bed with his personal trainer. Sure, he was no Brad Pitt, and he didn't light fireworks inside my body, but I had thought he was genuine. I thought we cared about each other. Damn, I think I fell in love with the idiot. To find out it had been happening for months broke something deep inside me.

Unlike me, Ella seems ecstatic at the idea. She's pleading at me with her big brown puppy dog eyes. She wants this. Of course she does. This fly away fairy doesn't have anything to hold her back. She doesn't have a job, and she's still dossing with me, sharing my double bed in my shared crappy rented flat. I blame our hippy parents. They never gave her any structure and I'm always the one left to try and teach her about the real world.

'Come on, Pheebs.' She grins. 'We could save this pub, become badass landladies and then sell it for a mint! You've always loved watching *Homes Under the Hammer*.' She waggles her eyebrows. 'You *know* you want to...'

I suppose it could be fun. A new adventure. God knows I haven't had one in years. And really, what's the worst thing that could happen?

'Oh, what the hell. Where do I sign?'

CHAPTER TWO

Monday 17th August

*T*wo weeks later we're packed up and are driving the short distance from Dublin airport to Ballykielty. We've just survived the most horrendous flight. I know it was our first time on a plane, but the pilot had to be drunk with that landing. I thought I was going to die. Mum and Dad would have a fit if they found out we flew. Bad for the environment, they'd say. Carbon footprint and all that.

The only rental car they had left at such short notice was a Kia Picanto. It's so bloody small we barely get our luggage in. I'm used to driving an automatic so I keep stalling. My Sat Nav starts going crazy when we pull down a long country lane about an hour later.

'*Next...n-n-n-next....n-n-n-n-next...*'

I hit it with the palm of my hand. Stupid thing. That's what happens when you buy one on the cheap from a guy called Dave in the pub.

'That thing is seriously freaking out.' Ella giggles, her

feet up on the dashboard, as relaxed as can be. I'm sure I read somewhere that if you have a crash like that you can crack your spine right in half. Not that she'd care if I told her. She'd say something like, *if the universe wants that for me, then who am I to disagree?*

What I should be worrying about is the potential massive mistake we've made by agreeing to do this. Not that I am. Of course not. Well... okay... I'm a *little* apprehensive. I have £15,000 saved from being a thrifty bitch all my life. We've decided that if *really* needed too we could use that to make it more sellable. But I'm hoping that the solicitor was just being a big drama queen and its actually in an acceptable condition.

I grab my phone and start tapping away, trying to bring up Google maps, but that's on the blink too. What the hell is wrong with the signal out here? I know it's a country lane, but we're hardly out in the sticks. We're only ten minutes away from the motorway.

'What's the name of the road again?' I ask Ella who's contentedly staring out of the window at the passing trees.

'Cock Lane or something?' she says vaguely, not even turning to look at my slightly panic stricken face.

Cock Lane? We're moving to Cock Lane? That's kind of hilarious in itself.

'Right next to Loughdrum apparently.'

Loughdrum? What kind of place is that? I should have spent more time researching this. Instead I was going on a licensing course, at our solicitors request, quitting my job, and packing up our entire lives.

This road doesn't seem to ever end, it's just never-ending lush greenery. If I wasn't so stressed I'd probably find it beautiful.

Oh wait, I slow down to see a small turning. I indicate

in and see a tiny sign, stating *Ock La,* barely visible from an overgrown bush.

Good enough for me. I turn in and finally catch sight the pub at the end of the road. Wow.

And not wow as in, wow its fabulous. Wow as in, *"What the fuck have we gotten ourselves into?"* It's an old building with ivy covering most of the sign and door. The grass to the left is so over-grown it must go up to our waists, and the tarmac car park is crumpled and cracked with age.

'This is it?' Ella asks, her eyes as wide as saucers; her lips turned down as if she just smelt fish.

'I... guess so.' I swallow, forcing down sheer panic. Ever the brave big sister.

'Well no wonder it's not selling. It's a shit tip!'

I frown at her, but know she's right. We just have to hope it's better on the inside. I mean nature has to take its course outside. Of course it does. The grass and ivy can't just stop growing, and it obviously hasn't been maintained. Poor Great Aunt Breda; she died in this place, all alone. My heart aches for her.

'Let's just hope the inside is better.' I park us up and get out. The fresh air hits me. It's strange not smelling distant pollution. My lungs already feel refreshed. 'Come on, let's get our stuff.'

I turn and take in our view. We're right across from a small children's playground, and beyond that Is a stunning lake, its crystal clear water shining against the sunshine. Wow. So there's one good thing about this place. It's too far to hear the water lapping, but I already feel more at peace just by being close to it.

We get our suitcases out of the boot. Well, I get *my* suitcase. Ella somehow managed to pack three which I leave her to get out herself.

With the sun setting behind us, the place seems to have an eerie air about it. It's so quiet, no other people for what I assume is miles. A bird tweets from a nearby tree. I shrug the eerie sensation off, knowing I'm just being silly. It's just because it's the unknown, I'm not used to this much quiet. I'm better when I know what I'm doing. When I have a plan.

I wrestle with the ivy over the red door, managing somehow to get myself tangled in it.

'Ella! Help!' I cry, terrified it's one of those plants that only get tighter the more you fight it. I'm sure they exist. Or did I see that in a film?

She rolls her eyes and laughs. 'Honestly, Pheebs, you can't do anything on your own.'

She's using the line I normally say to her; sarcastically. Sometimes I wish I wasn't such a know it all.

She calmly takes out a manicure set from her giant yellow handbag.

'I hardly think this is the time for a manicure,' I snap. God, this girl.

She glares back at me, unzipping it and taking out some tiny scissors. Ah, I see. Although I hardly think they're going to do it. But within seconds of her snipping, I'm free.

'Thanks.'

I take the long ancient looking key out from my pocket and turn it in the lock. It doesn't budge. Great. It's going to be one of those weird doors you have to do a secret bloody handshake to get into. I start wiggling it, then jump up and down while turning it different ways.

'Stupid fucking key!' I shout, quickly losing my patience. I blow the hair out of my sweaty face. After a whole day travelling I just want to face plant a bed.

Ella sighs and pushes me out of the way. 'Let me try.' She turns it and as if by magic it instantly opens.

What the hell? Apparently it only works for fairies.

'Just needed some patience.' She smiles smugly.

I snort and push past her. The smell of wet, old socks and urine invades my nostrils. Ugh.

'Oh my god,' Ella gasps, covering her nose with her hand.

I start to breathe just using my mouth, but I can still sense the stench trying to sneak its way up the back of my throat and into my nostrils. It's so strong, that for a moment I'm blinded by it. When I count to ten and open my eyes again I can see that the dark pub is anything away from a quick lick of paint.

It's covered in big, ugly cobwebs; so huge they could be leftover Halloween decorations. It's only the very real spiders that confirm they're not fake. Gross.

The walls look like they were originally painted white but now appear yellowed with patches of damp. Ah, that'll be the bad smell. Some walls are wallpapered, but are peeling so bad a quick tug and they wouldn't be. The carpet is sticky under our feet. I trudge through it to lean against the mahogany bar, the only thing that looks relatively tidy. Well, under the cobwebs. I lean my arm on it and turn to speak to Ella, ready to give her a motivational pep talk. Only the wood goes from beneath me, and before I know it, I've fallen flat onto the floor.

Fuck!

What the hell happened? I clutch at my throbbing side. I can't concentrate on any other potential injuries because Ella is wetting herself laughing.

'I'm fine! Don't worry!' I grumble, trying to stand up.

'I'm sorry,' she snorts, still hysterical. 'But we're only here two minutes and you've already done a Del Boy!'

I think back to that episode from *Only Fools and Horses* when Del Boy fell through the bar, and laugh despite trying to remain pissed off at her. Our grandad always made us watch with him whenever we visited. That's what I remember when I think of him. *Only Fools and Horses* and the smell of cigars.

'Okay, okay, that was kind of hilarious. For you.' I glare at her. 'It just shows that even the bar is broken. It looks like we'll have to spend a lot of cash on just making this place habitable. And we haven't even seen the living quarters yet.'

'Quarters?' She laughs, eyes dancing with amusement. 'You make it sound like we're being kept here against our will.'

'Might as well be,' I mumble under my breath.

'Come on,' she says cheerfully. 'Let's go explore.'

Behind the bar we find the toilets. The ladies has tiles missing and smells stagnant. I open every window I find. We don't even dare go in the men's. The stench from the door is enough to make us nearly pass out, so instead we run screaming into the kitchen.

It's a good size, professional looking I guess. Industrial fryers, a thing to keep plates warm and three huge fridges. I daren't look in them yet. I don't have the courage. If I find a disintegrated cucumber from months ago I'll vomit.

We walk from the kitchen into a back room which seems to be the only living space. More peeling speckled wallpaper and more damp patches. Great, just great.

We go up a steep staircase to the upstairs area. There's two double bedrooms. The whole place is stuck in a time warp, seventies veneer furniture to match. Even the bed sheets are dusty. Thank god I insisted on buying sleeping bags at the airport. Women's intuition my mum would call it.

There's a separate toilet and the bathroom has bars on the window. Well, that's safe. Not.

'It's not that bad.' Ella smiles, throwing herself down on top of a bed. A dust storm swirls around her. Eww. She looks up, batting the dust away from her face as she coughs. 'I take that back. It's bad. It's really bad.'

CHAPTER THREE

Tuesday 18th August

I roll over and inhale a mouthful of dust. My eyes spring open as I cough, trying to free my burning lungs. Ugh, it wasn't a nightmare. I'm still here. I push Ella, asleep peacefully in her sleeping bag next to mine, wanting her to wake and be upset like me.

'What?' she groans, eyes still closed. I don't know why she's so tired. She's the one who snores like a walrus.

'We need to get up and start working on this shit hole.' I clutch at my head, just the idea of what we have to do giving me a headache.

'Coffee,' she growls. 'I need a bucket of it.'

I whack her on the shoulder. 'We've got nothing here, remember? Now get that arse up so we can try and salvage this disaster.'

An hour later we're both dressed in our messy clothes and are attacking the living accommodation after finding a jar of still in date coffee granules. Great Aunt Breda must have been a coffee drinker. I already feel closer to her.

The way we see it, we've got to live here first and foremost. We've dragged the old sheets off the beds and made a large pile of them outside in the garden. We really should get a skip, but I have no idea who the local skip hire guy is, and we don't seem to get any internet coverage here, so for now this will do.

By the time we're finished, we've basically thrown everything out. We've peeled off all the wallpaper we can and scrubbed down the damp patches to the best of our very limited ability. It's not like we can afford to get someone in to actually treat it.

We dragged up the carpet to expose wooden floorboard. They're not the best, but at least slightly more hygienic. God knows what could have died on that carpet. Maybe even Great Aunt Breda. Ugh, I shudder. Why did my mind have to go there?

All that remains are the beds and mattresses, which I've hoovered to within an inch of their life, and some basic bits of furniture, which I'm thinking I can paint and shabby chic up. Yeah, like I'm ever going to have the time for that. A girl can dream though.

We drive into town to find the local hardware shop and buy some paint to spruce the walls up a bit. Ella insists on getting a plum purple for her room. I decide for a more neutral light green. I remember reading somewhere that it's calming. I need all the help I can get.

We grab some bread, eggs and milk from the petrol station and then head home. By the time we've finished for the day, we're exhausted. We found some magnolia paint in the back garage and decided in a moment of enthusiasm, and eleven coffees with little to no food, to paint the sitting room.

Yes the paint is on the walls, but where we started trying to cut in perfectly, now its sloppy. I don't even care anymore. We crash out together on my bed, the fumes of paint creeping up the stairs and sticking in my throat.

'Do you think we'll suffocate from the paint fumes?' Ella asks with her eyes closed.

'Probably. But I'm so hungry and tired right now, I honestly don't think I care.'

'Oh well,' she sighs. 'Tomorrow we should probably try to work on the pub.'

What the hell have I done? Muscles I didn't even know I had are burning in protest. Right now, that shitty temp office job is looking pretty appealing.

'Oh and I found this note stuck to the front door,' Ella says, handing over a piece of paper, barely moving her arm.

We have Suki ready for collection when you are. Our address is below.

Who the hell is Suki? And collection? Have we agreed to adopt a child or something?

'Weird, right?' Ella giggles, although even her giggle sound tired. 'You better go and see who the hell Suki is.'

Ah, she must be one of Aunt Breda's cats Dad mentioned. Great, I hate cats.

Wednesday 19th August

I put Google Maps up on my phone as soon as I've driven out of Cock Lane and get some coverage. I need to find this house to collect Suki the cat.

I finally find it and... wow! Up a long driveway is a

double fronted detached bungalow, with rooms built into the roof. Its bloody enormous. Who are these people anyway? How can they afford such a huge house? I must google the house prices round here. I'm so nosey.

I park up and walk to the door, nerves tingling up my spine. For all I know this could be some sort of psychopath out to kill me and Suki is nothing more than a fragment of their imagination. I tentatively knock, drumming my fingers against my leg as I wait.

The door eventually opens to show a woman with a round face in her fifties. She's dressed up in gorgeous cream trousers, with matching kitten heels, a blush pink cashmere jumper and a piny on over it. She grabs the bottom of it to rub her floured hands on.

'Yes?' she asks in the cutest Irish lilt. 'Can I help you?'

'Err... yeah. I got a note saying that I needed to pick up someone called Suki? I think it might just be a huge misunderstanding.'

Her eyes light up with recognition. 'Oh, of course. You're Breda's family. I'm Kathleen. Come in, come in.'

She kind of reminds me of Mrs Doyle from those Father Ted repeats; eager to please. Not that I'd say that out loud.

'Do ya want a cup of tea? What am I saying, of course ya do. You must be knackered after travelling all the way over from England.'

I follow her down the hallway into a large, bright and sunny kitchen. Cookies must be in the oven, the place smells of heavenly chocolate and vanilla. She's already filling up the kettle before I have a chance to tell her I'm fine.

'How was yer flight?'

'Fine, thanks.' I nod. 'It's our first time to Ireland.'

'You're fecking joking me!' she laughs, genuinely stunned.

I daren't tell her it was our first time on an aeroplane.

'Have yer managed to have a look around yet? I know we're no London, but we've got a fair bit to offer.'

'Oh, I'm sure its lovely.' I nod reassuringly. 'But we haven't had a chance yet. Too busy trying to clear up the pub.'

'Yeah.' She smiles and gives a small shake of her head. 'Poor Breda was too old to keep up with it the last couple of years. She did the best she could, God bless her.'

'How did you know her?' I can't help but enquire. She seems too young to be her friend.

'She went to school with me mammy.'

What the hell is a mammy? Does she mean Mum? I nod like I understand her.

'They were great friends, but she passed ten years ago. God rest her soul. I don't think Breda ever got over it really.'

'And she never married?' I can't help but ask.

'No. Breda always said she'd be happier on her own rather than settling for someone.'

She sounds like a bad arse feminist.

'Well...' I look around awkwardly. 'We didn't actually realise that we were also inheriting a pet. What kind of pet is it?'

Please don't say cat. *Please* don't say cat.

Her eyes widen comically. 'You mean ya don't know? Oh, Jesus. You're in for a shock, a grá .'

What does a gra mean? And what the hell is she going to present me with? A lizard? Oh god, what if it's a snake? I've heard they start to stretch themselves bigger so they can eat you while you sleep. Not that I'd ever consider letting it out of its cage. I shudder, knowing that I've just stored a future nightmare.

'It's not a...' I swallow down the fear clutching at my quivering throat. 'A snake is it?'

A smile explodes onto her face and she throws her head back, cackling a deep laugh.

'Oh god, no! Can yer even imagine?' She slaps her knee as if it's the funniest thing she's ever heard. 'It's probably just easier if I show you.' She disappears from the room before I have a chance to question her further.

This is getting weirder by the second. I hear her heels click down the hall and then click back. Ok, its clearly just a dog or a cat. I'm totally over-reacting and reading all of the signs wrong.

'Here she is.'

I turn round to see her holding a black and white creature with a small face and big bushy tail. That's a weird looking cat. Wait. I move closer and see its tiny claws. That's not... it can't be... can it?

'This is Suki the skunk.'

It is. It's a fucking *skunk*. How the fuck can this woman be expecting me to take a skunk? They belong in the wild!

'A skunk?' I repeat, my voice high pitched, the horror hard to hide. 'What the hell am I going to do with a skunk?'

'Oh little Suki here is lovely,' she coos down at her, adoringly. 'Don't you worry about that.'

I jump away from them. 'I don't care if she can sing like Diana-fucking-Ross! Skunks belong out in the wild. I don't want a disgusting skunk squirting its bloody stinky juice all over the place. I'm trying to get people in the pub, not scare them away.'

'Calm yer boots, lady.' She chuckles. 'Suki here has had

her anal scent glands removed, she's no problem as a family pet.'

'But... why? Why on earth would my great aunt Breda want a skunk?'

She smiles fondly down at it. 'This skunk used to visit her every day at the pub and try to get in. She soon gave in and took her to a vet so she could have her glands removed. You'll find she makes a lovely pet.'

I scoff. 'I bloody won't! I'm releasing it back into the wild. It can just go fend for itself.'

'No, you can't,' she says, her eyes creasing with concern. 'You don't understand. Without her scent glands to protect her she's not safe out there. She'll die.'

Oh crap. I don't want the poor thing to die. I'm not a skunk murderer. Yet.

'Can't you just keep her?' I attempt my sweetest smile. She seems fond enough of her.

'Afraid not. My cat Semen just can't stand her. I've had to keep them in different rooms.'

'You have a cat called semen?' I ask with a choke. Why?

'Yes.' She nods, like she has no idea why I'm smiling. 'After that English footballer lad, David Seamen. Anyway, Breda would want you to take good care of her.' She lands her into my horrified arms

I glance down into its creepy beady eyes, the feel of its claws on my arms.

'Good luck.'

I'll bloody well need it.

CHAPTER FOUR

So that's how I find myself driving around with a damn skunk in my passenger seat. I keep staring at it, half expecting it to lash out and attack me. Those claws are something else. Just the thought of them makes me itch. I better treat it nicely or the thing could kill me in my sleep. Crap, where is it going to sleep? Should I buy it a crate like a dog?

I drive around town, using Kathleen's direction, to find the nearest corner shop. I'm shocked to see that once we pass the hardware shop it's a proper busy bustling town. From the way we travelled here, I kind of assumed we were in some kind of backwards village, but once you're out of the country part you've actually got yourself a cute little town. I mean, the shop signs still confuse me, and the whole place looks about twenty years behind England, but it's still cute.

I parallel park as best I can, which is still pretty shitty, and decide to leave Suki in the car with the window cracked open. I doubt they allow skunks in shops, regardless of their scent glands being removed.

I must remember to get her some food, although what the hell a skunk eats I don't know. Something else to google before I get home and lose signal again.

I enter the shop, grab a basket and head straight to the coffee aisle. We're almost out and something tells me we're going to need the biggest bag they have. I take out my phone but its dead. Damn it.

I grab some essentials and microwave meals that are on special offer, then head for the till hoping to God the cashier knows what skunks like to eat.

The cheery man behind the counter takes my basket.

'Are ya new in town?' he asks, his brow wrinkled, eyes narrowed.

Dammit, they know I'm an outsider. I haven't even spoken yet.

'Yeah, we just moved into the Cock and Bull pub.'

His eyes widen, a big smile back on his lips. 'Ah, you're the English lass. Breda's family.'

'Yep, that's me.' I nod. News must spread fast around here. Small town mentality. 'We're doing the pub up. It'll be back open soon hopefully.'

He bursts out laughing, clutching at his sides, like it's the funniest thing he's ever heard. 'Yer joking. That place will cost you an arm and a leg to get going again.'

I smile weakly. Tell me about it.

'Hey, Ronan,' a voice shouts from the door. 'Have you seen some muppet's parking out there? It's fecking hysterical.'

Oh God, they are talking about *my* parking. I just know it.

I hear his footsteps round the corner and I deliberately don't turn to face him. My cheeks are on fire; my damn pale complexion is unable to hide the slightest blush.

'God, it's got to be a woman,' the bastard continues with a chuckle.

He's suddenly beside me grabbing some gum. I see the cashier try to discreetly wave his hands to try and tell him to shut up.

'What's your problem?' he asks the cashier.

I turn to take in the imbecile. Some cocky gorgeous bastard with jet black hair and dirty green eyes. Damn, why did he have to be so good looking? He could give Adam Levine a run for his money; all broad shoulders in a white t-shirt and jeans showing off his long legs.

'Wait,' he says, staring between the cashier and me with a cocky grin. 'Are you the girl that's left that poor fecking car like that?'

My shackles raise, my nostrils flaring. The obnoxious bastard.

'Yes, it's my car,' I admit through gritted teeth. 'I don't see what kind of business that is of yours? Or are you the car police?'

He snickers, eyes alight with amusement. 'Nah. Just a concerned citizen, worried for the half-witted female that thought that was appropriate parking.'

My mouth drops open. The arrogant bastard. I can't believe anyone could be so rude. I thought the Irish were supposed to be friendly?

I grab my change from the cashier. 'Well, this half-witted female doesn't appreciate your concern and would kindly ask you to fuck the fuck off!'

I pick up my shopping, spin on my heel, slamming the door behind me as I leave.

Fuck the fuck off? Why the hell did words have to fail me then?

I'm expecting Ella to share my shocked outrage about Suki the skunk being our new family pet, so when I walk in and her eyes widen, not in horror, but with adoration, I could collapse.

'Oh my god! How cute is that! Where did you find it?'

'I didn't find it anywhere,' I snap. Does she honestly think I'd bring in a wild skunk? 'It's Aunt Breda's pet. Sorry, now it's *our* pet.'

She bounces up and down on her heels. 'Oh my god, really?' She coos all over it and takes it into her hands. I'm glad to get the thing away from me. 'I'm assuming her scent glands have been removed?'

I stare dumbfounded back at her. 'Since when did you learn about skunk's scent glands?'

She smiles adoringly into Suki's eyes. 'I watched a documentary on the Discovery Channel,' she says, before adding in a baby voice, 'Didn't I, Suki. Yes I did.'

'Since when do you watch the Discovery Channel?' Who is this woman before me?

She shrugs. 'Okay, well maybe it was on in the background while I was at Alfie's house.'

'Ah.' That sounds more like Ella. 'Well since you're so invested in our new pet you can work out where the hell it's going to sleep and what it eats.'

'You can sleep in my bed, can't you,' she coos down at her, the way most people would to a newborn.

'There is *no* way she's sleeping upstairs. End of story.'

She turns and walks away, but not before I hear her mumble, 'We'll just see about that.'

CHAPTER FIVE

Tuesday 15th September

*A*fter nearly four weeks of hard slog, and attempting to raise a skunk later, its opening night. The place looks... well it looks passable. I made a massive dent in my savings to do it up as well as I could, but the truth is that it needs complete gutting and starting again. We don't have the budget for that.

Instead the mahogany bar has been cleaned and has pastel bunting hanging from it. Anything to try and brighten the place up. It's so dark and dingy in here, even when its sunny outside. We've bought some cute little mis-matched lamps we found in the local charity shop which we've dotted around the place to try and add some light. It looks like they're going to be on all day at this rate. I dread to think of the electric bill.

The top of the battered tables have been sanded down by us and painted white. The chair cushions have been replaced with vintage pastel ones from eBay and over the door are twinkling fairy lights.

The garden out back and to the side is huge; we haven't even attempted to attack it yet. Well apart from putting more fairy lights up against the fence. We've almost run out of money. Especially as we then had to go to Costco to stock up on some booze. We kept all of the stuff that was within their best before dates and got barrels of beer delivered from the brewery. Ella can even almost pull a pint without it being just half foam. Progress.

'Are you ready?' Ella asks, hovering her hands by the door lock.

I gulp down my rising panic, putting on a brave smile for her. Always the older sister.

'As I'll ever be.'

It would help if I wasn't so sleep deprived. Ella refused to confine Suki into the garden in a crate, stating that the poor thing would freeze to death in the September chill, so instead she has free roam of the flat. Ella tried to encourage her to sleep with her, but the damn thing is scratching at *my* door at two in the morning. I've tried to ignore her but she cries and whines until I let her in. I barely close the door and she's nestled under the covers. Gross little thing is actually starting to grow on me.

I stand behind the bar bracing myself for the rush of people. For a week we've been handing out flyers and putting ads in the local shops. Everyone must be gagging to see what we've done with the place.

Ella pins back the door letting in a cool night breeze. I'm still getting used to the weather here. I thought the UK was cold, but the air in Ireland has a special bite to it. One you feel deep in your bones.

I wait. And then I wait... no people. What the hell? Where is everyone?

'Everyone must be wanting to make a fashionably late entrance,' Ella says, nodding as if to reassure herself.

Yeah, that must be it. I mean, we did decide to do it on a Tuesday night. We figured people would be bored on a Tuesday and looking for something to do. Now what to do while we wait...

'Shot?'

~

By ten o'clock there's still no one here. And we may have be drowning our sorrows in sambuca and Sex on the Beach cocktails, while dancing to Rita Ora. She just always makes things seem better, doesn't she? I think I'm actually hallucinating when two men in their fifties enter in tennis gear. People!

Ella looks to me, her eyes lit up in wonder.

'Welcome, gentleman!' she sings like Julie Garland from the *Sound of Music*. 'Would you like to try one of our complimentary cocktails?' She points to the tray of Woo Woo's waiting. We've drunk all of the Sex on the Beaches.

They recoil as if she's just asked them to shit in a bowl.

'No thanks, love. We'll have two pints of bitter.'

Oh. Well that's a disappointment, but then I guess we were expecting more women to turn up. I can't really imagine these two with a cocktail. The idea makes me giggle.

Ella takes charge, pumping the bitter into the glass, overflowing the foam into the basin underneath. She really needs to practise more. When she presents it to them they look less than impressed.

'So you're the new girls running this boozer, then?' the

one with greying hair asks, completely un-impressed as they hand over their money.

'Yep, that's us.' I smile, trying to be friendly, and sober. 'I'm Phoebe, and this is my sister Ella.'

'Well you've done it up all wrong,' the other man states with a frown.

I narrow my eyes at him. Did he really just say that? I just assumed he was going to wish us luck with our new venture. Not insult us. This *"Irish are friendly"* rumour is a load of bollocks.

'Excuse me?' I ask, praying desperately that I don't look as put out as I feel. I don't want them to know they got a rise out of me.

'It looks like my granddaughter's bedroom,' he scoffs. 'All pink and girly.'

Ella looks personally offended. No-one offends her favourite colour.

'And what the hell is wrong with that?' she slurs, attempting to lean on one hip but missing it and almost falling.

'They'll be others up soon.' They smile at each other, as if sharing an inside joke. 'The town meeting has just finished.'

God, right now? I could do with just closing up. I'm a little inebriated, and all signs point to the fact I've lost all my money on a failing business. I fancy just falling into bed and drowning my sorrows with a hot chocolate. Hopefully it'll sober me up too.

Only that isn't how it goes. Suddenly there are hordes of people coming in, each one of them giving their very unwanted opinion on the new decor. We work our arses off to serve everyone, but it's hard while you're under a Sambuca cloud. Nobody wants our trendy cocktails, it's just a load of old men who want lager or bitter, and women who want wine. We get no young people of our own age.

A portly man with greying brown hair in his fifties walks in, eyeing up everything critically.

'Hi, can I help you?' I ask, with a grimaced smile.

He puts his hand out for me to shake. 'I'm Fergus. Owner of The Dog and Duck. Thought I'd come and introduce myself. Check out the competition.' He laughs, as if the idea is so ludicrous.

I politely shake his hand, recoiling slightly when I find it's sweaty.

'Well, it's nice to meet you.' It's not, but that's what you say, isn't it? 'What would you like to drink?'

'Oh, I'm not having one.' He laughs again, his beer belly jiggling all over the place. He's so bloody condescending. 'I just wanted to let you know that *when* your business fails, I'll buy it from you.'

Possibly the rudest man in the world. I hate him and his bushy black eyebrows. 'You seem pretty sure we're going to fail.'

He smirks, exposing crooked teeth. It makes him all the more menacing. 'Oh, I'll make sure of it.'

Jesus, the devil walks among us.

I fold my arms across my chest. 'I hope that isn't a threat.'

He smiles, but it comes across more frightening than friendly. 'Just being honest.'

'Anyway, it was up for sale for three years. Why didn't you buy it then?'

It would have saved me a whole lot of heartache.

'I gave Breda my offer, but the stubborn old bat refused to sell to me.'

How dare he insult her! The woman is dead for god's sakes.

'That's my great aunt you're talking about,' I snap, glaring at him.

'Just make sure you don't make the same mistakes. When you're willing to take up my offer, call me.' He turns and saunters out, like he already owns the place.

What a pretentious arsehole. I wonder whether Great Aunt Breda refused to sell just because it was him, or whether he put a ridiculous offer on the table? I intend to email the previous estate agent first thing tomorrow morning to find out. Their details are somewhere in the mountain of paperwork the solicitor gave us.

I don't have long to think on it because people start complaining. Half of the pub wants the music turned up, while the other half want it turned down. It's basically impossible to please everyone.

I hear Ella yelling at the other end of the bar. 'How dare you! My beer is *abso-fucking-lutely* fine, thank you very much!'

I look down at the pint of bitter she's pulled. It's at least half foam. Oh dear.

'I'm just saying, love, you need to get rid of that foam. I'm not paying for the foam.'

God, how did I not notice him before? He's gorgeous. His plain grey t-shirt shows off how tall and slim, but muscular he is. His arms are covered with black tattoos. He leans further into my view so I can take in his face. He's got jet black hair and dark green eyes. *Wow*. Wait... why does he look familiar?

'Get out!' She picks up the pint and I know instantly what she's going to do.

Oh God, Ella, no. No, no, no, no, *no*.

She chucks the pint, of mostly foam, all over him. Shit, Ella. Way to scare the customers away.

I rush over and grab a tea towel, trying to pat him down. He smells good this close, apart from the bitter. It's only now it dawns on me that this is the arrogant prick from the local shop who told me my parking was rubbish. Maybe he did deserve the pint in the face.

'I'm so sorry. Ella!' I shoot her an evil eye.

'Don't apologise to this wanker. You're barred, mate!' she shouts, attracting a small crowd of onlookers. 'Get out.'

'Ella!' I scowl at her. 'Shut up. The customer is always right.' *Even if I do hate this guy.*

'Not this time. Go on.' She throws her arm back and motions towards the door. 'Get the hell out.'

He grabs the tea towel from me and dries his face. 'Gladly. I wouldn't stay in this shit hole if you paid me.'

Everyone watches him as he flounces through the door. Oops.

'Way to make a scene, Ella,' I chastise. I might not like him, but we're hardly in a position to be turning people away.

'Oh whatever,' she slurs. 'I'm going to bed.' She turns and runs off, leaving me completely alone with the crowd of people.

'Ella!' I call after her, watching her unflinching back as she ups and leaves me.

The crowd stare back at me, waiting expectantly for how I'm going to handle this. How *should* I handle this? I have no idea. I can't help but feel ganged up on, all of these people against little old me. Why do I suddenly feel like I could burst into tears? Hold it together, Phoebe. *Hold it together.*

A lady in her sixties goes to sit down on a chair, all the

drama obviously being too much for her. I wish I could join her with a pint of vodka. Really drown my sorrows. She sits down but something cracks loudly, before I know what's happening, she's hitting the floor. Shit!

'Aaagh! My back!' she yells with a pained cry.

I run round the bar. By the time I'm there she's surrounded by a small crowd. I look behind her to see that the chair is broken, snapped clean in half. Damn rickety old furniture, it's probably riddled with woodworm.

'I'm so sorry.' I try to help lift her, but she throws me off.

'Get off me. My back could be broken. You can't just have furniture falling apart.'

'I'm so sorry. I thought it was okay.' *Don't cry, Phoebe, don't cry.*

'Well it wasn't,' she snaps, clutching at her back as her husband helps her up. 'And I'm going to sue.'

She turns to limp out, the entire pub following her, casting disgusted glances my way. I sink down against the bar, pulling my knees into my chest. What the hell have we done?

CHAPTER SIX

<u>**Wednesday 16th September**</u>

I wake up hungover to hell. My head is banging and my throat is as dry as the Sahara. Suki is sprawled out next to me, her little black shiny nose pressed against my bum.

When I first thought about owning a pub I thought we could just wake up at 11.30 to open up at 12, but no. I need to re-stock the bar, clean it, get the cash out of the safe and throw away that battered chair. Ugh, and we could do all of that and still not get one person through the door. The idea is exhausting.

By the time me and Ella are opening up, I'm already shattered. Every limb in my body is crying in protest. I'm not used to all of this manual work. We can only hope that today is a good day, and we actually take some money. God knows we need it.

Ella managed to find the details for the previous estate agents so I go for a quick walk to get internet coverage and send a quick email asking what Fergus's offer to Great Aunt

Breda was. I shouldn't have raised Ella's hopes before I knew what the offer was, but with being hungover I wasn't thinking straight.

As soon as we unlock the door, two men wander in. Well, look at this! Barely opened and already we've got two eager customers. The tall one walks straight towards the toilet. The other short guy stands by the bar. I go round, ready to serve him.

'Hi, what can I get you?'

Now I look more closely, I see that he's not actually looking at me. He's staring past me. I turn around to see what he's looking at. There's nothing there. I look back at him. He lifts his hand up and looks like he's typing numbers into some invisible ATM machine. What is going on here?

'Err... are you okay?'

No response. Ella walks up to us, frowning.

'What's up with this dude?' she asks, not caring if he overhears.

'Sssh!' I hiss. I don't want to offend the guy. 'Actually, I'm not sure if he can even hear us?' I lean closer and wave my hand in his face. 'Hello?'

'He's fucking nuts,' she states

'They're from the looney bin down the road.'

Who said that?

We both spin to see the arsehole from last night sat at the end of the bar. Jesus, when did he sneak in?

'Are you a ninja or something?' I blurt.

His brows meet, obviously confused by my random choice of words.

'I mean, you snuck in here without me hearing.'

Tiptoed more like.

He rolls his eyes. 'I just walked in, it's not my fault

36

you're unobservant.' He has tattoos all over his forearms and hands; my gaze is drawn down to them.

'What are you doing here anyway?' Ella demands, arms crossed over her chest. 'I thought I couldn't pull a decent pint?'

'You're right.' He nods with a grin. 'You can't, but I thought I'd give you a chance to apologise.'

'In your dreams,' she snorts, hands on her lips.

I grab hold of her arm and whisper in her ear, 'Apologise now. We can't afford to lose customers.'

She throws me off her and stomps to where he's sat on a bar stool. 'Sorry,' she mumbles, like a child forced to apologise.

'I forgive you.' He smiles and shows off perfect teeth. Of course they're perfect. 'Now can I order a coke or should I ask your sister to handle that?'

'Phoebe! Your customer,' she calls, going back to asking the weirdo what he wants to drink. I begrudgingly walk down the bar to him.

'Nice to meet you, Phoebe,' he says, his voice a deep Irish husk. He smiles, all cavalier, leaning back on his bar stool as his eyes roam over my body. I half hope the stool will fall down. He has the most perfect jawline covered in stubble and cheekbones many women pay good money for.

I get a glass and start pouring from the machine.

'And what is it they call you?' I ask, with an equally smug grin. 'I mean, apart from the town arsehole of course.'

I can't help but throw that in.

He smiles, as if pleased he annoys me. His lips are annoyingly perfect and plump. Nice cupid bow too. Never seen that on a guy before.

'I'm Clooney.'

I burst out laughing. This guy must think I'm a real

idiot. 'Yeah, right. I'm sure your name is Clooney. George Clooney, right? Pull the other one.'

He raises one eyebrow. 'What the feck's wrong with ya? My name is Clooney. Do ya want to see my driving licence?'

I raise both eyebrows in challenge. 'You'd have to for me to even consider believing you.'

I know this guy's winding me up. I can see it in the amusement dancing in his eyes, which are actually more a forest green up close. If he kept his mouth shut he'd seem so dark and mysterious. Instead he's an idiot.

He looks to Ella. 'And there I was thinking *you* were hard work,' he calls over to her with a chuckle.

She turns and flounces away, having apparently given up on the guy still staring into space at the bar.

He thrusts his hips into the air so his crotch is worryingly close to my face. Ah, he's getting his wallet out of his jeans. Calm down, Phoebe. He's not trying to sexually assault you.

He takes out his driving licence and throws it down onto the bar. I roll my eyes. Not even handing it over to me. Rude prat.

He could still be bluffing and hoping that I don't pick it up. Fuck that, I'm checking.

I pick it up and fuck, his name is Clooney Breen. His photo is hilarious. His hair is longer and pulled over to one side. Total emo haircut.

'Nice picture.' I chuckle, handing it back and busying myself with cleaning the bar.

He smiles, looking at it fondly. 'I was going through my Justin Bieber phase.'

I snort. 'Please tell me you're joking.'

'Of course I'm joking.' He chuckles but then stares at

me with brows pulled tight together. 'And you English are always saying how dumb *we are*.'

My back's up straight away. 'Did you just inadvertently call me dumb?'

He stares back. 'Are you deliberately using big words so I think I'm wrong?' He smirks.

Ugh, this guy.

I shake my head. 'I don't care what your name is. To me you'll always be Small Town Arsehole.'

'Suits me, sweetheart. Although I've *never* been referred to as small.' He winks.

'Do *not* call me sweetheart. You don't know if my heart is sweet or sour.'

He grins. 'Ah you're right, so you are.'

The way they speak here gives me a headache. It like they add in extra words for no reason.

'Yeah, you're more a Poodles.'

'Poodles? You're calling me a poodle?' God, Irish people are weird.

'I am. You're more a prissy poodle, looking down your nose at everyone.'

'No I'm not!' I have to change the subject before he chooses to call me Poodles forever. 'So, what were you saying about those men?' I glance down to the one still stood at the bar.

'They're from the funny farm down the road. Out on day release.'

'Funny farm?' I scoff. 'That's not very politically correct. I'm sure you meant mental health facility.'

He chuckles. 'Okay, Poodles. If that sounds better to your sensitive English ears.'

'They're really let out on day release? Is that safe?' Could he be winding me up?

He shrugs. 'They've never caused any actual harm and most don't get as far as the high street. They just like to explore around and then they're rounded up to go home.'

'Weird. Are they on day release every day?'

He smiles. 'Worried about your business, Poodles? Don't worry, I'd say they make the place look more busy.'

God, this guy is rude.

A tall skinny man in a grey suit walks in and steps up to the bar. Thank God for the distraction. I walk over, a big smile on my face.

'Hi. What can I get you?'

'I'm from Environmental Health.' It's only then I notice the clipboard in his hands. 'I'm here to check the cleanliness of the property.'

The cleanliness? Shit! The bar might be clean but the kitchen is a wreck.

'Oh, well we're not actually selling food yet,' I try to fend him off.

'I'm aware.' He nods, no hint of a smile. 'You still have a responsibility to keep the premises clean.'

Shit. We're done for.

'Don't worry. I know my way.' He walks around the bar towards the kitchen.

'Um...' I push myself in front of him. 'Let me just clean up first.'

One of the weirdo's takes this moment to come out of the men's toilet holding a toilet brush.

'I don't know what happened, but the toilets after flooding.'

'What?' Blood hell. Just what I need.

The suit gets out a pen from his satchel and hovers it over his clipboard. 'This really isn't a good start.'

'You can't hold some lunatic blocking our toilet with a huge turd... or shoe for all I know, against me.'

He ignores me and pushes the door open into the kitchen which we've been using as a glorified dressing room. All of our make-up is spread over the kitchen counter. Shit.

'Well this isn't good at all.' He tuts, writing something down. Somehow, I doubt it's a smiley face.

~

Clooney disappeared while I received a full telling off. I feel like a naughty pupil at school. Ella only reappears, carrying Suki like she's some fashionable chihuahua, after the suit has given me a copy of our report. God, they're strict with rules. There's a list as long as my arm of things we need to improve. We also have to take a food hygiene course, paid for by ourselves. If we carry on like this, I'll have to use that emergency credit card in my knicker drawer.

'Where the hell have you been?' I demand.

She jumps at my tone. 'Sorry! I was in the garden, trying to figure out what we're gonna do with it.'

Daydreaming more like.

'Meanwhile, I was getting my arse kicked by an inspector. Is this how it's always going to be? You swan off while I do everything?'

'Woah, over-reaction or what!' She waves me off with her hand. I wish I could be as carefree as her. Even for a day.

'Whatever. We're not even serving food but we've still got to keep everything clean.' I'm getting a headache at just the thought of it.

She shrugs, arms folded over her chest. 'Well then, why don't we?'

'Why don't we what? Keep it clean? '

'Not that, dummy.' She rolls her eyes. 'Why don't we serve food. Hire a chef and get him to keep everything in order.'

'We can't afford to employ anyone.' We can't even afford to do the course.

'Well the way I see it we have to spend money to make money. Look at the location of this boozer. It's hardly a grab a pint on the way home kind of place. We need to make this a food destination pub. We could be loaded come next week!'

God, she's like a female Del boy. But maybe she's right. We could do with getting more people through the door. I suppose in this kind of business you do have to spend money in order to make some.

'Okay. First thing tomorrow we advertise for a chef.'

'Or Cheffer.' she smiles, completely serious.

'Huh?' God, she's exhausting.

'Well we don't want to be sexist. Include female chefs too.'

My God. How can I be stuck in Ireland with the one person who thinks a female chef is called a cheffer? Send help!

CHAPTER SEVEN

Monday 21st September

*B*y Monday we're interviewing for chefs. I still haven't heard back from the estate agents, so I'm not holding my breath on being able to get out of this place anytime soon. I was expecting a slightly bigger turn out than three people to interview for the job, but I suppose it is a small town.

We walked down the road last night and managed to get on the internet. Someone had written on a message board to ask chefs to make an omelette when interviewing them. Apparently it tells you a lot about a person. I don't even like eggs, so I have no idea how we'll judge them.

The first man hadn't been to culinary college, had no previous work experience and his omelette looked more like under cooked scrambled egg. That was an easy no.

The second applicant was a woman who stank of body odour. As soon as she came into the room we decided she was a no. We only had to look at each other. I don't care which food college she studied at, nobody wants food cooked by someone who can't even keep themselves clean.

The third applicant sits before us now. A long skinny man with glasses and a bald head apart from the little tufts around his ears. I don't get why men don't just shave it, rather than clinging onto those few pathetic hairs.

He's sitting with his arms crossed over his chest. I don't have to be a body language expert to see that he's not that friendly.

'So...' I look down at his CV. How the hell do I pronounce this? 'E-og-han?'

He grits his teeth. 'Owen.'

I'm confused. 'Oh sorry. It says here E-og-han.'

He clenches his jaw. 'That's how they spell it here, in Ireland.'

'Oh. Oh...of course it is.' Why the hell would they spell it like that? The Irish make no sense.

Well that's a good start.

'So... could you tell me a bit about yourself?'

I look to Ella. She's glaring at him like she just smelt gone off fish. So the feelings mutual; we don't like this guy.

'I'm a chef. What else do ye need to know?'

Well he's bloody blunt.

I look down at his CV. There's lots of pubs listed here. He can't have worked at all of them, can he?

'You've got a lot of previous experience here. Can I ask why you've never stayed at a place over a couple of months?'

'Because the owners were eejits.' He still has his arms over his chest, his face set in a grimace. This man is horrible. He must have been asked to leave every job.

'So what you mean,' Ella interrupts, 'is that you find it hard to get on with people?'

He narrows his eyes at her. 'Food is my thing. Not people.'

I glare at Ella, we need to at least be polite and not lower ourselves to his standards.

'Well, on that note can you make us an omelette?'

He frowns. 'That's it. You just want an omelette? Not something more complicated?'

'Yes please. Just the omelette,' I insist, my jaw tense. Right now I'd prefer to crack a raw egg over his head.

We leave him banging about in the kitchen and walk back to the bar.

'Well he's a damn loon.' Ella laughs.

I bite my lip. 'Yeah, but who else do we go with?' I reason. 'The other two are a definite no.'

She raises her eyebrows. 'We haven't tasted his omelette yet. It could be shit too.'

'Let's just give him the benefit of the doubt, yeah?'

The more I think about it, the more I think Ella's right. We need to be serving food here to bring in a crowd that's going to pay the bills until we can sell.

'Oi!' he calls from the kitchen. 'I've got your omelette.'

I grit my teeth and follow Ella in. On a plate in front of him is the most beautiful looking omelette I've ever seen. Dammit. Well, it might look nice, but it could taste awful.

I grab a fork and take a bit, popping it into my mouth. My god, it tastes amazing, and I don't even like eggs. Damn, we're gonna have to hire this tool.

Ella takes a bite and her eyes say it all. She agrees.

'This is amazing,' I admit. 'When can you start?'

'I'll start tomorrow.'

It doesn't escape me that he *told* us rather than answered the question.

'I assume you girls have a food licence?'

We turn to each other. Ella's confused face mirrors mine.

'Food licence? I thought if we hired someone you'd have all of your qualifications.'

He flares his nostrils. 'Jeyses, you girls know nothing. Even if you're not preparing food you need to take a food and hygiene course in order to get a food licence. Surely you've been told that.'

Oh crap. We just assumed if we hired a chef we wouldn't need to actually take the course ourselves. That was the whole point of hiring one In the first place.

'Right.' Ella nods, biting on her bottom lip, forehead creased.

'And... how would we go about taking these courses?'

He huffs. 'I'll give you the details of the course. If you're at least booked on we should be able to serve food in the meantime and not get in trouble.'

'Okay great, thanks.'

Look at him, already being helpful. He might end up being great after all.

CHAPTER EIGHT

<u>Wednesday 23rd September</u>

*W*ell the chef is... different. Okay, he's a total arse. Seriously, he doesn't even say good morning, he just grunts. He's a bit like a pit-bull, but his food is amazing. He's got quite a few customers through the door. Plus he's helped us book onto that food hygiene course and he does keep the kitchen clean.

After a fairly busy lunch time I tell Ella I'm going for a quick walk to clear my head. Get away from chef more like. It's annoying to admit, but on a sunny day it is actually beautiful here. There's still leaves on the trees, turning yellow and orange and waiting to fall. They rustle in the breeze and blow some of my stresses away with their sound. I close my eyes and take a deep breath. It's nice to get away from everything for a minute.

My phone pings. Ooh I must have walked far enough for my 3G internet to work.

I take my phone out and spot an email from the estate

agents. I open it up eagerly to see if they've sent the details of Fergus's previous offer. I scan down to find the amount.

Wait... that's got to be a miss-print. He can't have honestly offered that pathetic amount of money? No wonder Great Aunt Breda refused it. It would barely cover the savings I've blown trying to do up the place. What a bloody cheek!

I spin and power walk back to the pub, my anger quickening my pace. I throw the door open in rage and Ella balks the minute she sees me.

'What's up your arse?' she asks as I storm through to the bar.

'Nothing,' I snap. I'm too irate to talk about it.

'Well, we've run out of fifty cents pieces,' she says, slinging a twenty euro note into my hand.

I go to the safe to get some, fury still coursing through my veins at the cheek of Fergus. Jeez, this old thing is so bloody heavy. It takes both hands to open it and that's with my current rage generating some unexpected strength. I swap over the twenty euro note for the fifty cents pieces I got from the bank and go to shut it when the chef starts shouting.

I swing round towards the sound, but not before an intense pain cripples my left hand. I look down to see that I've slammed the door of the safe shut on my thumb. FUCK! *Fuuuuuuuuuuck!*

I try to open it with my right hand but I don't have the strength. It's too hard with only one hand and the other pulsating in agony.

'Help!' I cry towards the chef, my finger throbbing so bad I'm considering just chewing it off, *127 days* style.

He's too busy whinging about having burnt his finger. Bloody idiot!

I'm going to have to do this myself. I take a quick deep breath. You can do this, Pheebs. You don't have much of a choice. I use all my strength to wrench the door off my thumb and gasp in relief once it's free.

Oh my god, the top of my thumb is completely dented and pale, as if all the blood has been drained from it. The throbbing pain is unbelievable, almost blinding me.

I rush into the kitchen, clutching my hand. I need to alert someone before I pass out. I'm already starting to feel light headed.

'Help!' I hiss to the chef.

He looks down at my hand with raised eyebrows. 'What do ya want me to do?'

'Something!' I howl, now feeling sick and woozy.

God, he's useless.

I run out to the bar to find Ella. She's not behind the bar. Where the hell is she? She's never here when I need her.

I look around, but there's just that idiot Clooney at the bar. Damn. He's the last person I want to ask for help.

'Ella. Ella?' I manage to get out, my voice wobbly. God, this pain is so immense its clouding my brain, not allowing me to even form a sentence. My throat clogs. I'm going to cry any minute.

'Haven't seen her,' he says with a shrug. 'Been ageing here, waiting for a drink.'

Trust him to bring it back to himself. Can't he see I'm in agony?

'Need. Her.' I thrust my thumb into his face, unable to explain properly.

'Ugh, what did you do?' he asks, jumping up from his stool, his face contorted. I look down at my hand, the nail is starting to go blue.

'Safe. Shut. Help.' God, I can barely think, but I can feel tears forming in my eyes.

'You need to get to the hospital.'

'Duh!' And the award for stating the obvious goes to...

He grabs his coat. 'Come on, I'll take you.'

Dammit, where the hell is Ella when I need her? I nod, knowing I don't have many other options.

'Wait, I need to lock up the pub,' I whimper looking around desperately.

'Where are the keys?'

God, the pain is intense now. I'm going to pass out. I can see purple spots.

He takes one look at me and shakes his head. 'Fuck locking up. I'm sure Ella will be back.' He grabs my arm. 'We're going now.'

The next thing I know he's pulling me outside and bundling me into a Ford Fiesta. The only way to see through the earth-shattering pain is to scrunch my eyes shut and take deep breaths. I'm thrown around in the car, glad he thought to put my seat belt on. I chance opening my eyes to see that he's driving like a maniac.

'Slow down! I don't want to be killed in a car accident.'

His forest green eyes turn murderous. 'I'm just trying to get you to the hospital before you lose the thumb.'

'Lose the thumb?' I squeal, starting to feel sick. 'I could lose my thumb?'

A smile creeps across his lips. The sadistic bastard that he is.

'Okay, you probably won't lose the thumb.' He chuckles, like this is funny. 'But I'm guessing you'll be wanting some pain relief asap?'

Dammit, I hate that he's right.

'Okay, fine!' I roar. 'Just get me there.'

'We're here, Poodles.'

I ignore the ridiculous nickname, annoyed he's remembered it, and attempt to get out of the moving car, my nostrils flaring with rage. Its bloody hard one handed.

'Woah, what the hell do you think you're doing?' he shouts, grabbing my shoulder and pulling me back. 'Wait for me to park, you eejit.'

I hate how he calls me an eejit. I pout and throw myself back fully into the seat, clutching at my hand, seconds feeling like hours.

I impatiently wait for him to park. Annoyingly it is a perfect parallel one. I could never park that well. He runs around the car, to open the door for me, but his gentlemanly gesture does nothing to dampen my hatred for him. Not when he acts like an arse ninety percent of the time.

'Come on. I'll take you to A & E.'

I'd argue, but I have no idea where I'm going, and the pain is unbearable. If it wasn't for his arm around my waist guiding me, I think I'd be stumbling around like a drunk.

By the time we've found the desk and he's telling the receptionist about my injury, I'm starting to feel weak. It's like all my blood has fallen to my feet. I chance a look at the thumb and immediately wish I hadn't.

The nail is almost black, the thumb swollen to twice the size and the skin around it purple. Shit, he wasn't joking when he said I could lose it.

My eyes flutter, the blood suddenly rushing around my head. My head feels as heavy as a bowling ball, the effort to keep it up zapping all energy from me. I lose the battle to keep it upright. The last thing I see is the floor.

CHAPTER NINE

$\mathcal{W}$hen I open my eyes, I'm on a bed and nurse is shouting, 'Phoebe?' in my face.

'Huh?' I croak, my throat dry.

'She's awake,' the nurse says to someone over my head.

'Thank God,' someone else says with a big sigh. I turn my head to see its Clooney. An ice pack falls from my forehead.

'Did I pass out?' I still feel sick and as weak as a kitten. My forehead throbs.

'Yeah.' He nods, shaking his head as if I'm a massive inconvenience.

'Right,' the nurse says, pulling up a chair. 'Let's have a look at this thumb shall we?'

The second she touches it I jump and my other hand reacts, slapping her on the side of the head.

'What the hell?' She holds her head, her mouth hanging open in shock.

Oh my god. Did I really just slap a nurse in the face? What the hell is wrong with me?

'Phoebe!' Clooney shouts, a smirk on the edge of his lips.

'I'm so sorry!' My cheeks heat with embarrassment.

'Now listen here, missy,' she says sternly, narrowing her eyes at me, 'We won't take that kind of abuse here. It might work in England, but here in Ireland it'll end up with you seeing the guards.'

'Guards? You have security guards here?' I look to Clooney, my stare wide and wild.

'She means the police.' He clutches at his forehead as if I'm giving him a headache.

They call their police guards? Well, that's a bit weird.

'I'm so sorry. I honestly didn't mean to slap you. It was just an instinctive reaction. I'm just in so much pain.'

It hurts so bad. I really need to be nice to the nurse with the potential drugs.

'Instinctive if you're from a the mean streets of London,' Clooney mutters under his breath. Why is he still here? He could have just left me with the nurse.

'Sorry. I promise I won't do it again.' I smile, pleading with her not to give up on me. Poor woman's just trying to do her job and I'm slapping her silly.

She looks warningly at me before going closer to inspect it again. The second she touches it, my hand flips out and slaps her again, this time on the shoulder.

'Shit.' What the hell is wrong with me?

'WHAT did I just say?' she snarls, her gaze enraged.

'I'll hold her,' Clooney says, jumping up and stepping to my side. He grabs hold of my able hand. 'Squeeze my hand instead of smacking the nurse, will ya?'

I smile weakly at him. Despite everything, I am grateful he's here. 'I'm just crap with pain, that's all. Can I get some gas and air or something?'

The nurse sighs, but begrudgingly goes off to find some.

'Hey, why didn't she offer that to me in the first place if it was an option?'

He glares at me. 'Maybe because most Irish folk wouldn't be having a shit fit over a smashed thumb.'

My nostrils flare. He has *no* idea what kind of pain I'm in.

'Oh, well I'm *VERY* sorry if my injury isn't *Irish* enough for you! What would make you sympathetic? If I'd sprained my wrist drinking Guinness? Or been kicked while milking a cow?'

He lifts his eyes to the ceiling. 'God, you're a pain in the arse.'

I can't help but suddenly feel emotional. He doesn't even want to be here. I want Ella or Mum, and neither of them are here with me. The last thing I need is him making me feel shitter about myself. Garry's cheating already did a number on my self confidence. I don't need more men making me feel like crap.

'Then just go.' I throw his hand away. 'I don't need you here.' I even sound defeated. Do *not* cry in front of him.

He snorts. 'I beg to differ. You'll beat the nurse black and blue if it's not for me staying. That and you'll get yourself put into a strait jacket by the guards.'

'They wouldn't put me in a strait jacket.' Typical man, calling a hurt woman hysterical.

'Trust me, the minute you'd start talking they'd be sure you were insane.'

I bite down a growl, knowing that I do actually need him. How annoying, having to rely on a man. I ignore the burning at my throat, push back the stinging in my eyes, and steel my jaw.

The nurse arrives back with the gas and air. 'This

should calm you down a bit.' She has a hopeful look in her eyes before smirking quickly at Clooney.

I take a few deep breaths of it. It makes me feel a bit weird. My mouth feels tingly and almost numb. I feel a bit wasted, but a good wasted. Okay, let's do this.

'Right, make sure to hold her,' the nurse instructs Clooney. He takes my hand again. 'Here goes nothing.'

~

Three hours later we burst back into the pub to find Ella behind the bar.

'Pheebs! Where have you been?' she demands. Her forehead is puckered, as if she's aged ten years.

'In the hospital,' I huff, holding my bandaged thumb up for her to see. 'Didn't Eoghan tell you?'

'No?' she shrugs. 'I've been ringing you, but I found your phone in the back room. I thought you'd been kidnapped.'

'She could have been,' Clooney interjects, surprisingly hostile towards her. 'Where the hell were you? I've just spent the last couple of hours holding her down, along with two other nurses, so she didn't kick a doctor in the face while they cut her thumb nail off.'

Ugh, just remembering that scalpel is enough to make me vomit. My thumb throbs at the memory, my stomach wobbly as jelly.

'They took your nail off?' she asks, face recoiled in disgust. 'God, why?'

I burst into tears at the memory. 'There was too much swelling.'

She gags. 'No wonder they had to hold you down. Didn't you have any pain relief?'

'That's why I had to hold her down,' he explains. 'She kept saying the injections weren't numbing her.'

'So they kept piercing my fucking finger with that needle! God, it was agony.'

'What a nightmare,' she says, her face scrunched up in disgust.

Well she obviously wouldn't have been any help anyway.

'Whatever. I'm going to bed.' I just want this day to be over.

'You can't,' she says, her eyes panicked. 'We still have the night shift. We need to lock up, do the tills and put everything in the safe.'

God, just for today I really wish I hadn't got myself in this mess.

'I could always help out.' We both turn to face Clooney.

'*You?*' I can't help but sound horrified. 'Why would *you* help *me?*'

He scratches his neck. 'That's why I was in here earlier. I was wondering if you had a job going.'

Ugh, God. I knew he didn't just want to help out of the goodness of his heart.

'Just go,' I growl. 'We don't have enough money to be taking anyone on right now.' I turn, more than ready for my bed. The place can burn to the ground tonight for all I care.

'Then how about I move in?'

I turn to face him, the stirrings of a headache dancing around my temples. 'What?'

'Yeah,' Ella snorts. 'At least buy her a drink first.'

He chuckles. 'I mean, you can pay me with lodgings and food.'

I stare at him, trying to work out his angle. I'm too tired right now to care.

'Fine, whatever. Help out tonight and we'll talk about it properly another day.'

CHAPTER TEN

<u>Thursday 24th September</u>

*C*looney kept to his word last night and helped Ella with everything. Suki the skunk spooned me to sleep and for once it was nice to have her company. Almost like she knew I was wounded and could do with a cuddle.

Eoghan produces amazing food. There's no denying that. The smells that come out of that kitchen are incredible. Unfortunately, there's also no denying that he's an unreasonable, moody, arrogant bastard.

'Service! Service now!' He yells from the kitchen.

I look to Ella, both of us rolling our eyes. I know it's my turn.

'I said SERVICE!' he hollers.

Jesus, anyone would think the pub was rammed and he's rushed off his feet. It's only our second order of the day, and it's a cheese sandwich. It's hardly going to get cold.

I walk into the kitchen and force a friendly smile. It's hard after the restless night's sleep I had. It turns out I like to sleep on my hands. It's unbelievable how many things you do every day that involve your thumb. It still hurts like hell but the pain medication they gave me is taking the edge off.

Strangely I dreamt of Clooney's tattoos. I tried to focus on them yesterday while they were attacking me with the scalpel. All of them are black which somehow makes them appear classier. I remember spotting a butterfly, a dove, a rose and a song verse amongst other stuff.

'Did you not hear me calling?' Chef snaps, throwing a tea towel over his shoulder.

He looks ridiculous, all dressed up in his white chef outfit, blue apron and stripy hat. He's said it is kitchen regulation. Who am I to argue with him? I haven't a clue and to be honest, anything that stops us closing down is a good call right now. I must remember that when I want nothing more than to pummel him in his stupid face.

Word is ever so slowly spreading that we're serving food and I don't want to stop the good news from circulating. If we carry on like this, we'll be building up a small lunch time trade.

'Sorry,' I practically spit through gritted teeth. He still hasn't apologised for not helping me yesterday when my thumb was about to fall off.

'Table five,' he barks, not even looking at me. 'If you can handle that.' He's a bitch through and through

'What was that?' I can't help but ask.

I know I'm not supposed to bite, but he riles me up like no other person I've ever met. Well, apart from that Clooney guy.

Me and Ella have a theory that Eoghan was ridiculously good looking when he was younger, so he had never needed to or had bothered to form an appeasing personality. Now he's in his fifties, ugly as sin, *and* a miserable bastard.

'Just checking you're up for the job. God knows you've only been doing this five minutes.'

I clench my fists around the plate. Do not throw the plate at his face. There are no other local decent chefs.

'I think you'll find that I am more than up to the job, and that I am, in fact, your boss. It would be nice if you'd pay me a bit more respect.'

He curls his upper lip. 'I only give respect to people that have earned it.'

That's it. I just can't stand this dickhead anymore.

'You know what?' I put the plate down, my hands shaking with rage. 'I've just about—'

'Phoebe!' Ella says, appearing from nowhere and giving me the wide eye. 'Why don't you go tend to the bar and I'll manage things here.'

I actually bite my tongue and walk to the bar, my fists clenched, needing some time to calm down. He brings out the violence in me.

I watch Ella serve the food to the customer and then walk back to me with a knowing smile.

'Don't worry,' she whispers with a wink as she gets back behind the bar. 'I've got a plan.'

She'd have to have a magic wand to make me feel better.

'Oh really. And what is this clever little plan of yours?'

She wiggles her eyebrows up. 'We're going to hit two birds with one stone.'

'Please speak in clear English. I'm too tired and stressed to try and decipher what you're on about.'

'We are going to steal the chef from our biggest rival, The Dog and Duck.'

The Dog and Duck is the only other pub in the town and sits smack bam in the middle of the high street. Far easier for people to pop in for a pint. It's also owned by that cocky bastard Fergus.

'I cannot believe we're doing this,' I whisper hiss to Ella as we hang around the back that evening. 'Closed the pub and are waiting for a chef to come out to the bins so we can try and persuade him to join our pub.'

'Our *failing* pub,' Ella corrects me. She's dressed head to toe in black like that'll make us less noticeable.

'Yeah, remind me to do the sales pitch.' I snort.

'I'm just saying. Trying to remind you how much we need this.'

I grit my teeth. 'Ella, don't for one minute think that I don't realise the stakes here. I'm the one that's rinsed all of my savings on the place.'

'Don't do that,' she snaps, shaking her head, her jaw tense.

'Do what?'

'Treat me like I'm some little bimbo. Like my opinion doesn't matter just because I didn't have savings to go into this.'

Well, now I feel wretched. I suppose I do put her down and dismiss her an awful lot. She doesn't deserve my negativity. I feel like I've been in a bad mood since I found Garry in bed with that tart.

I take her hand. 'I'm sorry. I'm just hassled.'

'We're both stressed,' she says, flicking her long brunette locks into my face.

I hear the rustling of bin bags. 'Ssh, he's coming.'

She grabs my arm, her eyes wide. 'Just remember if we're caught by anyone you're deaf and I don't speak English.'

I watch as the chef appears, cigarette hanging from his mouth, carrying two black rubbish bags to the industrial bins at the back.

'Hi!' Ella calls, rushing over to him. 'Excuse me, Mr Chef!'

Oh dear god. What a way to start. He slings the rubbish into the bins, takes the cigarette between his fingers and stares at us.

'What the feck are ye girls doing back behind here?'

'We were actually hoping to speak to you,' I say with what I hope is a friendly smile and not a desperate grimace.

'Ah,' he nods, as if clocking on, 'you're the new English girls.'

I suppose our accent does give us away.

'What the hell do ye want with me?'

I clear my throat. 'We were wondering if you'd like to come work for us?' I ask with a hopeful smile.

He stares back at us, his face impassive. I think he's considering it. Then he throws his head back and laughs. Not just a little chuckle, no he laughs like he's heard the funniest joke in the world. Bloody rude if you ask me. Just a simple no thank you would have sufficed.

'This is a serious offer,' Ella insists, still hopeful. 'We have very competitive rates of pay.'

We do?

'How good are we talking, here?' he asks, his interest piqued. 'Because I'd only ever consider leaving here for double my salary.'

'Err...' Ella stutters, looking to me for help.

'We can do that,' I nod. I mean, I have no idea *how*, but I'd beg, borrow and steal to get him in the hope that he'll bring us in more money, and that I won't want to strangle him daily.

He barks another laugh. 'I'm only messing with ya. I wouldn't leave this place. I've been here five years.' He leans back over the fence. 'Here, Fergus, come hear this.'

Oh great. Just what we need. Some more humiliation.

'I've heard it all now,' Fergus says, appearing from around the corner. He meets our eyes with his icy hard ones. 'Just when I thought English girls might have some class, you girls go and surprise me.'

I sigh, an overwhelming sense of wanting to burst into tears and run home dragging me down. Only our home is in the pub that's failing. My flat mate Valerie would have found another flat mate by now. If I don't somehow sort this pub out, I'm literally homeless. It's not like I can rely on our hippy parents.

'I think the best thing for ye girls to do would be to cut your losses, sell up to me and move back to England. God does love a trier, but enough is enough.'

'Come on, Ella,' I pull on her arm, needing to get away from the humiliation.

She turns and begins to walk with me back to the car.

'Just like their aunt Breda. Mad as a fecking hatter.'

Oh no he didn't! My nostrils flare, my fisted hands so tight my nails are cutting into my palm. Before I know it, I turn and march up to him.

I point my finger in his face. 'You mark my words, you will regret underestimating us.'

I turn and walk back to the car.

'Great.' Ella sighs. 'So, what's the plan now?'

'I have no idea.'

CHAPTER ELEVEN

Friday 25th September

'*I* can't believe we ever thought we'd be able to get away with that,' I say to Ella the next morning as we're re-stocking the bar. We don't really need to, having only sold a few, but it beats the boredom.

She sighs. 'At least we can say we tried.'

We also got home to find Suki had chewed at the leg of one of the tables. Separation anxiety according to Ella.

'By the sounds of it he bloody deserves us stealing his staff. Saying we'd fail before we'd even begun. Cheeky bastard.'

It's just confirmed we'll have to put up and shut up with our chef.

'We'll be the bloody local laughing stock by lunch time. He's sure to tell *everyone*.' I rub my hand over my eyes, for a second forgetting my bandaged thumb. It zings with pain whenever I touch it. 'It's just so humiliating.'

'Yeah, it is,' a male voice says above us.

We both jump up to see Clooney leaning over the bar, that sexy cock sure smile on his annoying lips.

'How the hell did you get in here?' I snap accusingly. I was sure I'd locked the door.

'Breda hid a key above the door. I'm surprised you haven't removed it yet. Dangerous, that.'

'Yeah, thanks for breaking in to show us how unsafe we are.'

He rolls his eyes. 'Anyway, I'm here to talk about the job.'

'Job?' Oh, the job he was going on about the other day. It already feels like a lifetime ago. I'd completely forgotten. 'I'll say it again. We don't need anyone.'

He smiles, undeterred. 'I've told you I'll work for lodgings and food. And I have experience. From the sounds of it, you need a bit of local charm in here. The whole town is talking about you trying to steal The Dog and Duck's chef.'

I turn to Ella, narrowing my eyes accusingly. 'I told you.' I face him again, studying his face to see if he's genuine. 'Why would you being here be helpful then?'

Since Garry I struggle to trust people.

'Isn't it obvious?' His eyes twinkle. I have a feeling that twinkle turns a lot of perfectly intelligent women stupid. 'I'm loved around here. You get me behind the bar and your takings will be up within the week.'

I scoff. He's such a pompous dick. 'You are so bloody full of yourself, it's ridiculous.'

'Ooi!' someone shouts behind us. We all turn to see Chef walking in, his face red and blotchy, his eyes squinted. Jesus, what's happened to him? 'You two. English dickheads.'

Woah, did he actually just call us dickheads? To our face? We're women. How rude.

He rolls his lip, basically snarling at us like a wolf. 'The whole fecking town is talking about you trying to recruit another chef. I've never been so fecking mad in all my life.'

'Alright, mate,' Clooney says, standing protectively in front of us. 'No need for that.'

'There's every need for it, Clooney!' He peers round his broad chest. 'You bitches can stick your fecking job where the sun don't shine.' He throws his uniform down on the bar and storms out, slamming the door behind him.

Well shit. Now we don't have *any* chef. Just when we thought we might be turning a corner and actually making some profit eventually.

'So,' Clooney says, a shit eating grin on his face. 'Looks like you'll be needing a new chef. Seems like I'm moving in at just the right time.'

I grit my teeth. 'I can't just give you the job. I'll have to interview you first.'

He grabs a bar stool and perches on it, without a care in the world. It's infuriating how sexy he looks doing it, those muscles on his arms moving under the tribal looking tattoos. Luckily I could never fancy someone so sure of themselves. Garry was a little shy and he still ended up doing the dirty on me. A guy like this must have a different woman every night.

'Fire away, Poodles.'

Poodles? Really. Why does he feel the need to call me that, dammit? All I need is this idiot winding me up twenty four seven.

I square my shoulders and attempt to be professional.

'Mr...' shit, I can't remember his surname.

'Breen,' he adds for me, a sweet yet mocking smile on his face. He knows I'm out of my depth. He can smell the fear, like a pit-bull.

'Breen,' I repeat with a nod of my head. 'Right, I'll need to ask you some questions.'

He rolls his eyes. See, right there is exactly why I should never employ this guy. He has no respect for anyone.

'Did you bring a CV with you?' I ask, trying to sound as official as possible.

I look up to see him staring at me incredulously. 'Do I have to have a CV for working in a boozer?'

'Yes,' I snap. I just have the overwhelming urge to pummel him in the face. 'I need to know about any previous experience.'

He nods. 'Well I can tell you that. I've worked all me life in The Dog and Duck.'

'Our rival pub?' Ella asks, her forehead puckered.

I shoot her a quick *calm down* look. It *is* the only other pub in town.

'You mean from turning eighteen, I assume.'

'Sure,' he says with a shrug like he finds me annoying.

'Can I get a reference from there?' Not that I actually want to speak to that man Fergus ever again.

'Probably not.' He smiles, as if keeping a secret. 'You see, the reason I left is a bit of a sore point.'

So he *is* the irresponsible dickhead I had him down for.

'Set the place on fire, did you?' I snarl, a smile edging my lips.

'No, actually,' he retorts, looking like he wants to stick his tongue out at me. 'I just fell out with the owner.'

'Oh.' Finally something I agree with. 'Well, I can understand that. The man's an arsehole.'

'Hey, don't speak about me Da like that!'

My mouth drops open. 'Your Da? Oh, wait, do you mean your dad? He's your *dad*?'

'Yes.' He nods, as if it's no big deal. 'He's my dad.'

He's the rivals son. What the hell is going on here? I call bullshit. This is such a set up. He's clearly been sent here to spy on us.

'So you expect me to believe that the rival pub owners's son wants to work *here?*'

He frowns, as if not understanding why that would be a problem. 'Yeah.'

Ella puts her hand on her jutted out hip. 'So you're not being sent here as a spy?'

'Jesus, no.' He sighs, like *we* are massive pains in the arse. 'I've fallen out with me Da and I need a new job and place to live. This place kills two birds with one stone. I could do this job with my eyes closed.' He looks to me. 'Far better than you and that fairy sister of yours.'

'Hey!' Me and Ella shriek in unison. I'm the only one allowed to call her a fairy.

'I'm not going to give you the job if you're just gonna slag us off the whole time.'

He sighs heavily, suddenly appearing tired. 'Look, I need a job. I guarantee you'll go through every eejit in the town and I'm your best bet.'

God, I hate how he's right. Plus, I did like how he tried to protect us when Chef—ex Chef—lost the plot. I hate to admit it, but it would be nice to have a man around. Just in case anything happened. Booze and people can be a terrifying combination. Garry used to turn quite nasty after too much to drink.

'All I ask is that I have Tuesday nights off.'

I look to Ella. She folds her hands over her chest and shrugs. I can't believe I'm going to hire this tool.

'Okay, fine. The jobs yours. But I warn you now.' I stick my finger at his chest. 'If I find out you've been feeding information back to your dad I'll kill you. They say a woman scorned and all that, well they've never been scorned by a Bellerose sister. Let me tell you, you don't want to find out.'

Ella shoots warning devil eyes at him.

He puts his palms up in defeat. 'Consider me warned.'

'And no bringing women home.'

'Fine,' he forces out through gritted teeth. He sighs, as if pulling himself out of his bad mood. 'And if this sweetens the deal, I can tell you that Dad's been telling anyone who'll listen that you're barmy, just like your Aunt Breda.

'What?' My nostrils flare. Yes, I might not have ever met her in the flesh, but damn it, she's family and no one should talk about anyone like that.

'That's it. This is WAR.'

CHAPTER TWELVE

<u>Monday 28th September</u>

*C*looney is just getting himself acquainted with the kitchen the following Monday when a short heavy-set man with a clipboard turns up. Not another clipboard guy. They're never bearing good news.

'Health Inspector,' he announces. 'My colleague was here the other day. I'm sorry to say that there's been reports of rats on the premises.'

I scoff a laugh. 'Really? Rats? Who the hell...' I trail off as I realise exactly who would have told them that. That bastard Fergus from The Dog and Duck.

'I'll need to see your kitchen immediately.' He pushes past me and walks towards the back.

I run in front of him and open the swing door to see Clooney walking towards me, his eyes grave.

'Phoebe, there's a—'

He's about to show me something when I shout at the top of my lungs 'Inspection! There's an Inspection Officer here.'

He quickly puts whatever he was about to show me behind his back.

'Ah, hi Lenny.' He puts on his cock sure smile, which I'm confident regular people find charming.

Lenny smiles back. 'Clooney.' He nods. 'I didn't know you were working here.'

'Yeah, brand new. Mind, is this just a regular inspection or...?'

'We've had a report of rats,' Lenny says, already inspecting the shelves.

'Rats,' Clooney repeats, shooting me wide worried eyes. He flicks his jaw behind him.

I follow it to see him holding a dead rat in his hands behind his back. Dear fucking god! We *do* have rats! How the hell did that happen? And why oh why does he have to be holding a dead one while we're being inspected?

I raise my eyebrows at Clooney, cricking my neck to the left to try and signal for him to get it the hell out of here.

'Clooney,' Lenny says, making us both jump. 'I'll need you to show me round the kitchen.'

'Well, I'm still learning the ropes, myself actually, Lenny.'

'Still,' he insists. 'If you're going to be in charge of the kitchen I'm going to need to talk to you.'

He looks expectantly at him. Well shit, he can hardly show him around with a dead rat in his hands.

I'm going to have to... *gulp*... take the dead rat from him. Ugh, I can see its slimy tail. It's the grossest thing I've ever seen. I fight the urge to jump up and down on the spot screaming. Where the hell is Ella when I need her? I know she'd find it cute and cuddle it before holding a funeral and burying it in the back garden.

She's not here though. I need to suck it up and get on

with it. For both our sakes. I can't have us being shut down before we've even got going properly.

I stand right next to Clooney. I need to distract Lenny somehow. I place one hand behind my back and then point to something behind Lenny.

'Look!' He turns and I quickly try to take the rat from Clooney's hands. Ugh, it's still warm. I shudder from the feeling, unable to take it from him.

Lenny turns back. 'What? I can't see anything.'

'Sorry,' I try and joke. 'Thought I saw a rat.'

His eyes flash in horror. 'I thought you said you don't have a rat infestation?'

'Oh, we don't. Just trying to be funny. That weird English sense of humour of mine.' *What the hell is wrong with me?*

He quirks one eyebrow up, obviously finding me a bizarre weirdo.

'Lenny, can you please...' Quick Phoebe, think of *something*. 'Tell me your qualifications for this job?' Anything to keep him talking so I can get this dead bloody rat in my hands.

He steels his jaw, obviously shocked at the audacity of the English woman asking. He starts rambling off his qualifications while Clooney places the dead rat carefully into my squirmy hands. His fingers touch mine and I grimace. It feels strangely intimate to be touching him, which I realise is ridiculous. The man has held me down while I got my thumb fixed. The awkwardness almost distracts me from the dead thing in my hands. It's hard to clutch it with my bandaged thumb. It's heavier than I thought it would be.

When I have hold of it, I nod at a rather bemused Clooney.

'Actually, Clooney,' Lenny says. 'Have you completed a food and hygiene course?'

'Err...' he looks to me. 'No. I didn't actually get one.'

He shakes his head, making a note on his clipboard. 'Well then we'll have to book you on before you can be serving food.'

Crap I didn't even think to ask if he had that. Perfect time to run away, while he's distracted.

I turn and run through the pub, out the door and down to the lake. I throw the dead rat into the bushes and then before I can rationalise with myself, I run down the short pier and jump into the water, needing to feel clean again.

I plunge down deep into freezing, cold darkness and scramble to emerge, quickly realising this was a stupid idea. I finally open my mouth and gasp in some oxygen to my burning lungs. That's when everything hits me all at once; the dead rat in my hands, the leaving England, being tied to this failing pub, humiliated in front of the town, having my thumb nail cut off, Garry cheating on me, probably getting shut down by health and safety. It's all so un-bloody fair.

I throw my head back and let out a scream. An ear piercing screech that echoes around the trees and off into the distance. I'm out of breath from the exertion but feel strangely better. It was quite satisfying.

I swim, my limbs heavy and tired, to the edge and struggle to get out. It's not easy with my wet clothes weighing me down. It's not like it has a convenient ladder or anything. I have to throw myself onto the wooded pier and drag myself up.

I'm so exhausted once I've lifted myself out, I just lay on my back and stare up at the clouded sky, trying to catch my breath. I've never felt so hopeless in my life. My whole life

I've battled and sought out responsibility, but now I feel it crushing against my shoulders, dragging me to the floor.

I don't think I could stand if I wanted to. Not that I do. Right now I'm content with just staring at the grey clouds. I don't believe in God, my parents insisted that I wasn't to buy into a mass-produced religion only there to make us feel guilty, but sometimes, I really wish I did. Wish I could tell some stranger in the sky all of my problems and feel a glimmer of hope that someone is trying to sort shit out for me.

Instead I just have myself to rely on. Always myself. Sometimes I wish I had someone. Someone stronger than Ella, who I could rely on for a change. I can't rely on our parents that's for sure.

'Phoebe!' I hear my name shouted in the distance.

I attempt weakly to raise my head, but I can't be bothered. Every bone in my body is tired of forcing myself through this bullshit we call a life.

'Phoebe!' A voice calls again, this time closer. 'Shit, Phoebe!'

I turn to face the voice, but a shadow is already leaning over me. I look up to see Clooney frowning down at me.

'Shit, you're freezing. Did you fall in?' He takes his leather jacket off and wraps it round me. It smells of him; a mix of cinnamon, mint and cigarette smoke.

I try to answer him, I really do this time, but it's like the words won't form on my lips.

He scoops his arms under my body and then I'm heaved upwards and into his chest. His body feels deliciously warm. I feel myself curling into it like a cat as he rocks me to sleep.

He bangs the pub door open with his back reminding me to stay awake.

'Phoebe?' I hear Ella say on a gasp. 'Quick, take her upstairs.'

I feel the thudding of him running up the stairs and then I'm placed on the floor of my room.

He starts grabbing at my long sleeved t-shirt. What the hell is he doing? I try to stop him, but it's like my brain isn't communicating properly with my body.

I hear a strange noise close to my ears. It's only when I zone in on it, I realise it's my own teeth chattering. He throws my t-shirt over my head and then he's unbuttoning my jeans.

'What the hell happened to her?' Ella asks him, arriving with towels.

'I think she fell in,' he says, yanking my jeans down to my ankles.

I want to tell them I jumped in. That they're being ridiculously over protective, but all I can hear is the chattering of my teeth. I'm thrown into bed in just my bra and knickers and wrapped tightly with my duvet.

'What are you doing?' Ella asks him. I can vaguely make out the rustle of clothes.

'She's not warming up quick enough.' I can hear the worry in his voice.

Next thing I know the duvet is yanked back and his body is on top of mine. It's so warm it feels almost scorching to my frozen skin.

'Ella, go find any hot water bottles and blankets. Anything to help her get warm.'

He wraps his arms around my body, pressing me into him. If I wasn't so cold I'd push him away, but I allow him to press up against me. I feel myself thawing out enough to cling onto his body. My hands are shaking, my bandaged thumb throbbing. He rolls over, bringing me with him so I'm lying on his chest.

I press my face unashamedly against it. I listen to his heartbeat as my breathing turns from shallow and husky to more relaxed and even.

'Are you feeling warmer?' he asks.

'Yes,' I nod, suddenly feeling embarrassed by the whole situation. I mean, I'm in my bra and knickers on top of him in my bed.

His hand starts stroking my back lazily. 'You gave me a real fright there.' He sounds genuinely worried.

I lift my heavy head up to look at him. 'How did you know I was so cold?'

He scoffs. 'Phoebe, your lips were blue and chattering, and you could hardly move. Most people don't go for a swim in the lake in September.'

I try to push myself up and off him, but he grabs my arms and pulls me back onto his chest.

'You're still freezing. How did you fall in?'

I squirm away from him, humiliation heating my face.

'I didn't fall in,' I admit, bringing my hands up to hide my face, when I should in fact be hiding my body.

'You got in willingly?' he asks, trying to hide his smile.

I nod. 'I was a little freaked out after holding a dead rat in my hands!'

He smiles at me, but this smile is different to the other cocky ones he's previously directed my way. This one almost looks... affectionate? Jesus, I must be concussed.

'I got a hot water bottle,' Ella says bursting into the room. She spots me sitting up. 'Ah, thank god you're looking better.'

I take the hot water bottle from her and turn back to Clooney.

'You can put your clothes back on now,' I say, needing his hot, naked body away from me before I do or say something stupid.

I don't have the time or patience for a man in my life right now. Let alone one as self assured as him.

He steels his jaw, his shoulders tensing. 'Gee, thanks for saving my life.'

I shrug. 'Any excuse to get a girl naked.'

He scoffs. 'Don't flatter yourself, Poodles. And this is my bedroom now.' He puts his hands behind his head, showing off a bronzed six pack. 'I'll expect your shit out of it by the end of the day.'

And just when I think he might have a redeeming quality he goes and shits on it.

CHAPTER THIRTEEN

<u>Tuesday 29th September</u>

*C*looney relished in me packing up my things and having to share a bed with Ella. Keeps joking that we can sleep with him if we want. I'd rather die than get into bed with that man whore again. I can't believe we've had our near naked bodies pressed together. No, what I really can't believe is the horny dreams I've had about him since. Ella said I was moaning last night. I hope to god he didn't hear through the wall.

Clooney has actually been worth his weight in gold business wise, even if he can't work in the kitchen until we do our hygiene courses. He managed to get himself booked on the same course as us. He's so good at pulling pints and I hate to admit it, but he has brought some people in. His little fan club of young women who flutter their eyelashes at him is sickening, but as long as they're spending their money, I'm happy.

It's yet another slow afternoon so I decide to start asking

him questions about his tattoos. Strangely I want to find out everything about him.

His left forearm has two playing cards on fire, surrounded by roses. The fumes of the smoke run up his arms to beneath his t-shirt sleeve. A large intricate butterfly takes up his entire hand. He has a tiny king of hearts symbol over his ring finger. Obviously fancies himself a lothario.

He has the smallest star on his little finger. It actually looks like a Jewish star. He's not Jewish, right? I don't think I've ever met someone Irish and Jewish. Plus, I'm pretty sure they're forbidden from getting tattoos.

'What do they all mean?'

He looks up, bunching his eyebrows together.

I point to his arms. 'Your tattoos I mean.'

'Oh. That would be telling.'

O...kay. So he's not a sharer. Why would someone get tattoos that everyone can see and then refuse to talk about them? Sounds like attention seeking if you ask me.

His other arm has some kind of quote on it above a beautiful illustration of mountains and a lake. It kind of looks like our lake actually, but then I suppose they do all look the same. A big dove and its open wings cover his wrist and part of his hand. He has a single rose down his index finger, and he has some sort of words written down the sides of the others.

'What do they say?' I ask, pointing to between his fingers.

He glares at me, but parts his fingers so I can read *Peace, Respect, Loyalty and Love.*

'Wow, that's deep, bro,' I joke in a ridiculous impression of a stoned surfer.

He stares back at me blankly. I think he's angry.

'So, why did your dad chuck you out?' I can't help but ask him, trying to change the subject.

I hate that I'm nosy enough to ask.

He crosses his arms over his chest, his brows pulled in. 'I'd rather not talk about it.'

He looks adorably stubborn with his arms folded tight across his chest.

Damn me for wanting to dig, but I do.

'That's probably what a spy would say.' I hope that by antagonising him he'll answer.

He tilts his head. 'Are all of the English as nosey as you?'

'Are all the Irish as evasive as you?' I counter back.

We stare toe to toe with each other, both of us fiercely glaring. My chest heaves from the anger he creates in me. It's moment like this I hate that he's practically seen me naked.

His face dissolves into a smile, like he finds my anger amusing.

'Anyway, people keep asking if you've got the sports channels.'

Ugh, he's so cryptic.

I look at the old TV on the wall. 'I don't even know if that thing works.'

He nods towards it. 'I can check it out for you, but I know if you want to get sports channels in here it'll cost you about two thousand a month.'

'Two fucking grand?' I raise my voice. 'You must have that wrong, bloody hell!'

He shakes his head. 'Afraid not.' He walks off to collect some glasses from the end of the bar left by his little fan club.

'But...' I notice the elderly man behind the bar and turn to listen to what he has to say.

'But what?' I ask in clear desperation when he doesn't impart his advice straight away. Clooney could be onto something with getting sports channels. Encourage more people in. But we could never afford that.

'Well.' He clasps his pint of bitter, lowering his voice to a whisper. 'If you get it installed in the flat and then funnel it through, you'll just pay the regular amount.'

Ooh, I like this idea.

'Is that allowed?' I whisper back, careful not to be over-heard by Clooney.

He sips his bitter. 'Do you care? People want the sports. It'll bring them in.' He looks around. 'And God knows you need it.'

I think about it. He's right. If we carry on like this we're not even going to be able to pay the electric bill.

'Okay. How do I go about doing it?'

'I'll speak to my son. He'll fit it for you. Nice looking lad too.' He winks.

I grimace. Oh dear. I hope he doesn't think by him doing this favour I'm now engaged to be married to his son. Is that how it works around here? You trade a favour and then you're betrothed?

I quickly scribble my number down on the back of a beer mat and then shoo him away when I spot Clooney coming back behind the bar.

He squints his eyes between us both. 'Everything okay?' He asks, a hint of a smirk playing on the edge of his lips.

Okay, play it cool, Phoebe.

'Yes, of course it is. Would you just chill out and leave me alone?' I huff before flouncing away from him.

What is it about Clooney that turns me into a ridiculous teenage girl that can't think clearly?

~

Thursday 1st October

Today we've closed the pub, dropped Suki off to Kathleen's, and driven to Dublin to drop off our hire car and then attend our food hygiene course. We don't really need the car now with Clooney owning one and it's another expense we could do without.

'I don't know why they made me do this,' Clooney complains as we walk out of the course, having completed and passed our assessments. 'I'm well used to the kitchen and Lenny knows it. Unlike you two who can't even make toast.'

'Hey,' I snap, shoving him on the shoulder. 'We passed, didn't we? According to them we're as equally qualified as you.'

He smiles condescendingly. 'Just because you can ace a quiz doesn't mean you can cook.'

'He's kind of right,' Ella agrees with a scrunch of her nose.

He grins back at me smugly, as if to say, "*See, even she agrees.*"

'So your taxi mate is collecting us, right?' I ask as we walk onto the street. I can't see anyone waiting. He ignored my advice for him to drive his car to take us home. Said he might fancy a drink at lunch.

He grins mischievously. 'Well, actually, I have a bit of a surprise for you.'

My stomach does a somersault. I hate surprises. I like to know what I'm doing and when I'm doing it.

I stare at him, unamused. 'What the hell are you talking about?' After the too long course, all I'm looking forward to is soaking in a hot bath, and not listening to Clooney talk in riddles.

He locks his forest green eyes with mine. 'I thought I'd show you what Dublin has to offer.'

'You're taking us out?' Ella asks with an excited gasp.

He grins, turning and winking at me. 'Yep, we're going on a bar crawl, Dublin style.'

What did that wink mean? And why did it make me tingle down below? I don't even like this guy, let alone fancy him.

Ella jumps up and down enthusiastically. 'Yay!'

He throws his arm around my shoulders. 'Come on, Poodles. I hate when you're mad at me.'

I can't help but smile back at him. I still want to be outraged, but damn, when the idiot touches me, I go stupid.

'Okay, but we can't be out late.'

Seven hours later we're in some random bar in Dublin, getting more free drinks from yet another bar tender Clooney knows. I've lost count of how many drinks we've sank. Dublin is fun! It's just like central London except everyone is friendly and you're not so scared of getting beaten up in the toilets. Ella is dancing on top of the bar while I watch, happily content, sat next to Clooney.

I know I'm drunk, but every now and again Clooney will touch my leg or my back when he can't hear what I'm saying over the music. It's turning me crazily on, the throb between my legs growing intense. It's official, I need to stop drinking cocktails, they're bad for my brain.

He looks down at his phone, his eyes widening. 'Shit, Conner's here. We need to go.'

I motion for Ella to get off the bar. She begrudgingly does when I shout that she can finish my cocktail. Then Clooney and I take an arm of hers each and all but carry her out while she moans in protest.

Clooney leads us to what looks like a van.

'Hey Connor,' he shouts into the front window. 'I think Ella might be better riding up front with you.'

She giggles, leaning down to say hello to the good looking redhead. 'Well, *hello,* Connor. Damn, are all Irish boys as dreamy as you two?'

'Are you sure?' I ask him with a laugh. 'She might be pregnant by the end of the journey.'

We chuckle as we place her into her seat and put her seat belt on.

He takes my arm and opens up the side of the van. I expect seats, but to my horror it's just a regular worker's van. Its full of tools and leftover pots of paint.

'What the hell, Clooney? I thought you said he was a taxi driver?'

He avoids my eye gaze as he climbs in. 'He is, of sorts.' He turns back to look at me, trying to gauge my reaction.

'What the hell does that mean?' I ask, swaying from side to side. It's hard to act responsible when you're this drunk.

'Just get in, will ya?' he reaches his hand out to me.

'I don't know ab—' He grabs my arm and yanks me in. I nearly land on top of him. 'Clooney!' I screech, pushing myself up.

Luckily for him my thumb bandage is now off and the pain has all but gone.

He reaches behind me and slams the door. 'Ready to go,' he shouts to Connor. We speed off before I even have a chance to sit down.

'Clooney, this guy is not a taxi driver.' Women are always told not to get in unlicensed taxis, but then I suppose Clooney does know him.

'Well, he kind of is in Ballykielty.'

'How is that?' I can feel my patience draining away.

'Because we only have three men that do taxi service, and the other two are normally in the same pub you're calling from and getting pissed themselves.'

'Oh my god.' I can't help but bark a laugh. 'Well at least this guy is sober.'

'Yeah, he's the best drunk driver of the three.'

My eyes nearly pop out of my skull. 'What?'

We're all going to die.

He grins, the skin round his eyes crinkling. 'I'm joking with ya.'

We go around a corner so sharply I'm thrown into Clooney's lap.

'Jeysus, buy me a drink first,' he chuckles, looking down at me.

'Clooney!' I push myself up but end up pushing against his dick in his skinny jeans. Crap. Do not think about the huge bulge you just touched.

We go around another corner, this time Clooney is thrown onto me. I'm pinned against the side of the van, petrified the door is going to fall off any second. We'll both be abandoned like roadkill.

I push him off me. 'Your friend is a fucking maniac. Tell him to slow down.'

'Ah, Connor is fine. Leave him alone.'

How can he be so dismissive of our safety?

'Leave him alone? Are you serious—'

We're both lifted off our bums as we go over some sort of bridge I'm guessing.

'Jesus!' I shout, grabbing hold of Clooney's hand instinctively. 'Please get him to slow down or I'm gonna have a heart attack.'

He just laughs like we've willingly gone on a roller-coaster.

'If I'd have known he was this bad a driver I'd have drunk a hell of a lot more.'

He chuckles as we're thrown to the left. 'Not possible.'

CHAPTER FOURTEEN

<u>Friday 2nd October</u>

*W*ell we just about survived our ride home last night. I ended up clasping onto Clooney's hand and shirt, scrunching my eyes shut, the remainder of the journey. I'm ashamed to say that it felt good to be so close to him. He's just so strong and manly, it's easy to feel safe with him.

Sharing a space with him is getting tenser by the minute. I keep finding him staring at me when he thinks I'm not looking, and then quickly looking away when I do. I still can't work out if it's because he thinks that I'm an idiot, or because he finds me interesting. Pretty even. See what I mean? Clooney turns me into a teenager. A very *hormonal* teenager. I don't know why I keep blushing from his attention, I don't even like the guy. You can't fancy someone you don't even like, right? If Garry has taught me anything its to stay away from men, especially womanisers.

Suki has started to follow him around and sit by his feet. It seems no females are safe.

As promised, that guy Dermot's son, managed to get the sports channels fitted and funnelled through into the pub while we were out on the course yesterday. His son didn't produce an engagement ring either which makes me feel better. I'm now terrified I'm going to be caught and put in prison. I mean, is it considered stealing? Or fraud even? I lied to Clooney and said we were on a free trial. All I know is that I'm past caring. If we carry on much more like we have been, we're just going to be sinking further into a hole. Desperate measures and all that.

With Clooney now being in charge of the kitchen the menu has changed to just soup, sandwiches and jacket potatoes at lunch. Still more than me and Ella could manage. In the evenings he plans to open for two hours with a special he hopes to talk the customers into. I say customers; currently just his fan club seem to be here, hanging off his every word. It's actually embarrassing watching them drooling all over him. In fact, now I think about it, that's probably why he's staring at me. Trying to work out how I'm immune to his charms.

He's been telling everyone that tonight we're playing the Irish rugby match. I've even taken a few phone calls from people enquiring.

Clooney's cooked a few pizzas and laid them out on the bar with cocktail sausages and curly fries. We've managed to bring in a crowd of about fifteen extra people. I just hope to God they all plan on getting slaughtered drunk.

Clooney beckons me with his finger. I follow him into the kitchen, an excited tingle travelling up my spine whenever he asks for time alone with me.

'What's up?' I ask. I press my lips together to stop myself smiling like a goon.

His eyes glint mischievously in the light. 'I have a plan.'

I frown, knowing instantly this spells trouble. 'How worried should I be?' I start biting my nails.

He grabs my hand and drags me out the back door. 'Come on.'

Like a fool I follow him. I know he's trouble, but I just can't help but be taken in by him; if only for tonight. Something happens when he touches me, even just to hold my hand. He lights up some sort of girly giddiness inside me. I remember us both practically naked in bed, skin to skin. It makes me shiver just to think of it. The urge to feel his arms wrapped around me again is getting stronger by the day, as if he's cast a spell over me.

He notices the shiver and frowns. 'Shit, I forgot our coats. I keep forgetting you're not used to this weather.'

I nod, rubbing my palms up and down my arms. Better to go with that over feeling turned on. It's practically Baltic out. It doesn't help that I've developed a slight runny nose since nearly catching hypothermia the other day.

He looks at his watch. 'I don't think we have time. Here.' He takes off his flannel shirt and hands it to me, leaving him in just a light grey v neck t-shirt. A small bit of dark chest hair is visible. I stare down at the shirt like a dummy. He can be so sweet sometimes.

He grabs my hand again and pulls me into his car. By the time he's got in his side I've put on his shirt. It's warm and smells amazing. Smells of him.

'Where are we going?'

He grins, his eyes glinting in the glow of the street lights. 'You'll see when we get there.'

I sigh. More damn surprises. 'Are you taking me off to murder me?'

He smirks. 'I have a feeling any killer worth his salt would answer no to that question.'

'Whatever. Just tell me,' I plead. 'I hate surprises.'

He holds the steering wheel with one hand. 'Jeysus, you need to chill out, Phoebe.'

Is there anything worse than being told to chill out? I don't think so.

'You need to stop being so damn stubborn and just tell me where you're taking me.'

'Jey-sus.' The skin around his eyes bunches in annoyance. 'I'm taking you to my dad's pub. We're gonna play a little prank on him. Payback for the whole rat in the kitchen thing.'

My mouth drops open. 'I thought with him being your dad you wouldn't want to get involved in our drama?'

His jaw tenses. 'Phoebe, the man chucked me out. Believe me when I say there's no love lost between us.'

Then why won't he tell me the whole story?

I shrug, attempting to appear casual. 'He's still your dad though. My parents drive me mad, but I can never imagine hating them. Disliking them, maybe.'

His jaw tenses. 'But I'm guessing your parents never chucked you out of your own room?'

'True, I suppose.' I nod, looking out of the window.

Little does he know we never had a house to be chucked out from. We spent our entire life being driven around in a minivan on our way to rallies or protests and being home-schooled by our hippy parents. Hardly the supportive environment most kids have growing up.

'So what are we doing?' I ask as we park up and get out at The Dog & Duck.

He grabs my hand again and pulls me behind him. 'Be quiet.'

He's so bossy, but damn, when this guy holds my hand and directs me with his Irish melodious voice, it tricks me into thinking he can be adorable. I know his type. I've dated his type. Charming and attentive, but ready to drop you the minute you sleep with them. Hell, I couldn't even trust boring and reliable Garry.

We sneak up towards the back of the pub and through a gate I've not seen before. He turns the torch on his phone and hands it to me.

'Here, you'll have to hold it still.'

'Still for what?' I whisper hiss, glancing around us. I might not know what we're doing, but I already know I don't want to get caught.

He walks up to what looks like a fuse box and opens it.

'Hold it still,' he snaps. It's only then I realise my hands are shaking. I'm not used to being a vandal.

He switches all of the fuses off and we watch as the pub gets plunged into darkness. People shout.

He takes the phone back and hands over his keys. 'Here, pull the car to the front and wait for me behind the hedge.'

'What are you ...'

It's too late, he's already rushing into the pub with the torch. I don't have time to question him further so rush into the car, rearrange the seat because he's a tall lanky bastard and then drive to where he instructed.

I hear lots of commotion before he runs over to the car and jumps in.

'Quick, go! Step on it.'

I manage not to stall and speed away.

'What the hell was that all about?' I shout as soon as we are around the corner.

He grins. 'Just telling them all that we're showing the rugby in our pub.'

I bark a laugh. 'God, Clooney, you really have no shame, do you?'

He pouts his lips. 'I'm trying to help you here.'

'I know.' I cringe. I can be such a bitch, but I'm just so bloody stressed these days. Plus, I have weird mixed emotions about him calling it *our* pub. 'Sorry.'

'And yes, I do have no shame.' He winks, sending a thrill of excitement down my spine. 'It's much more fun like that. Now pull the car over and let's swap, you aren't insured.' We do, and with that we are back on our way home to our pub.

CHAPTER FIFTEEN

<u>Saturday 4th October</u>

I wake up and yawn straight away. The pub was the busiest it has ever been last night. True to his word, not long after we got back Clooney managed to bring most of the Dog and Duck back to ours, desperate to watch the rugby.

They were all over the moon to see he wasn't lying when he said we had the sports channels. It was manic. Everyone drinking like it was going out of fashion. The way a pub should be.

The only annoying thing was that Suki kept escaping into the pub whenever we went to get change from the safe. Chasing around after a skunk never looks good.

By the time we'd tidied up it was gone midnight. We practically crawled into bed. God, Ella can snore like an old sailor. The amount of times I lost it and shouted at her to *shut up* was ridiculous. She'd just snort like a little pig and roll over, managing to be quiet for a few seconds only to start the cycle all over again. I swear her snoring is worse in Ireland.

At about two a.m. I heard Suki scratching at Clooney's door. She's clearly found a favourite.

The thought of having to re-stock the pub, do a line clean and open up again has me feeling sick to my stomach. I drag myself up, get washed and dressed and then head downstairs. Ella is still dead to the world, regardless of how many times I've shouted that she's a lazy bitch.

I take a calming deep breath and go down to the kitchen. The smell of sausages hits my nostrils. I look up to see Clooney making sausage sandwiches. There's three plates set out. For all of us. Wow. I didn't even think he was awake.

'Here she is,' he says cheerily, over the frying sausages spitting in the pan. He has a lazy smile on his lips, Suki at his feet. 'I was just gonna call the both of you.'

I snort. 'Don't bother with Ella. She's dead to the world.'

'More sausages for me then.' He grins, passing my plate over to me.

I start shovelling it into my mouth, eager to get started on the bar. Damn, this is good.

He stares at me, eyes wide. 'Jesus, you're eating like you just got let out of prison.'

I cough a laugh. 'Sorry,' I mumble through a mouthful, covering my mouth so he doesn't see my chewing. 'I just know I've got a lot to get done before opening up.'

'Like what?' he asks with a frown. Whenever he frowns he gets this adorable little dent between his eyebrows.

'Like restocking the bar, doing a line clean.' I sigh just at the thought of it.

'I've already done it,' he says casually, shovelling another mouthful of sandwich into his mouth.

'You what? Bloody hell, what time did you wake up?'

He grins. 'I've never been very good at sleeping in.'

What a weirdo.

'Well, it turns out you *are* pretty handy.'

He wiggles his eyebrows. 'Oh, you have *no* idea.'

I snort a laugh. Attractive. Trust him to turn it back to sex.

'If your fan club are anything to go by, I believe you.'

His forest green eyes crinkle with a cocky smile. 'I can't help it that the ladies flock to me.'

He's so full of himself.

'Hey, as long as they're buying drinks, I couldn't care less.' I could, but I won't tell him that. Desperate little skanks.

He drops a small bit of sausage for Suki. She quickly gobbles it up, only to immediately spit it out.

'Don't feed her. Not that she seems to like your sausage.' I freeze, widening my eyes when I realise what I just said.

He chuckles. 'I think you'll find that she's the first ever female to refuse my sausage.'

We're interrupted by someone banging on the front door. Thank God. We turn to stare at each other with raised eyebrows.

'Who the hell is that?' he asks, already standing up.

We both abandon our sandwiches to go and see who's making all the racket. It's a man I've seen in the pub before.

We open up the door. 'Sorry, we're not open yet,' I say with a polite smile.

He scoffs a bitter laugh. 'Oh, trust me, I'll never be coming here again. My wife is at home, sick as a dog. She's got food poisoning from the prawn sandwich she had here yesterday.'

'What are you talking about?' Clooney asks, eyes narrowed. 'Those prawns were fine.'

'Well, clearly not.'

Suki chooses that moment to push her head out of the door, nosing to see what's happening.

'And you have a skunk in your kitchen?' he asks in wide eyed horror. 'I'm reporting this to environmental health.'

'No!' I yelp, trying to run after him. This is the last thing we need. 'Please, surely there's something we can do between us to sort this out?' I smile sweetly.

He looks at me, his eyes hard and unforgiving. 'Can you go back in time and not poison my wife?'

My mouth moves hopelessly up and down, no words able to come out.

'Exactly!' He turns and storms off to his car.

I turn back to Clooney. I couldn't feel more deflated. 'Just when I thought we were getting somewhere.'

The overwhelming urge to crush my head against his chest and let him comfort me is strong. I resist, reminding myself that Clooney is not even my friend, let alone a potential boyfriend.

'Oh shite, it's not over yet.'

I frown up at him. 'Huh?'

I turn to where he's staring and find his dad pulling up and storming out of the car. I still can't believe these two are related.

'Oi! You two!' His face is red and blotchy, his teeth bared like a pit-bull.

'Oh shit.' Is it too late to run away?

'Don't worry,' Clooney says, moving in front of me like a well-built shield.

It's not the first time he's used himself to protect me. It's strangely sweet. I don't think I've ever had a man stick up for me like that.

Fergus barrels up to us, his beer belly swinging wildly.

'I know it was you two! Don't try and deny it,' he roars, pointing his finger accusingly at us.

'I don't know what you're talking about,' Clooney says, puffing out his chest.

'Don't play silly bastards with me, young man. I know it would have been your idea. Even she's not stupid enough to try that herself.'

'Hey,' I protest weakly, from behind him. Way to look like a strong independent woman.

He looks straight at me, his brown eyes protruding. 'Be warned, girl. He can put on the charm, but he's nothing but a bad-un.'

What the hell is he talking about?

'Leave her alone,' Clooney growls, 'and get off her property.' His clenched fists shake with rage by his sides. 'You're barred.'

Fergus gets right up in Clooney's face, his angry eyes bulging. 'You've messed with the wrong man, son. I would have thought after what you did you'd be trying to get me to forgive you, but instead you go and declare war. Big mistake.'

He turns and flounces back to his car. He really does look nothing like Clooney and he definitely doesn't have his charm. Could he have been adopted?

What did he mean? After what Clooney did?

'Come on,' Clooney says, grabbing my hand and pulling me back into the pub. He reaches across and pulls the lock on the door again. 'Are you alright?' he asks, his brows snapped together.

It's only now I realise I'm shaking. It's pathetic how one

aggressive man can turn me into a quivering wreck. Then, I suppose I was brought up around peace loving hippies. The only aggression I ever saw was aimed at the animal testers or the government. Whoever we were trying to protest against, not each other.

'Come here.' He grabs my shoulders and pulls me into his chest, squeezing his arms tight around me. I give myself a moment to revel in his warmth and scent. I can make out chamomile and orange today, but I have a feeling I'd have to sniff him from head to toe to work out his full signature scent. It's everything I need and everything I shouldn't want.

I push him away gently, reminding myself that he's the one that caused this bloody situation by his prank last night. But then I suppose he was only trying to help us, bring in some more business. Still, I need to ask him what he did to get such scathing verbal abuse from his own father.

'What was he talking about?' I ask carefully, pulling away slightly to look up at him.

He avoids my eye-line, his arms dropping to his side. 'What do you mean?'

I steel my shoulders. 'You know exactly what I mean. What did you do to him?'

He sighs and starts to walk away. I follow. I hate when people try and be dismissive. I stop him and raise my eyebrows in question.

He sighs, his shoulders deflating. 'I didn't do anything to him. I hurt myself far more than I hurt him.' He turns to walk away.

What the hell does that mean? Hurt himself?

As if knowing I'm not going to drop it, he turns back to me, his eyes clearly tortured by something.

'Look, Phoebe, I really don't want to talk about it, and I'd appreciate some privacy in this place.'

I sigh, realising quickly I'm not going to get anywhere. Not until he trusts me more. Something tells me that the Clooney everyone sees and fawns over isn't the real Clooney at all. He has demons beyond that chirpy persona and for some reason I want to gain his trust. I want to find out what those demons are and attempt to heal him. An unrealistic hope, probably. Which means I'm in big trouble. I just hope that I don't hurt myself while I attempt to find out.

CHAPTER SIXTEEN

Tuesday 6th October

*W*e started the morning being served with court papers. Apparently the lady that fell from the broken chair is taking us to small claims court for compensation. Wants five thousand euros. Good luck, love. You can't get blood from a stone and all that.

Even with Sky TV, we're not going to survive carrying on like this. With our small lunch time trade now ruined thanks to those bad prawns, and another visit from environmental health, insisting we must keep Suki strictly in the accommodation, it's beyond dire.

If it wasn't for all of the money I'd invested, I'd be long gone. My life bloody savings have gone into this place. I can't just close up and write it off. I have to know I've done everything in my power to make it work before walking away.

So I've decided that I'm going to get a day job. I can surely earn more money with a full-time job than I can standing around here hoping people come in. Plus, it'll be easier to avoid Clooney, who makes me feel things I shouldn't. Added bonus.

I've gone to the local library and printed off my updated CV and trawled the high street. I've gone into the temp agency and asked in every shop, but apparently no-ones hiring. The only place left to check is the one place I *really* don't want to work. The funeral directors.

I push open the door, the bell above the door jingling. A bit too cheery for a place that discusses death, but whatever. The smell of moth balls hits me. I wonder if that's because death smells like moth balls? Must google before I get home.

I walk to the man behind the desk in a black suit. I smile brightly, attempting to appear friendly.

'Hi, my name's Phoebe Bellerose. I'm just dropping in my CV in case you have any work going.'

Recognition dawns on his face. 'Ah, you're the English girl, Breda's great niece, right?'

Jesus, everyone knows everything around here.

'That's right.'

He frowns. 'I heard you were trying to get the pub going again?'

'We are.' I nod. 'Except... well, until word spreads, I kind of need a day job.'

He smiles sympathetically. 'Well, you're in luck, missy.'

Does anyone like being called missy? Does he think I'm five years old.

'We need someone new. You know what they say, this business never has a lull.'

I suppose he's right. People are always going to die. What a depressing thought.

'So... what would that be doing?' I ask carefully, dreading his answer. Hopefully it's just answering the phones.

'A bit of everything really. We're a family run business so we don't like people claiming it's not their jobs. A bit of funeral planning, now and again driving the hearse and the occasional prepping of the passed.'

'You mean... the dead people? I'll...' I swallow, praying my stomach doesn't empty its contents out onto their carpet. 'See the dead people?'

He looks at me with his lips pursed. 'Of course you'll see dead people. This job isn't for the faint hearted. Are you going to be able to handle it?' He raises one eyebrow in challenge.

Do I have much choice? What's my alternative? Starve to death at the pub and be found eaten by that skunk Suki.

'Of course.' I nod, trying to look determined and unafraid.

He nods with a smile. 'Then the jobs yours. You start tomorrow.'

I grimace. 'Great.'

Only I could end up working in a funeral directors.

'Although, there is something we'd like to check first.'

I start playing with my injured thumb. The nail is beginning to grow and I've found myself fiddling with it when I'm anxious. 'Oh?'

He nods. 'Come with me.'

I dubiously follow him into the back where a dead person is laid out in a coffin. Shit. It's a man in his seventies or eighties. His skin is slightly yellow and he seems shiny.

'Doing this job, you need to learn to be around the dead.'

I nod, trying not to inhale the musty smell they've tried to hide with fresh flowers.

'I'd like to leave you alone with Lochlan here, to see how you cope.'

I point at the dead person. 'Lochlan?' He nods. 'Seriously?'

He nods again, his eyebrows pinched together. 'It might sound extreme, but it quickly weeds out the people who aren't serious about the job.

Shit, it might weed me out before I've even started.

'Can't you just believe me?' I smile as sweetly as I can.

He smiles reassuringly. 'You can do it. I'll be back soon.' He leaves, closing the door behind himself.

Shit. I'm sharing oxygen with a dead man. Okay, the main thing is not to panic. I pace the room, desperate not to look at him. Not to think of the dead person. Only, of course, that's all I can think about. The elephant in the room. Or the dead person in the room in my case.

You know what? I'm avoiding the obvious. He's right, if I'm gonna work with dead people, I need to learn to look at them. I walk slowly towards him, taking a deep breath with every slow step. My stomach does somersaults, my mouth dry.

I look down at him. He could be mistaken for being asleep if you didn't know. Whatever they've done to him is good.

I think about what life he had. Who might miss him now that he's gone? Did he have a family? Grandchildren? Did he take them up on his lap and read them stories? A tear runs down my cheek.

Did he smell of Werther's Originals? My eyes fill with tears when I think of the potential life this man had. How we all end up the same, dead in a coffin, put into the ground. Before I know it, I'm all out sobbing. This poor man.

I find a box of tissues on the nearby table and take one, dabbing at my eyes and blowing my nose nosily. I take another deep breath. The main thing is that he now has a dignified end. That he's looked after here. That his family are able to grieve him properly.

I lean back over the coffin. 'Rest in peace, Lochlan.'

He does looks at peace. Then his arm jerks out towards me. Oh my fucking god. My heart tries to escape out of my throat. I scream. The bastard is fucking alive! Either that or possessed by the devil. I run to the door and try to open it but it's locked. I bang my fists against it.

'Let me out! This guy is still alive!'

The walls start closing in on me, my breaths hitched in my chest. This is it. How I'll die. Only I could be killed by a still alive corpse possessed by the devil.

I sink down the door, hands pulling at my hair.

'I need to get out of here.' I rock my body and rub my arms.

The door suddenly opens, leaving me to fall onto my back. I look up to see the same guy and another younger man bent over, holding their stomachs, laughing.

I quickly scuttle up to standing. What the hell is so funny?

'Sorry,' he says, trying to pull himself together. 'It's just that we watch through the cameras and we've never quite had someone react the way you have.'

'He moved!' I cry, pointing towards a very still Lochlan. 'His arm moved. He's still alive.'

He walks calmly over to him, not worried in the least. 'I can reassure you that he is dead. Feel his pulse if you don't believe me.' *I'd rather bloody not.*

'But then why—' Did I imagine that? Have I lost my mind?

'Gasses releasing from the body can cause involuntary

movements,' he explains. 'One of the many things you'll learn working here.'

I frown back at him. 'You mean, you still want me to work here?' Surely they can see I'd be a damn petrified liability?

He grins. 'Of course. We find that if people are forced to have their first freak out it gets it out of the way. Now we can crack on and train you. Can you start tomorrow?'

CHAPTER SEVENTEEN

<u>Thursday 8th October</u>

So working in the funeral home isn't actually the worst. I think after yesterday anything seems tame in comparison. It's a bit like party planning, only I'm planning a party for a dead person and everyone is quite sad.

I think they've eased me in with doing this after my freak out so I haven't had to see anymore dead people yet. Just lots of crying relatives, which does get you down after a while, but luckily I'm good at being sympathetic.

The only annoying thing is that I don't trust Ella at the pub by herself. Thank God Clooney is there. Any kind of responsibility I give her, she screws up. I found her drunk when I got back last night. I get it, its bloody boring, but she needs to snap out of it and be a team player.

Today I'm driving the hearse, transporting a coffin to the church. That's right, my first time driving the hearse and I have a dead body in the back. It gives me the heeby jeebies just thinking about it. I'm going with denial. Just taking a drive to church.

Seamus, the fifty odd owner that locked me in the room, is in with me at least, instructing how fast to go and where to turn. Luckily they aren't letting me go faster than 20mph.

We've barely pulled off when I hear it.

'No-one to wave me off. Bloody typical.'

I turn to look at Seamus. He stares back at me, his bushy eyebrows raised. 'Keep your eyes on the road, please, Phoebe.'

'Sorry,' I mumble, shaking my head. I'm sure he spoke. I must concentrate. I feel like I'm taking my driving test again.

'And look at this coffin. Cheapest in the range.'

Okay, I'm sure I heard something that time. I turn around, looking to see where it's come from. It's as if it's coming from behind me. Seamus is staring at me again, lips pressed flat.

'Sorry, Phoebe, is there a problem?' he asks, his voice raised.

That's when it hits me. It's a joke. Of course it's a joke. There's no body in the hearse at all. This is one of those jokey initiation things just like being in the same room as the dead guy. Niall, Seamus's son, must be in the coffin saying this stuff, pissing himself laughing. The cheeky bastards. Pair of right jokers I'm working with.

'No problem.' I giggle. Alright arseholes, I'm game.

'If that cheeky bitch of an ex-wife of mine dares to show her face at the church I'll have a good mind to haunt her.'

I burst out laughing. Seamus turns to stare at me incredulously. 'Phoebe, what on earth is so fecking funny?'

'Oh come on!' I heckle, laughing so hard the odd snort

escapes. 'The jigs up. I know its Niall back there.' I turn to face the back. 'You can come out now, Niall!'

He frowns and scratches his neck, really committing to the prank. 'Phoebe... what do you...?'

'Come out, Niall! The joke's up!' I clutch at my stomach, tears starting to run down my face.

'Phoebe!' he shouts. 'The road!'

I spin back just in time to spot someone in the middle of the road. I slam the brakes on, emergency brake style, desperately trying to stop before hitting them. Scrunching my eyes shut, I hope to God I don't kill someone.

When I open my eyes again, my heart racing so fast I feel it pulsing in my ears, I see we're okay. The person is stood frozen to the spot in front of the hearse panting erratically. Its only when I focus on them that I realise its Clooney's dad, Fergus. I turn to see that the coffin has smashed against our head rests and has chipped slightly.

I turn to Seamus with a grimace. 'Oops.'

'*Oops she says,*' the voice comes again.

'Ugh, if Niall would just shut up I wouldn't have crashed in the first place!' I jump out of the car, choosing to ignore Fergus shouting about how he could have been killed. This farce has gone on too long.

I open up the back in search of Niall. He must be lying next to the coffin. I search around but he's not there. What the hell's going on? Is there some sort of secret compartment I'm not aware of? Or maybe he's actually in the coffin.

'What are you doing?' Seamus asks, suddenly at my side, the skin around his eyes bunched up tight. He waves at the family limousine behind us.

'Open the coffin!' I demand, hand on my hip. 'I know Niall's hiding in there. I think we can both agree this has gone beyond a joke now.'

'Phoebe!' he reprimands, his neck red. 'I am NOT opening the coffin,' he hisses. 'Niall is NOT in there. I have no idea what you're talking about.'

'Who the hell is Niall?'

'I can hear him. I can hear you!' I shout defiantly at the coffin. Why are they doing this to me? It's gone way beyond a joke now.

'What on earth is going on here?'

We both turn round to see Niall standing behind us, head tilted to one side. I look behind him to see he's been driving the following car filled with mourners.

'The family are distraught. Now what on earth's going on?' Niall demands.

'Not that they'd give a feck.'

I clutch at my temples, a headache forming. What is going on? Let me get this straight.

'Are you seriously telling me you can't hear that?'

They both look at each other, exchanging worried glances.

'Are you okay, love?' Seamus asks

Shit, *am* I okay? Do I have a concussion? No, I was hearing the voice before I almost hit Fergus, wasn't I? Right now the only possible out is to go with the feeling sick excuse. Maybe I can make out I'm delirious from a fever.

'Err... yeah, I think I'm feeling a bit...' I fake a cough. 'Ill.'

'I think so too.' Niall nods at his dad. 'Why don't you go home for the day.'

CHAPTER EIGHTEEN

I'm still shaking. What a bloody day. I'm more confused than ever. How the hell did I hear that weird voice? What is going on with me? Am I having a breakdown or something? I suppose it's possible. I have been through a traumatic event. Being cheated on and then soon after choosing to leave the country to take on a failing business. Yes, in fact I'm surprised it hasn't happened sooner. I reckon a good night's sleep will sort me out. I just need to learn how to de-stress.

For once I'm actually glad to get back here. It might be failing but at least its home for now. I open the door to the pub and nearly fall over when I see that its packed. What the hell is going on here? Have I walked into the wrong pub by accident? I lean back, but no, it's our names above the door. Unless this is part of my hallucinated episode?

I walk in to see Ella with a frown on her face, looking unnervingly worried as she serves a man. When I take a closer look I see that the guy looks like a traveller.

I go round and walk behind the bar placing my hand bag on the floor.

'Look,' Clooney says to the guy, his chest puffed out. 'I saw the ten euro note myself. It wasn't a twenty.'

'Well I'm fecking well telling you that it was,' he argues, slamming his fist onto the bar, his face reddening.

Shit. I look around to see they're all travellers. I try not to be biased towards people from different cultures, but I don't have a good feeling about these guys. My guts are twisting as I take it all in. Where have they come from?

'Just give him the money,' I whisper to Ella. She begrudgingly hands over too much money, her shoulders up around her ears.

I grab her and pull her out back to the kitchen, grabbing my handbag on the way. 'What the hell's going on?'

She leans on one hip, arms crossed over her chest. 'I have *no* idea. We've just suddenly been over-run with travellers. They've been a nightmare from the minute they came in. Saying we've short changed them and given them the wrong drinks.'

'Shit.' This is just what we bloody need. I lift my hair from the nape of my neck, suddenly sweaty with panic. 'We have to get rid of them.'

'No shit,' Clooney says, appearing in the doorway and crossing his arms over his chest. That position shows off his perfect triceps and tattooed forearms. 'But you have to be careful with this lot. You can't just bar them. They'll kick off.'

'You shouldn't have left the bar. They could be robbing us right now!'

I start walking back towards it. I need to grasp some sort of control over the situation. I stand behind the bar looking over their faces. What can I do to get rid of them?

The front door opens and all three of us peer round to see who's walking in. If it's more travellers I'll possibly cry.

As if my prayers have been answered two police men walk in, or guards as they call them here. Everyone in the place turns to stare at them. An eerie silence descends on the place.

'We'd like to speak to a Phoebe Bellerose please.'

Crap, there was me thinking they were here to help us.

'Erm, that's me,' I confirm as calmly as possible. My wobbly voice betrays any possibility of that. My cheeks burn as every traveller in there stares at me. Yeah, like *I'm* the dodgy one right now. 'What's this about?'

'We'd prefer to speak to you in private, please,' the taller one says, eyeing up the local travellers with caution.

'Err... of course. Come through the back.'

Ella's eyes nearly pop out of their sockets in a speechless attempt to ask what's happening without actually using words. I shrug and lead them through to the back room. When I open the door Suki runs around in excitement. They look at her warily.

'Don't worry, she's friendly and without her anal glands.'

Words I never thought I'd say.

I invite them to sit on the sofa and sit myself down on the chair by the table, wiping my clammy hands on my trousers. Suki jumps up onto my lap, clearly thinking she's a support animal.

'So, what's this all about?' I ask, twiddling my hands.

The taller guy clears his throat. 'We've been informed by Mr Breen that you tried to run him down today.'

Oh for God's sakes. Clooney's dad trying to cause trouble again. Can he not see that I'm clearly capable of putting myself in it without him getting involved?

I sigh, slouching over. 'I didn't *try* and run him down. He stepped out in front of the hearse and I had to emergency brake to stop in time. The car didn't even touch him.'

'So it definitely wasn't deliberate?' he asks, his lips pursed, his pen and pad at the ready; like he's expecting me to confess and he doesn't want to miss anything.

'Of course not!' Do they really think I would do that?

He nods. 'It's just that he owns the rival pub and claims you have a grudge against him.'

'Ha!' I snort. 'If anyone has a grudge its him. He's not stopped trying to cause problems for me. He even tried to get us shut down for rats that he'd planted in here.' I realise I've been flailing my arms around and quickly put them behind my back in an attempt to look calm and controlled.

'Well,' he looks to his shorter colleague, 'your story seems to tie up with Seamus and Niall's, so we're happy.'

'Oh. Okay.'

That was easier than I thought it would be. Thank God they didn't mention me accusing them of hazing me. That would make me look *really* unhinged.

'Now, do you have any idea how I can get rid of them lot out the front?' I ask, my stomach still in knots.

He pursues his lips together, his eyes sympathetic. 'Unless they've broken the law, not much we can do, I'm afraid.'

I sigh and cross my arms over my chest. 'Great.'

I'll have to think of something myself, although I have no idea what.

I put Suki in our small private courtyard garden we cleaned up and then lead them back out to the bar to find another massive guy arguing with Clooney. The idea of him being hurt makes me feel sick to my stomach.

That's when the idea pops into my head.

'Can I get you lads a drink while you're here?' I ask loudly to the officers.

They look to each other. 'We shouldn't. We're still on duty.'

I clear my throat. 'Well make sure to tell ALL the guards back at base to come here. Fifty percent discount if you're a guard.'

Worried faces spread over the pub. They won't like guards drinking in here. That'll ruin all their fun.

'No way.' They grin at each other. 'That's great and bound to get them in the door. Thanks.'

Way to keep them on side too. Two birds, one stone.

They're barely out the door before everyone downs their drinks and scarpers. A lightness releases over me as my stomach un-knots. Thank God.

'Good thinking,' Clooney praises, his eyes warm but drained.

I nod, the relief taking any last energy from me. I really need this day to be over.

'I'm going up for a lie down.'

I jog up the stairs, but trip on a loose floorboard. God, this place is falling apart. I go to slot it back in place when something catches my eye. I lift it off fully to find some dusty books in there.

I carefully pull them out and read the first page. 'Breda Bellerose.'

These are Great Aunt Breda's? Why the hell would she have hidden them in a step? I flick through to see that they're diary entries. I suppose that makes a bit more sense as to why she hid them, but still. I mean, didn't she live alone? Why would she want to hide them? Worried Suki the skunk was going to read them? Maybe she *was* nuts.

I check the dates finding that they go all the way back to

when she was a teenager. Ooh, I hope there's a good bit of gossip in here. Maybe even some dirt on my righteous parents.

I take it back to my room with me, shaking it to disperse some more of the dust. I lie down on my bed and turn eagerly to the first page. I should feel bad invading her privacy, but it's too intriguing to ignore.

$\sim$

5th February 1951

It happened again today. I don't know what's happening to me. Hearing voices. God knows if anyone ever found out, even found this diary, I'd be locked up in an asylum.

Ma had just told me that Eileen in the village had passed away last night. I went to school with her daughter Niamh, so I took up Ma's offer of going with her to offer our condolences. I don't know why. I hate when people die. I never know what to say and because of that I've always avoided it and feigned sickness so I didn't have to go to funerals. But today I went.

Niamh answered the door looking like she'd been crying all night. I awkwardly offered her my comfort and then we were asked if we'd like to see Eileen. I had no idea you could see them laid out like that. You'd never believe how normal she looked. Just as if she was sleeping.

Niamh took me right up to her and that's when I heard it.

'Hello there, Breda.'

I nearly jumped out of my skin. I was sure Niamh had said it and so I confronted her about trying to scare me. She said I was wrong and called me an oddball. Mammy had to apologise for me and take me home, but all the while I could hear Eileen talking to me.

'I can't believe you can hear me Breda. You've got the gift, just like your Grandma had. You can hear the spirits.'

Am I an oddball? Can I really hear spirits or am I going mad? I daren't mention it to someone for fear of them locking me up. I had to persuade Ma that I was tired and hearing things on the way back. But I'm sure. As sure as I can be. I heard Eileen.

Well fuck a duck. Great Aunt Breda heard spirits? Is that what I heard today? A voice of the deceased?

I pause for a moment, my head cocked to one side. 'Aunty Breda?' I call softly. I mean, if this is true, she might still be around, maybe she could help me with the pub...

Nothing...

Nah. What am I thinking? Great Aunt Breda must have been off her rocker. I'm fine. *Totally* fine. Just in need of a good night's sleep.

CHAPTER NINETEEN

<u>Monday 12th October</u>

*A*fter a rather slow, and thankfully uneventful, day at the funeral home I'm completely drained. I decide to treat myself to a bubble bath. A bath always makes everything feel better. It helps that it's also a rebellion against my parents.

We were never allowed baths. Well, our camper van didn't have one anyway, but our parents, being the eco warrior protesters that they are, insisted we only ever have showers and even then they could only last two minutes. I know how wasteful a bath is. How many showers you could have with all of the bath water. But right now, I don't care. I need a hot bath to soothe my tired, weary muscles.

Plus I'll end up taking it out to the garden in a watering can to water the already overgrown garden. I hate that I can't just let it go down the drain wasted. Stupid saving the planet soul.

I ease myself into the too hot water, careful not to wet my thumb. Although healing it's still sensitive as hell, especially in different temperatures. Not that it's looking great; the nail has started to grow back. I should really book a doctor's appointment to get it checked over, but I haven't even registered with a surgery yet. I've no idea where the nearest doctor's surgery even is.

I manage to get my body submerged and dunk my head under the water. I might as well wash my hair while I'm here. I hold my breath, liking the feeling of shutting everything out. Under here there's no pressure to succeed. It's just me and the water. The only thought in my head, a simple reminder to breathe. This is the only type of meditation I'll ever be able to do.

Something makes the still water jump and I sit up abruptly, expecting to find Suki has barged her way in. I stare back at Clooney, his eyes bulging out of their sockets. What the hell is he doing in here? I put the sock on the door. I told him this bathroom didn't have a lock. The sock on the door is code for occupied. His eyes lower and I'm reminded that I'm naked.

I clutch my breasts. 'Agh! Get the fuck out!' I scream, ducking down lower in the water.

He snaps out of whatever trance he's been in and turns around, scrambling at the door handle. He finally finds it and yanks at it so hard that the handle comes off in his hand.

He turns around to me, holding it out, eyes almost popping out of their sockets. I duck my chest further into the water.

'Dude!' I shout. 'What the hell?'

'Sorry!' he shouts back, turning so his back is facing me. He tries in vain to reattach the door handle, but it's clear it's not going to work. The strong bloody idiot.

'Didn't you see the sock on the door?' I screech.

'Obviously not.' I can feel him rolling his eyes.

'Really?' I snort sarcastically. 'How convenient.'

'Please.' He turns to face me. 'If I wanted to see a naked woman, I'd just call any one of the girls on my phone.'

I manage to cover my boobs with a face cloth and if I pull my body close to the edge of the tub, he won't be able to see my lady bits.

'Ugh, you're such an arrogant pig,' I cry, but my heart is pounding. 'Pass me my towel, keep your eyes turned that way.' I stab my finger to the door.

He smiles smugly, before turning back around. 'I'm just telling the truth.' There's a pause. 'What towel?'

Oh my fuck. I haven't forgotten my towel too? The moment he says it, I know. I can vividly remember laying it on the bed.

I sigh. I can't even have a bath in peace. 'Whatever. Call one of your skanks now to come and let you out. I was *trying* to relax in here.'

He pulls his phone out of his pocket and frowns. 'Shit, it's dead.'

'Oh for God's sake. So neither of us can get out of here?'

He bites his bottom lip. It's annoying how sexy it is.

'Afraid not. We'll have to wait until Ella comes up. Well, unless you can get through those bars.' He points towards the metal bars over the windows. I knew those bars would end up causing me direct pain.

Here I was thinking they'd be a fire hazard. I never considered being trapped in here, naked, with Clooney.

He sits down on the floor, his back leaning against the bath, and sighs heavily.

'This isn't ideal for me either, you know,' he says, his voice tense.

'Ugh, whatever.' I'm sure he's been in worst situations. I sigh, attempting to let all of my stress out in one heavy breath. It only proves to make me feel more hassled, every muscle in my body taut. I mean, if the guy turned around right now, he'd see my cooch. And I haven't even bothered to shave my lady garden—for a while. Like since I broke up with Garry. He'll think I live like this all the time, like a bloody cave woman with a forest instead of a neatly tended garden. Damn it.

'Why are you so bloody stressed anyway?'

I sigh again. Doing a hell of a lot of sighing at the moment.

'Let me think. I've ploughed all of my savings into a failing business, I've moved to a country that seems to hate me and now I work with dead people.'

I don't dare tell him I might be able to hear them too.

'Well, shit,' he says with a chuckle. 'Sounds like you need to get laid.'

My jaw drops open at the bare faced audacity.

'Oh my god, is that your answer to *everything*?' I exclaim. 'Meaningless sex?'

I don't know why I expected anything more from him. He's nothing more than a man-whore.

He shrugs. 'It doesn't have to be meaningless.' His tone has turned serious.

Shit, what does he mean by that?

'And it doesn't even need to be full sex,' he continues. 'You just need an orgasm.'

Oh my god. The cheek of this man.

I snort. 'Well, good luck.' Why has my voice turned husky? 'I can't even get myself to come, let alone a man doing it for me.'

Jesus, why am I telling him this? I need to stop blurting stuff out in front of him. He makes me so stupid.

He turns to face me from under his dark lashes, locking

his intense forest green eyes with mine. A shiver runs through me.

'Sorry, did you just say that you've *never* had an orgasm?'

Jesus, why must I be such an over-sharer? As if being naked doesn't make me vulnerable enough. I might as well tell him. Maybe if I open up he will too and I'll find out the deal with him and his dad.

'Face to the wall,' I demand, my voice low but full of authority. He tuts but does as I ask. 'No. I'm pretty sure I've been close before, but I've just never been able to get there fully. You know, those over the hill, falling back to earth, soul shattering kind of orgasms you read in books or women's magazines. Part of me thinks it's all just a load of bollocks and it's not even real.'

He snorts. 'Oh, it's real alright.'

I scoff a laugh. 'You mean, you haven't even considered that those women you sleep with aren't faking their orgasm?'

'Trust me, no one is that good an actor.'

Such a cock womble.

'*Really?*' I want to dent his massive ego. 'I'm sorry, but I doubt very much that any of those were real.'

He turns to face me again, those eyes making promises he can't keep. 'I'm telling you.' He searches over my face as if looking for something. 'Why the hell would they keep coming back for more?'

I raise my eyebrows. 'To flatter your ego no doubt.'

He raises his eyebrows, as if to say *really?*

I decide to continue, to let him know how real women operate.

'They probably hope that one day you'll amend your ways and they'll be the special girl to change your mind and consider a relationship. A girl will always want to change a bad boy. It's the oldest story in history.'

His eyes glare at me. He's so close I can feel his minty breath on my face. 'I'm telling you right now. I could give you an orgasm in minutes.'

Is he offering?

'I don't believe you,' I whisper, suddenly breathless. Damn it, why am I turned on right now? I'm supposed to be insulting him and now I have him offering me an orgasm? I feel my nipples pucker under the face cloth. I pray he doesn't notice.

His jaw stiffens in annoyance. 'Just shut up and turn around, will you?' he growls.

'Why? What are you going to do?' Panic grips at my throat. My heart thumps inside my chest. It scares me how much I want him. How I crave to feel his bare skin on mine again.

His eyes darken. I'm not sure if it's with lust or annoyance. 'Just fucking trust me for more than ten seconds, will ya.'

CHAPTER TWENTY

I begrudgingly turn, nervous anticipation bubbling in my stomach. Am I really doing this? Daring him to give me an orgasm so that I can prove him wrong?

I jump, splashing the water, when he puts his hands on the top of my shoulders, goose-pimples breaking out all over my body.

'Calm down,' he murmurs. There's an amused lilt to his tone. 'I'm just going to give you a massage.'

Oh thank god.

'You think you can give me an orgasm from a massage?' I ask in challenge. Why am I encouraging this? *Because you secretly want it.*

'Do you ever just shut the fuck up?'

I clamp my lips shut, wanting to turn and punch him. But there's still a tiny part of me excited by his hands on me. Damn, anyone's hands on me. It feels like forever since I've had a reassuring touch.

'Just try to relax, okay?' He squirts some liquid soap

onto his hands and places them on the top of my shoulders, massaging in warm circles. It's annoying how incredible it feels. He must have been one of those lads at school who was good at everything he tried.

He starts trailing one hand slowly down my spine. It makes me shiver even though the bath water is still roaring hot. The butterflies in my stomach come alive. Don't freak out, Phoebe. Just let yourself feel this.

His hand reaches down to my hip and squeezes. It makes me jump, a buzz zinging through my body, ending up low below the water.

'So so tense,' he says against my neck, chuckling a hoarse and low sound.

I try to actively relax myself, not wanting him to call me uptight. I take a discreet deep breath. He mirrors his hands, soothingly shifting them upwards and then down again on my sides. The guy is good, he must have taken a massage course or something.

I feel myself start to relax against his touch. Maybe it's not so bad letting him help me. He might just stop at the massage after all.

His hands slowly move closer to my hips, his tentative touch teasing me. It's making me feel ridiculously hot and needy. Damn him, it just makes me want to be touched more.

His fingers travel lazily in figures of eight up my spine and rest at the top of my shoulders. Is he going to stop? Please God don't stop. There are things heating inside of me that I didn't know existed.

His fingers skim over the curve of my shoulders and focus on my upper chest, slowly moving from my collarbone down to the very tops of my breasts.

It's such an almost touch, not really making contact

where I want him, where my nipples are already erect and begging for release. My breasts heave up and down in time with my erratic heartbeat. One hand trails slowly down the centre of my chest, careful not to touch them, and then swoops from my stomach around to my back again.

My god he's a tease. He repeats this four times, until I'm basically wanton with lust, pushing my breasts desperately out every time he's near them. Right now I don't care that it's Clooney with the magic hands. I don't care how much he specifically is turning me on, or how my control is slipping away. Every nerve ending in my body is electrified.

I'm basically panting like a dog when he finally relents and greedily grabs a boob in each hand, squeezing hard. I cry out, unable to help myself. I can practically hear him smirking. Arrogant arsehole. I feel my cheeks redden but I'm too turned on to care that much. Why am I letting him do this again? I don't want to embarrass myself or let myself be vulnerable around him, but it's too late now. It feels too good.

He teases one nipple between his finger and thumb while he massages the other like he did my back. It's hard to concentrate on anything at all, with two very different sensations happening at the same time. I feel delirious and out of control, my brain in serious danger of overheating.

His breath is on the back of my neck, his breathing laboured too. He's enjoying himself. It's quite a revelation. This isn't just him providing a service. He's into it too. I know if I turned to look at him right now, he'd have hunger in his eyes.

My legs fall open in front of me, the excited heavy pulsing overwhelming me, making me do things I wouldn't normally. Dammit, I really should have tended to my lady garden. That's a life lesson. Keep yourself tidy. You never know when a sexual experience will surprise you.

He grabs hold of my waist, bringing me back to the present, and turns me to face the taps. I don't want to make eye contact with him. Don't want him to see the vulnerability I know is in my eyes. To break the spell I'm under. I've never felt this close to release before and I don't want him to stop.

I don't get a chance because he dips his head and takes one of my nipples in his mouth. I cry out, so loud I'll be surprised if the entire town didn't hear me. His hot tongue is delicious on my highly alert, sensitive, goose pimpled skin.

I don't have time to be embarrassed. Before I know it, his fingers are travelling down past my belly button and through my ridiculously bushy lady garden, teasing at my entrance. Shit, this is it. He's touching my bits. How the hell did we get here?

The minute his finger travels inside me I cry out, throwing myself back, as if possessed. As if an electric current has passed through me. He puts his arm around my shoulders, holding me up so I don't drown.

A second finger fills me. I feel myself pulse around it. Fuck, he's good at this. Never before have I been made to feel like such a sexually desired goddess. I shut my eyes and drink it in.

His thumb massages my clit ever so gently, causing my heart rate to accelerate to a dangerous speed. It's so unlike anything I've ever had with a man.

But this guy... wow. No wonder he's a much-wanted man whore. He's a bloody professional. I can see why women turn stupid around him. If they've felt this themselves, or even heard the urban legends, well, it's enough for him to get the reputation he has. It's so well deserved. I'm already considering buying him a medal.

I look down at his tattooed forearm, his fingers dipping in and out of me. It looks so crazily hot. Turns out that king of hearts tattoo *is* well deserved.

He takes my breast into his mouth again. By now I'm jumping around involuntarily so much it pops out in seconds. I'm so squirmy. I almost want him to stop, the building pleasure unbearable.

He trails his tongue up to my neck and then starts nibbling at my ear. I'm not normally an ear girl at all, but this I can get on board with as he lazily plays with my lobe.

My breath hitches in my throat, as if impossible to purge it from my lungs. Another moan escapes my lips.

I'm suddenly so hot and full of sensation that I can feel myself falling, as if I've just jumped off a cliff. You know those dreams, where you wake up having fallen and you're a trembling mess? Well that's me right now. I cry out, as if willing for someone to catch me.

'Oh god, oh god, oh god, oh GOD!' I scream, holding onto the helpful grab rails, my head spinning like I've drank too much alcohol.

'Let yourself go,' he whispers into my ear, the sound of his rasping voice making my skin tingle. Combined with all the different sensations, it's enough to push me over the edge.

I can't remember how to breathe, my toes curl. I scream something that could never be confused with an actual word. I physically push myself back so hard he drops me and I'm under the water, basking in the most beautiful after glow. Every part of my body feels fantastic, soothed by a comforting warm balm, I could drown right now, and I honestly wouldn't care less.

He pulls me up, a smirk on his face as he skims a light touch over the contours of my face. I stare dumbly back at him in awe.

'I told you so,' he teases playfully, his voice still loaded with lust.

I smile sleepily back. I must look like a half asleep geek right now, beaming back at him, but I don't care. That was amazing. Epic. Beyond all the adjectives.

'I've never been so happy to be wrong,' I whisper, my voice barely audible.

He smiles back at me, pushing my hair out of my face. It's a tender moment considering what we just did. The urge to kiss him has me leaning forward eagerly. He glances down at my lips.

The door swings open, hitting hard and loud against the wall. We both jump apart guiltily. Ella is stood staring at us both, eyes nearly exploding from their sockets.

'What the hell is going on here?' She demands, looking between the two of us, her jaw aghast.

'Ah, thank god,' Clooney says, jumping up for the door. 'I've been locked in.' He runs like the room's on fire.

I try so hard not to be hurt that he ran so quickly at his first chance, but the guy gave me my first orgasm. He'll always hold a special place in my heart because of that.

Ella is still standing against the open door, her face searching mine for an explanation.

'Well, are you going to explain, or what?' she demands, tapping her foot impatiently.

I shake my head, hoping to bring myself back to reality.

'I don't have time now. Just grab something to put in the door until we get it fixed.'

I want to be alone to bask in all of the strange sensations

running around my body, before my sensible reality comes crashing back.

She disappears for a second and then comes back to slot a book in the door jamb. 'That'll do it. But this is *not* over. I want details and I want them soon.'

CHAPTER TWENTY-ONE

Tuesday 13ᵗʰ October

*M*e and Clooney are avoiding each other. It's been easy while I'm working at the funeral home, but with living with him and working together in the evenings, it's still been tough. Neither of us have been able to look the other in the eye since the bathtub incident.

Ella didn't believe me when I said nothing happened. Said she knew I'd had an orgasm just from the glow of me. I just played ignorant and said we'd almost kissed. Far more PG. I've never discussed sex with her and I'm not about to start now. Especially about the guy we both live with.

The fact that we didn't kiss on the lips, but did all of that other stuff just makes it even weirder. I can still feel the tingling sensation in my skin as he touched me. My stupid crush on him has only developed. Whenever there's some little tart flirting with him over the bar, I can't help but want to glass her in the face. A tad dramatic some would say, but that's how crazy he makes me feel. Why the hell did I have to fall for a fuck boy? Someone so obviously unattainable.

To add to that stress, it seems that I've officially lost my mind. Ever since the scenario with the hearse I've been hearing voices whenever a new body comes into the chapel of rest. I've tried desperately to ignore it but... well, they've started to notice. Okay, I know I sound mad, but stick with me here.

Let's just say for a crazy second that I'm hearing their spirits or ghosts, whatever you want to call them. Well, I try to ignore them, but they've started saying things like *'You can hear me, can't you?'* It's getting harder to evade them.

I don't know whether they talk to each other or what, but it's starting to scare me. I mean, should I go to the doctor? Get some anti-depressants or something? I feel perfectly fine otherwise. Have I inherited the gift? Not that I'd call it a gift, more like a bloody curse.

I spent the last few days devouring great Aunt Breda's diary and she got herself into some sticky situations over this supposed *gift*. I could definitely avoid any extra drama in my life right now.

Anyway, as I walk into the pub that night I'm ready to pour myself a large glass of wine and sink into a hot bubble bath. Dammit, Clooney has ruined baths for me. I can't think of one without the other. Instead I find Ella already sat at the bar, a finished bottle of wine next to her.

'Ella?'

She grunts back. Now I look closer I see her shoulders are drooped and her eyes distant. Clooney raises his eyebrows behind the bar as he dries a glass with a tea towel. 'She's been like this all afternoon.'

Ugh, just what I need.

'For Gods sakes, Ella. We can't be drinking the small profit we're making,' I say, exhaustion making me almost slur. Here I am working all day and she can't even keep it together.

'What's the point?' she says with a sniff. Her eyes are blotchy, her mascara smudged underneath.

'Point in what?'

She spreads her arms dramatically. 'This whole thing? Let's face it, it's not working here. We should just cut our losses and go back home.'

I scoff. 'That's easy for you to say. You haven't just spent your life savings doing it up.'

She slumps further into her bar stool. This is just like her to make everything about herself. All of it is *so* Ella. When something is too hard, she just quits.

'We're stuck here aren't we?' Her chin starts wobbling. 'We're going to die here and be eaten by the stupid fucking cows.'

She's so dramatic. She saw *one* cow.

I choose to ignore her. I'm already feeling down. I can't cope with this too. I walk behind the bar and pour myself a glass of cold white wine.

'*So, don't panic...*'

I look at Clooney. Did he just say that? It didn't sound like his voice. He's looking at me with narrowed brows.

'*But I followed you home from work.*'

Oh for fucks sakes. You have *got* to be kidding me.

'*I really hate to bother you at home, but I need you to pass on a message to my wife.*'

'Go away!' I shout in frustration, forgetting I'm around actual living people.

Clooney jumps out of his skin. 'What? I'm nowhere near you, you fecking maniac.'

I shake my head. 'Sorry, I didn't mean you.'

'Did you mean me, then?' Ella asks, full of self-pity. 'My own sister wants me to go away.'

'I'm afraid I can't go away.'

'Who were you talking to then?' Clooney asks, his eyes raking over my face, trying to work out what my problem is.

'You see, I need you to pass on a message.'

Dead people making me look nuts again.

'Um... myself?' I offer weakly. It's hard to keep up with two conversations at once.

'It's a pretty urgent message, you see.'

God, will he just fuck off? I'm trying to look normal in front of alive humans.

'Yourself?' Clooney asks, amusement dancing in his eyes. 'You were telling yourself to go away?'

'Yes, okay,' I snap through gritted teeth. I don't have the time or energy to come up with something better. 'Anyway, you can finish your shift now if you like.'

'My wife can't find my will. She's turned over the house looking for it.'

'Alright, thanks.' He smiles, bewildered.

'But I hid it in the dog food container. I need you to let her know.'

I attempt to wave the ghost off, motion for him to piss off without having to speak.

'You sure you don't need me to stay?' Clooney asks, looking at Ella in alarm.

'Only I need you to let her know urgently.'

'Go away,' I snarl through my teeth.

Clooney's eyes widen in alarm and is that... a bruised ego?

'Alright! There's no need to be rude. I'll go.' His voice is scored with hurt.

'Sorry, not you.' I sigh, exhausted, rubbing my temples trying to release the stress.

'Who, then?' he demands, hand on his hip. He looks like a sexy teapot. I bet he's into tea bagging too, the dirty bastard.

'Can you go see her tonight?'

I rub my forehead. 'Ugh, I've just got such a headache.'

'Okay, well... I'll be off then.' He turns to leave, obviously thinking I'm some maniac. Maybe I am.

'Please. I'll leave you alone as soon as you've told her.'

'Actually,' I shout after Clooney. 'If you could stay while I run an errand, that would be great.' I grimace a smile.

'Jeysus woman, make up your fecking mind.'

CHAPTER TWENTY-TWO

*a*s I trudge back into town, I'm heartbroken to think I've upset Clooney, even if I didn't mean to. That hurt look in his eyes will haunt my dreams. He's sure to think I'm a nutcase. Hell, that ship's probably long sailed. But this voice following me has given me an address and said to ask for his wife Colleen. The way I see it, if a Colleen opens the door that's confirmation enough that I'm not imagining it all.

I stop outside a row of small terraced houses painted pretty pastel colours.

'It's the one with the ivy.'

'Yeah, and I'm sure she's going to want to talk to the random woman at her door.'

'My Colleen can be a bit suspicious, but we'll talk her around.'

Great. I can't believe I'm potentially being bossed around by nothing more than a figment of my imagination. I knock on the door, dancing from foot to foot. This is crazy. I'm acting insane, but at this point I'll do anything to quieten his voice. He's a real chatty Cathy.

The door swings open to reveal a guy about my age. Ah, not a Colleen. See, I'm losing my mind.

'Ask for Colleen.'

'Uh hi... does Colleen live here?' I ask with an apologetic grimace.

'Yes,' he says, narrowing his eyes suspiciously at me, 'who are you?'

'My son. He's just as suspicious as his mother.'

Great. So I'm gonna have to beg two people to listen to me.

'My name's Phoebe Bellerose. I have something to tell her.'

He searches critically over my face. 'O... kay. Follow me.'

I smile and follow him through a lounge and into a small, bright kitchen/diner that smells of freshly baked bread. There's a woman with short brown hair and glasses sat at the table, her face etched with worry.

'My Colleen.'

It suddenly dawns on me that this woman has lost her husband and he's lost his Colleen. You can hear the affection in the way he speaks her name. How heart breaking to have lost each other. I can't even find one decent bloke. The thought of finding the love of your life, but only to lose him again, makes my heart ache for them.

'Colleen?' I ask, trying to smile sympathetically—not that easy.

'Yes,' she confirms with an apprehensive nod. 'Sorry, but I do I know you?' Realisation dawns on her face. 'You're Breda's great niece, aren't you?'

Accent gave me away again.

'Yeah, sorry.' I shrug, bouncing on my heels, already wanting to run away. 'This is going to sound really weird.'

She frowns back at me, then at her son.

How exactly do I put this? *Your dead ghost of a husband contacted me because apparently I'm now someone who talks to dead people.*

'Um... I knew your husband.' I swallow, my mouth dry.

Her eyes cloud over with fresh tears. 'Frank,' she says, beginning to sniff. 'You knew Frank?'

'Yes.' I nod. Funny, his voice doesn't sound like a Frank. More like a Mick.

'How did you know him?' she asks, with a squinted gaze.

'Um... we met in the pub.' My hands tremble by my sides. I despise lying.

She glowers at me. 'Really? That's strange. Frank wasn't a drinker. Plus, he's been bed bound for the last three months. I thought you and your sister had just moved here.'

Jesus, help me out here Frank! He's decided to go quiet on me.

'Well, anyway,' I say quickly, attempting to move it along. 'He wanted me to tell you that his will is hidden inside the dog food container.'

She pouts before crying out a laugh. 'Sorry?'

'Yeah,' her son joins in. 'What on earth are you talking about? Why would he put it there?'

'Seemed like a good idea at the time.'

Not now Frank.

'I have no idea,' I shrug, already walking backwards, more than ready to get the hell out of here. 'But I just wanted to come here and tell you that.'

'Wait,' she instructs, warning me with her eyes to stay in place.

She gets up and walks slowly over to the kitchen sink. Looking back at me, her head tilts, as if sizing me up.

I gulp. If this guy has set me up and there's nothing there, I will die of shame. Like this isn't weird enough.

She opens a cupboard underneath the sink, pulls out a metal tin and roots through it. She looks back at me, then back into the tin. She pulls out an envelope, rips it open and pulls out a document that I'm guessing is the will. Thank God for that.

'Why did he tell you about this?' she demands, appearing paler than a few minutes ago.

'Err...' I stammer, every fibre in my being telling me to turn and run. 'He just kind of... mentioned it in passing.'

She narrows her eyes at me. 'He... mentioned it in passing? Why on earth would he mention in passing the place he had hidden an important document? And like I said, he's been bed bound for three months.'

Oh God. I suppose a guy wouldn't just mention that in passing, not if he can't even leave the house.

'So when exactly did he come in?' She puts one hand on her hip. 'And what date did ye girls move here?'

'Err...' Oh God, this is awkward. 'I can't remember specifically.'

'I have to say,' the son says, eying me accusingly. 'I find this all very strange.'

Like I don't.

'Me too.' Colleen nods.

'She was always suspicious.'

'Anyway, I really have to go!' I spin on my heel and practically run to the door and out of there. I start the walk back to the pub on shaky legs, praying to God he'll now leave me alone.

'Are you happy?' I shout. 'Will you leave me alone now?'

'*Yes. Thank you so much. I'm ready now.*'
'Well go towards the bloody light, *please!*'

I'm so relieved when I get back to the pub, my shoulders un-hunch the minute I walk through the door. I just want to sit down and let out a loud sigh. That or get a hug from Clooney, which I know is completely off the table.

I don't know why I want his comfort specifically. Probably because I know that Ella is currently a mess. Something about him is just so strong and stable. I'll have to just settle with Suki.

My God, it's so nice only having my own voice circling round my head.

I look around to see Clooney sat down on a table surrounded by his friends. They're playing cards. I study him for a moment, before he notices me. It's weird seeing him relaxed in the company of his mates. His shoulders are loose, laughing as they share a joke. It's nice to see the laughter lines around his eyes.

It makes me realise that I've not actually seen Clooney laugh properly before. He's always smiling smugly or snorting a laugh, but this is pure unfiltered joy emanating from him. I want to sit down and soak it in, let some of it rub off on me. I can't remember the last time I laughed like that.

'Hey.' He smiles, when he notices me. It's like I blossom every time he looks me over; every muscle in my body springing alive at just the memory of his tongue on my skin.

'Hi.' I quickly snap myself out of it, hoping he didn't catch me staring dreamily at him. I can't help but want to try my hardest to earn that laughter from him.

'All sorted?' he asks, eyebrows raised.

God, he's gorgeous; olive skin against a simple white t-shirt, those biceps covered in tattoos. He's extremely lickable.

'Yep,' I nod, looking around for Ella. 'Is she...?'

'I put her to bed,' he nods with a breath-taking smile. 'She was pretty wasted.'

I smile back gratefully. I look down at the table they're sat at and notice that there's money on the table. Why can't guys just put their stuff in their pockets? I suppose its these skinny jeans they all insist on wearing. Talk about try to steal our style.

Wait, are they using that money to bet? Is this a proper poker game? Are they gambling on my property?

'Are you... gambling?' I blurt, feeling stupid as soon as I've said it. Of course he's not. He wouldn't be so irresponsible. He knows the rules of a boozer.

Clooney looks back at me wide eyed. 'Yeah, just a friendly game. Why?'

'Why? Because you're gambling on my property. That's totally illegal.'

He scoffs a laugh. 'As if. It's only a harmless game.'

'A harmless game that could totally lose me my licence.' I can hear how hysterical I sound and it makes me cringe.

His mates turn to stare at me. Maybe I *do* need to get a strait jacket.

He stands up and ushers me to one side. 'Pheebs, chill,' he says soothingly, hands up in defence.

'Don't Pheebs me! You don't even know me. You don't get to nickname my full name. And especially when you couldn't give a shit about whether you lose my licence or not.'

Here I am working myself to death and he could ruin everything in one evening.

'Err... we should go,' one of his friends says, already on his feet, reaching for his jacket.

'No, you're fine,' Clooney snaps back. 'Sit down.'

His friend drops into his seat, looking between us with a loud swallow.

'You're not going to lose your licence over a stupid little game between friends. This is Ireland, not London. You're not likely to be raided any minute. It's not an episode of EastEnders.'

'Oh, and you think you have the right to make that decision for me, do you? Right after we've told every guard in town that they get fifty percent off?' His eyes flicker in realisation. 'Yeah, I bet you forgot about that little fact, didn't you?'

He runs a hand through his hair. 'God, you're dramatic.'

'Dramatic?' I repeat, stern-faced. 'You have *no* idea what I've put into this business. I can't just allow you to flush it down the toilet.'

Why am I taking my bad mood out on Clooney? I hate myself, but it's like I can't stop.

'You're doing a good job of that yourselves,' he says under his breath.

'Hey fuck you, Clooney.' I spin on my heel and storm to

the back of the bar and into the kitchen. I can't even look at him right now, I'm too mad.

'Wait!' he shouts. I'm half in the kitchen when he takes me by my arm.

'No!' I throw him off me, my rage giving me super strength. 'Why am I even shocked? You're not on our side. You're on your dad's side. You were probably sent to fuck everything up in the first place.'

He flinches, his eyes squinted at me. 'Hey! I have my friends out there spending money on *your* booze. Do you think my dad would like to know they're here, rather than at his?'

I open my mouth to respond, but realise he is right. Damn, I hate being wrong. I know deep down I'm pushing him away because I'm scared of how he makes me feel. Scared of being hurt again.

'I mean, yeah," his voice softens, "maybe I didn't think through the poker game, but fuck, Phoebe.' He grabs a fistful of his t-shirt. 'Of course I'm on your side. I want this place to work. Not just to piss my dad off, but because I want you guys to be successful here.'

He seems so sincere. It would be so easy to believe him, but I'm guessing all those women that slept with him believed all of his broken promises too. He's too charming to ever fully trust and let in. Not after Garry. I won't humiliate myself like that again.

'You promise?' My voice sounds wobbly, even to my own ears. I'm so pathetic. Way to look like a strong, confident woman.

He sighs, stepping forward, his wide green eyes imploring mine. 'I promise,' he says, his voice low and serious.

I relent. It's not like I have much chance up against that beautiful searing gaze.

'Okay, well then, I'm sorry.' I bite my lip. Something about Ballykielty has me losing any calm rationality.

He runs his hands through his dark hair making it stand on end. I imagine that's how he looks when he's freshly fucked.

'And I'm sorry for not thinking. It won't happen again.'

'Okay, thanks.' I smile, suddenly embarrassed to have got so cross with him. It's just with everything getting on top of me he was the closest one to lose it with. Ella's never here when I need her. I turn to walk into the sitting room.

'Oh, and Phoebe?' he calls after me. I turn around to see him at the kitchen door, his frame still tense. 'You said I don't know you well enough to call you Pheebs.'

'Err... yeah?' I nod, confused what his point is.

He smiles lazily, as if to himself. 'I already know you a hell of a lot better than you think.'

He turns and walks out. The worrying thing is that he's possibly right.

CHAPTER TWENTY-FOUR

<u>Wednesday 14th October</u>

J can't stop thinking about what Clooney said last night. Why the hell does he think he knows me so well? What kind of illusion is he under? He doesn't know me. Not at all. The man might have got me off in a bathtub but that doesn't mean he knows me. Knows my soul. My deepest, darkest fears and secrets.

I don't have to be in work until this afternoon, so I get to watch him jogging out in his tiny shorts for a run. I don't know how he can stand to be in shorts in this freezing weather, but I'm not complaining as I ogle his thick thighs and toned calves out of my bedroom window. I've turned into a little pervert lately.

'Really?' Ella teases, coming in with a cup of tea. I need it, she was snoring like a trooper last night. This sharing a bed lark is getting old real quick.

'I was just checking the weather,' I insist with a shrug before taking my tea from her. Suki trots in, stretching herself out on the floor like a small fur rug.

'Oh pur-lease!' Ella laughs. 'You fancy the pants of him.'

I take a sip of tea, biding for time. I know if I protest too much she'll call me a liar. I need to play this cool.

'I don't think I could ever properly trust him. Not after Garry.'

She sighs. 'Pheebs, how many times do I have to tell you? Not all men are like Garry. He was the reason he cheated, it had nothing to do with anything you'd done.'

'Then why do I blame myself? Why have I replayed every conversation we've ever had? Every sexual encounter. What if it's because I'm shit in bed?'

She snorts a laugh. 'You're not bad in bed. Garry was just a moron. He was never good enough for you.'

'Oh and Clooney is?' I raise my eyebrows.

Her face lights up in mischief. 'Isn't the risk worth it for him?'

She takes a biscuit out of her dressing gown pocket. Trust her to have a biscuit for breakfast.

'Do... *you* fancy him?' I can't resist asking.

This has been nagging at me for a while. I suppose I know in my heart of hearts that if she does, I don't stand a chance. She's always been the prettier, funnier sister.

She dips her biscuit in her tea. 'Nah, I prefer them blonde. Plus, you two have this whole vibe going on.'

'We do *not* have a vibe going on.' I can't help but feel a little glimmer of hope blossom in the pint of my stomach. I'm so girly and giggly at just the mention of him.

She grins, popping the biscuit in her mouth. 'You know you do,' she mumbles, her mouth full. 'You almost kissed the other day. I think he's into you.'

I shake my head. 'He's into anyone with a vagina. Don't think for one minute that I'm special.'

She smiles, as if hiding a secret. 'Whatever you say.'

~

For some reason I find myself rushing around getting break-fast, wanting to go back to hiding in my bedroom before he gets back from his run. I don't know why, but I'm nervous. I know it's dumb, but my body didn't get the memo from my brain.

He walks in, sweat dripping down his forehead, his t-shirt clinging to his broad chest. Damn, why does he insist on looking so sexy? It's as annoying as hell.

'Hey *Pheebs*,' he jokes, accentuating the nickname.

'Hi *Cloo*,' I joke back.

He smirks, like he finds me hilariously amusing. Not in a *ha ha funny* way, more a *isn't she cute like a bunny rabbit* way.

'That was a quick run.' God, why did I have to mention that? I butter my toast so I don't have to look at him.

'I didn't realise you were timing me.'

I chance a quick look at him. He's smiling, like he's got me all figured out. I hate that he assumes everyone fancies him. I hate that its true.

'All calmed down after last night?' he asks with a wide toothy smile.

'Yes,' I snap, cutting into my toast a little too hard. 'Although some would argue that I had every right to be upset.'

'Some would also be drama queens.'

I swallow, hating that I made such a show of myself last night.

'Anyway, I have to get going and get ready for work.'

'Yep. I bet those dead people are hard work. Maybe even *rigid.*'

I bark a laugh, despite wanting to stay cool. Jesus, I've got it bad. Laughing about a dead person joke. My cheeks burn, my body cringing at myself. Stop acting like an idiot, Phoebe.

His phone rings, apparently on a better network than us. 'Sorry.' He takes it and moves to outside the back door.

I can't help but listen in. Apparently, I'm obsessed with him now.

'Yeah. It's on at 2.30 p.m. Blue Ridge. Yeah, it's a sure thing. Put me down for fifty.'

What is he talking about? Not that I have time to ask. I've got to get to ready for work. I might as well turn up early. It's better than staying here embarrassing myself. I just hope to God I don't hear any voices.

I put on a brave face in front of Patricia, Seamus' wife. Luckily I don't seem to be hearing any voices today. Seamus and Niall are out doing funerals. Apparently I can't be trusted with them.

Around two o'clock she realises she's worked through lunch so I offer to watch the shop while she pops out to get something.

About fifteen minutes after she's gone, a teary middle-aged widow walks in, clutching at her tissue.

'Hi, can I help you?' I ask, using my friendly but sympathetic voice I've managed to master while working here.

'I'm here to see my Garrett laid out.'

Oh crap. I suppose I can't act unprofessional and tell her I don't know what I'm doing. They trained me for this the other day. I just need to go in there first, check his name bracelet and then allow her in.

'No problem. Let me just go check everything is set up properly.'

I run in, spotting Garrett in his coffin on stilts. I stand by it and try to reach for his wrist, but with the stilts it's too high for my short arse. Damn. I know, I'll get a chair.

I find one and drag it into position next to him. I jump up, lean over and brace myself. He's just a normal person that has sadly died. He's not going to come back to life. He's not going to jerk. This is fine.

I take a deep breath as I reach for his nearest wrist, attempting to just pull up his suit jacket sleeve to see. I don't want to actually touch his skin. I've never touched a dead person's skin before and I have no idea what it will feel like. Would it be cold? Slimy?

Ugh, where is this damn identity bracelet? I'm going to have to touch him. Deep breath, Phoebe. Do it for the grieving widow. You can hardly show her in for her to then announce that he's not her husband. That would traumatise someone for life, and definitely get me fired.

I place one hand on his, shocked to feel that although it is cold he's not beyond freezing and his skin feels kind of normal. I move his sleeve all the way up but still no bracelet. Damn, it must be on the other one.

That side of the coffin is pressed up against the wall. I have to reach over and take his hand, as if holding it.

'Sorry about this, Garrett. Just want to check you are who I think you are.'

I reach my hand up his other sleeve and finally feel it. Result! I pull it down to see his name written on it. Thank God. I fist-punch the air victoriously. Only... it seems I'm a bit too enthusiastic because I feel the chair wobble beneath me. Oh no.

My body is thrown forwards, my forehead hitting something squishy. I grab the sides of the coffin, steadying myself. I quickly realise I just head-butted the dead guy in his dick. Ugh, vom.

I push myself off him, falling onto my back on the floor. Jesus, Phoebe. Way to respect the dead. I dry heave a few times. This job is the worst.

I get back up to standing, straighten my clothes down, blow my hair from my face and attempt to pull myself together. You can do this.

I put on my sad face and walk back out to the widow, clutching my hands in front of me, just like they taught me.

'He's ready for you,' I announce, showing her through and leaving her to it.

When I get to the front desk, Patricia comes back in.

'Oh no, is Mrs McCarthy here?'

I nod. 'Yes, but don't worry. She's in with him.'

Surprise flits over her face. 'Did you make sure to check his identity bracelet?'

'I did,' I answer proudly. 'All done, just as you taught me.'

'Ah, excellent.' She beams back at me. 'I'll watch it back tonight and let you know anything you might have missed off for next time.'

'Sorry?' I laugh nervously. 'Watch it back? What do you mean?'

'I mean on our CCTV.'

Now I remember Seamus and Niall watched me on it when they put me in with that dead man, Lochlan.

'We have to have it. We went through a period a few

years ago where some nutcase was breaking in and trying to have sex with the dead.'

I gasp. 'That's horrific.' Not as horrific as when she sees me head-butt the dead guy in the balls.

'Indeed,' she nods, 'but we've found it helps with training.'

'Great,' I grimace. Yep, just great.

CHAPTER TWENTY-FIVE

'Hey,' I say, dumping my bag onto the bar after another long day at work.

Ella is already sat there with a large wine. I smile at Clooney. Never before have I wanted to run into someone's arms so much. It's like he's a magnet, some unknown force pulling me towards him. I have to fight it with all of my being, knowing that he's wrong for me. It's becoming exhausting.

'Can I have one of those too?' I ask him with a pout, motioning to Ella's wine.

'Jayses, you can get it yourself. I'm not your slave.'

I baulk, shocked at his sudden rudeness. Now I look at him properly I see that his shoulders are tense, his jaw tight. Where did this mood come from?

'What the hell crept up your arse?'

He glares back at me and goes to clean the other end of the bar. Moody, pathetic man.

'Lost a bet, I think,' Ella whispers. 'Some horse or something that didn't come in.'

I watch him stomping around the place. How could one

little lost bet affect his mood so greatly? Has he lost a lot of money? How could that be possible when we're not even paying him? Surely there has to be more to it than that?

~

Thursday 15th October

Clooney practically skips down the stairs the following morning, followed closely by Suki. What's he got to be so happy about? Especially after being such a miserable arse last night.

'Morning!' he sings.

'Why are you so happy this morning?' I ask with a snort. Attractive. Real attractive, Phoebe.

'Just feeling lucky.' He smiles, his eyes practically lighting up the room. What the hell am I missing? His moods are giving me whiplash.

'Well, lucky boy, fancy changing a barrel for me?'

He frowns and purses his lips. 'You really need to learn how to do it yourself, you know.'

I shrug. Every time I've tried to do it so far, I've been sprayed with smelly beer.

'Not when I pay *you*.' I smile sweetly, fluttering my eyelashes.

He smiles, a distant emotion in his eyes. 'You don't pay me at all.' But he walks off to do it.

That has me wondering again. With us not paying him how could he afford to put on a bet? Where did he get that money from? And why so happy now?

He's left his phone on the side. God its so close. I bet whatever he's happy about is on that phone right now. Some text from a leggy, slutty blonde. I really shouldn't look. I *really* shouldn't. But, God, it's just so close, calling out to me, promising answers.

Okay, one little peek won't hurt. I grab it and open it before I can stop myself, glad he hasn't got a security code. Instead of a normal text message there's a casino app open. He's happy because he's playing an online game?

'All changed.'

I quickly place it back onto the side before he spots it.

'Great!'

I spin round, pulse raising, thanking God I wasn't caught. That was close. There's no way I'd be able to explain myself out of that one. I'm ashamed of myself. All self-control disappears around this man.

I open the pub up and greet the man already waiting with a clipboard. Men with clipboards are never good news around here. I walk back behind the bar, wanting some kind of armour between us, hoping and praying he's just doing an annoying survey.

'Hi. What can I get you?' I ask, playing dumb and hoping he'll go away.

'Hello. I'm from Sky. We've been informed that you have sports channels on the premises, which is strange, because we only have you down for a personal residential account.'

My stomach hits the floor. Shit.

He arches one eyebrow, his jaw tensing. 'Can you tell me how that's possible?'

We've been caught. The games up. I knew it was a stupid idea. Knew we'd never get away with it. I was ridiculous to think we could do something without it coming back to smack us in the face.

'They... must be wrong?' I attempt with a crooked smile.

My voice sounds high and wobbly even to me. My hands start to tremble.

'Or.' He lowers his glasses. 'You're funnelling it from the personal service into the main bar?'

Oh God, he already knows. We're done for.

'Um... no.' I shake my head vehemently. 'I mean, I wouldn't even have any idea how to do that.' Which is kind of true.

That's it, Phoebe, play the dumb blonde card. If in doubt I can always pull that out.

He smiles knowingly. He's obviously seen this act before.

'That's no problem. I know how to check.' He spins on his heel and heads outside.

'Shit.' I run into the kitchen to Clooney, feeling sick to my stomach. 'A guy from Sky is here. What do I do?'

'Nothing,' he shrugs, obviously not realising the vastness of this problem. 'Probably just checking your connections are all in working order.' He narrows his eyes slowly. 'Wait, you're not illegally funnelling it, are you?'

'Err...' I couldn't feel like more of an idiot. Why didn't I listen to him?

His eyes nearly pop out of his head. 'What?'

Oh God. Now I've got to explain myself. I start pacing, my hands behind my back.

'Ugh, Dermot's son did it and he said it was no big deal, that loads of pubs do it,' I ramble. 'I mean, we could never afford the two thousand euros a month otherwise. Your dad's pub has it. If we wanted to stand any chance competing, we had to have it.'

'Fuck.' He leans back against the fridge, a hand through his glorious black glossy hair. 'You do realise he's going to fine you, right?'

'Really?' I ask meekly, not really wanting to hear the truth. I could quite happily bury my head in the sand for a few more hours. 'Don't you think he'll give us a chance? Let us off with a warning, it is a first offence?' I don't even sound like I'm convinced myself.

He takes my shoulders and steels his gaze. 'Phoebe, it's not like you've been caught speeding. This is Sky. You've been illegally watching their channels. This is serious.'

I gulp, bile trying to make its way from my stomach up into my oesophagus. I'm fucked. We are never going to be able to pay the fine. I'll end up in Irish prison being fed bad lumpy mashed potato for breakfast, lunch and dinner. I'll be someone's bitch. I'll have to kiss her and pretend I like it just so I have some form of protection. God knows I've never been able to fight. Although I really don't know if I'll be able to touch someone else's vagina.

The door bangs. 'Indeed, it is serious,' the man says, reappearing. His bald head is flushed. 'Here is your fine.' He hands over a notice. 'We expect it to be paid in full within thirty days. I've disconnected you and be warned that if we find you doing this again, we will be forced to take legal action.'

Shit. Clooney was right, but at least they haven't arrested us. I mean, it could be worse. I won't have to touch a vagina. Phew.

The guy turns and marches off, clipboard wedged under his arm. I look down at the paper and scroll my eyes down to the total of the fine. Seven thousand euros. Shit. We're totally screwed.

CHAPTER TWENTY-SIX

'Seven thousand euros! Are you fucking joking me?' Ella cries later that day, before throwing herself back on the chair. 'I'm gonna kill that guy!'

She means the elderly man Dermot who suggested it would be fine to illegally funnel it. Although, we're the idiots who believed him.

I narrow my eyes at her. 'Ella, the guy's in his seventies. It wouldn't be a fair fight. It's totally my fault.'

She frowns, narrowing her eyes at me. 'How did you work that one out?'

I sigh, slumping my shoulders. 'Because I talked you into it. You're easily swayed by me.'

'Ugh.' She rolls her eyes. 'So what you're saying is I'm a dumb arse that'll go along with anything you say?'

Well, now I've upset her. I can't do anything right at the moment.

'No, Ella, that's not what I'm saying. I just...'

'How are we going to find seven thousand euros?'

I sink down onto the bar stool, stroking my hair back off my face. I've noticed myself doing it lately. I think it reminds me of when Ella used to play with my hair when we were little. Simpler times.

'I have no idea.' I sigh, completely deflated. 'It honestly feels like it couldn't get any worse.' As soon as the words leave my mouth, I regret it.

All of the lamps go out and the background music stops.

'Just what we need, a power cut.'

'You paid the bill, right?' Clooney asks sarcastically.

'Of course I did.'

Err... I did, didn't I? Yeah, I'm sure I did.

'If you want to help find me some candles so we can stay open.'

Truthfully, I'm already considering just giving up and going to bed.

'Already on it!' Ella says, running out back. Never before have I been so happy for her candle obsession.

It turns out a town blackout is good for business. A load of people end up coming in, deciding to wait it out with friends and booze. For once we're actually busy.

The only issue has been that we've had to bring Suki out to the bar. She was terrified in the dark all on her own, whimpering like a baby. It's not like we could have trusted her with a candle. She could have burnt the place down to the ground. Not that I couldn't do with the insurance money. The customers all seemed to love it, cooing over her.

Finally, we ring the bell and start the clean-up. By the time I'm forcing a smiled goodbye to the last customer, all I want to do is curl up in my bed. Clooney has disappeared and Ella tells me she can't stay awake one more moment before practically running off to bed carrying a sleepy Suki. *Well, gee, thanks, sis.*

Clooney re-appears from the front, having had a cigarette. Is it weird that even when he faintly smells of smoke I find it alluring? Probably need some therapy if I'm being honest with myself.

'Ella snuck off to bed?' he asks with a nod of his head while he locks the front door behind him.

'How did you guess?' I retort. If it wasn't for him, I'd be doing so much more on my own.

'She's not made for this pub game,' he says, leaning over the bar, those beautiful tattooed forearms on display.

'No, she's just not made for *any* kind of hard work.' I scoff a laugh, instantly feeling bad for slagging her off. Sisters before misters and all that.

He smirks. 'You two did well tonight though, eh? Hopefully we'll get a few more back when the lights are back on.'

He starts blowing out the candles on the tables and then stacking the chairs on top. It's easier for us to hoover in the morning this way.

I copy him, starting on another table.

'Yep, just got to earn a cool seven grand before we can break even.' I hate that I'm so negative these days. I used to be such an optimistic person.

He rolls his eyes but ignores me, carrying on tidying away the tables. With every candle blown out the place gets darker, but my emotions get more heightened. When they're done, we work at opposite ends of the bar, blowing out the last few remaining candles.

Without any actual electricity I can start to feel another kind of current passing between us. Being alone like this, in the dark, well, it's doing strange things to my lady parts. Even my tongue feels like it's quivering, attempting and failing to come up with something to fill the awkward silence.

Not that Clooney's awkward. Far from it. Sometimes I honestly wonder if he has any idea how affected by him I am. I can be such a bitch to him, but it's just easier for me to push him away. I can't be doing with any complications right now and me making a fool of myself in front of a gorgeous guy is high on the list to avoids.

I glance up at him as he saunters closer to me, almost in slow motion. His broad muscular shoulders look even sexier in flickering candle light. My mouth dries at the thought of being so close to him in this dimly lit room.

Before I can reason with myself to run the other way, we're both going to blow out the same candle. He stops and laughs.

'After you,' he offers, curling his hand in a polite circle; his usual smirk licking the edges of his lips.

He makes me giggle like a girl when he pretends to be gentlemanly. Something in me knows he's anything but. I bet he's a beast in bed, throwing you down and yanking your hair to get you in any which position he wants.

'No, you go,' I manage to say, my voice hoarse. Like I work on a sex line kind of hoarse. I clear my throat, hoping he didn't notice.

When I meet his eyes, I know that he did. They're aglow with recognition and something I haven't seen before in his dark wide pupils. Is that lust? He licks his bottom lip, swallowing, causing his Adam's apple to bob up and down. God, how I want to feel that neck beneath my fingers. That olive, clear skin covered in sexy stubble. To have the heat of his body beneath me. Or above me. Or behind me. Jesus, Phoebe calm the hell down.

'No, I insist,' I whisper, my voice barely audible. 'You

do it.'

He looks down at the candle and then back at me, his eyes hooded with a question. What it is I don't know, but all I do know right now is I'd give up all my limits and self-respect just for a small kiss from him. I'd take all the awkwardness, the rejection, all of it, just to know if he wants to kiss me back.

He lowers himself over the candle, his dark eyes still locked on mine. He puckers his lips and blows out the candle, plunging us into pitch black.

Our panted breaths are more noticeable now that I can't see. His breath is coming closer to me, now so close I can feel it on my forehead. I suppose he is taller than me.

I wait, praying to God for him to make a move. To put me out of my misery.

His lips lower until his breath is on my own. This is it. He's leaning down to me. It's happening. Our lips are going to connect.

A clicking noise makes me jump at the same time as the lights come back on, so bright they're blinding. I look up to see him clutching his forehead as my own throbs as if I've been hit by a brick.

'Damn it, Phoebe, you head butted me.'

'Shit.' I can't help but giggle at the whole situation. He was coming in for the kill. That's the only reason I'd have been able to give him a head injury. 'Sorry,' I offer lamely with an apologetic grimace.

Now that the lights are back on, I know it's over. That brief insanity has disappeared. Our confusion reawakened by the lights.

'Time for bed, then,' I say, my voice tight and clipped. I spin on my heel and bolt before I can make any more bad decisions.

CHAPTER TWENTY-SEVEN

<u>Friday 16th October</u>

I couldn't feel worse about what happened with Clooney last night. I totally overstepped the mark. Well, *we* very nearly overstepped the mark. I mean, strictly, he's my employee. Yes, my employee that gave me an orgasm in the bathtub, but still.

I shouldn't be trusting him like this. I shouldn't be offering my wanton lips up to him. It's clear he's not a relationship kind of guy and I'm not a one-night stand kind of gal. Not that I haven't fantasied about it. Several times. But I know deep down that this is all temporary. I'm building this business up so that we can finally sell and move back to England. Back to our normal lives.

There's no point making the time I have with Clooney even more awkward by throwing myself at him every time there's a power cut. Not that I suspect that happens often, thankfully.

I'm just out of the bath, wrapped only in a towel as I

walk back to my room, my thoughts distant, when I literally bump into Clooney.

My eyes swoop upwards, along his partially naked body. He's only in some black boxer shorts showing off his broad muscular shoulders, slim but athletic torso with the smallest smattering of dark hair over his chest and down to his belly button. My eyes follow it to where it goes under his boxer briefs. I'm sure they call that a happy trail. Something tells me I'd be very happy if I got to the end of that trail. I finally find his face. He smirks, knowing I'm checking him out, his eyes lazily dancing over my bare shoulders.

My heart races, I'm not sure if it's the embarrassment of last night, or the secret hope that he'll lean forward, drop my towel to the floor and drag me by my hair into his room.

I shake my head, trying to get all those stupid intrusive thoughts out of there. It's then that I notice the small bruise on his forehead.

'Crap, is that bruise from my head?'

He smiles, exposing his perfect white teeth. I wonder if they're real or veneers. Knowing him he didn't even wear braces and he was just born with a perfect set. Well, not as a baby. That would be weird. Come on, Phoebe, back in the room.

'Yep. Turns out your head is full of bricks, not brains.' He grins playfully.

I scoff out a laugh, loving that we can get back to light-hearted banter so easily. 'Gee, thanks. No wonder you know how to get all the ladies. Such a charmer.'

I turn to walk back into my room.

'I don't go out to *get* the ladies,' he says after me. I turn to him. His eyes dance with mischief. 'They all come willingly.'

My eyes nearly burst out of my head. Is he talking about

last night? Making out I was *willingly* going to him? He is, he's trying to embarrass me. Make me out to be some sort of desperate clinger. This guy likes to make me squirm. Sadistic bastard.

My damn body doesn't understand these games. Heat flares along my cheeks. His grin becomes wider, knowing he's affecting me. Damn dickhead.

I spin on my heel and storm back to my room before he can make me flush any more. I get dressed quickly, but make sure to put on my best jeans and a nicer bra than usual.

I tell myself it's because I want to feel good about myself when I face him next. When I'm applying my make-up I think of it like war paint. Because I am at war. I'm at war with my own feelings. I will not let myself be vulnerable in front of that cocky bastard again.

I was hoping not to hear any voices today at the funeral home. Wow, I was wrong. As soon as I got into work, I heard Eamon. Eamon is a chatter. An annoying chatter. He won't bloody stop. Begging me to do him a favour. Only, this is a bloody massive favour that I have no intention of doing.

You see, Eamon's told me that he had an affair with his next-door neighbour for the last fifteen years. Yeah, just dropped that massive bombshell on me. Like it was nothing. Well Eamon wants me to announce to everyone at his funeral that he's been having this affair and that he wants to come clean before passing over.

Like that would go down well. He has *no* idea.

I've been to the toilet about fifteen times to try and reason with him. Niall and Seamus are bound to think I have the shits, but it's not like I can talk back to him in front of them. I'd be wheeled off to a looney bin in a strait jacket.

The drive to the church is tense, but for some reason Eamon has kept quiet. Maybe I've lost him. I hope so. Obviously I haven't been trusted to drive the hearse since *the incident*.

Patricia still hasn't mentioned the CCTV of me head-butting that corpse. I'm hoping it's because she hasn't seen it and not because she's scared to approach me.

The hardest thing about this job is looking sad all the time. Seeing friends and family of the deceased is depressing as hell, but sometimes, just because I know I can't, I feel the intense urge to break into giggles.

That would get me locked up for sure.

Seamus, Niall and the other undertakers take the coffin out of the hearse while I tell the friends and family to take their seats in the church. Six nervous men take the coffin and carry it in, to the sounds of *Hallelujah*.

'Ah, I wanted Gone Too Soon by Michael Jackson,' Eamon says in my ear. I nearly jump out of my skin it's so loud and sudden, but I manage to school my face back to impassive.

The coffin is carried to the front by men from his family and laid down. I stay stood at the back with Seamus and Niall, hands crossed in front of me, as I've been taught.

The priest starts his mass. That's when Eamon starts again.

'Please,' he begs. 'You have no idea the guilt I feel seeing her grieve for me like this.'

'I'm not doing it,' I whisper hiss. Niall turns to look at me with his eyebrows raised in questioning. I smile back as reassuringly as I can.

'You know I won't leave this world until everyone knows

the truth. I hope you're happy for me to be haunting you for the rest of your life.'

I look heavenwards. 'Why do you want them to know?' I whisper, attempting to cover it with a cough.

Seamus side eyes me.

'Because my wife is devastated. Its far better for her to be angry at me than to mourn me like she is.'

I suppose I do see his reasoning, but either way I'm not disrupting this funeral. I'll be fired first and foremost. Secondly, and possibly worst, the entire town will think I'm nuts. I know from Seamus and Niall that they have a grown-up son and two little granddaughters. This would break all of their hearts.

'I can see the light. I don't know if I'll be offered it again.'

Oh, for fucks sakes.

'Go towards it,' I whisper hiss under my breath.

'I can't. Not until the truth is out. Ah well, where do you live? I'm sure we'll be quite happy together.'

The thought of this Chatty Cathy living with me permanently has me walking forward before I have time to reason with myself. A few people turn to look at me, but quickly lose disinterest. Must think I'm going to the toilet or something.

'That's it, girl,' Eamon encourages. *'Now all the way to the front.'*

I go to move but stop myself. I can't do this. What the hell am I thinking? This is madness.

'Remember, I'll be here every day and night until you decide to tell my wife.'

Hmm, it would still be better for me to tell her tomorrow, away from the prying eyes of the entire funeral procession. Yes, I'll tell her tomorrow.

'*If you don't do it now, I'll just go into your body.*'

'What?' I whisper.

'*That's right. I'll possess your body and do it. It'll be a shame if they think you're the devil incarnate and lock you up in the loony bin, but that's a risk I'm willing to take.*'

Fuck, this guy is going to ruin my day one way or another. I think of the scene in Ghost where that man goes into Whoopi Goldberg's body. Ugh, I could not handle that. Just rip the band-aid off. Get it over and done with.

I walk towards the front. The priest slows down his talking and stares at me, horror dawning on his face. I ignore every fibre of my being telling me to sit the fuck back down.

I turn to face the horrified crowd. Seamus and Niall are staring at me, open mouthed. Eamon's family and friends start whispering to each other.

'Hi, everyone.' I do an awkward wave, swallowing down the lump in my throat. 'I'm so sorry to interrupt, but... I kind of... have a message.'

'A message?' Someone shouts from the back.

'Yes,' I nod frantically. 'A message for Ciara.'

A lady, I'm assuming Ciara, squirms in her front row seat.

'Could I have a word with you privately?' I ask.

CHAPTER TWENTY-EIGHT

Saturday 17ᵗʰ October

*O*f course I've been sacked. I don't know why I was shocked. Maybe I was holding out some small bit of hope that they'd take pity on me. But no, turns out, when you tell the grieving widow that her husband of forty years has been having an affair, it doesn't go down too well.

I don't think I'm cut out for it anyway. With this weird *being able to speak to the dead* thing, it was never going to end well.

I can't tell Ella the truth, she's already depressed and can't cope as well as I can. She never has been able to. Always been babied by my hippy dippy parents.

As I dry myself the next morning after a bath, I remind myself that I'm a strong, independent woman. I repeat this mantra to myself as I blow dry my hair, angrily shaking it about like it has personally wronged me.

Right, this is it. Time to open up the pub. My hair is bouncier than usual due to all of the angry fluffing. I quickly try to calm it down with my hands. I don't know why I'm crushing on such a Neanderthal.

I take a steadying deep breath. You can do this. Now is the time to go face the public and hope they're not all talking about the weirdo who ruined Eamon's funeral. Suki watches me and yawns before slumping her head down on the bed and going back to sleep.

I bound down the stairs and into the kitchen, but as soon as I open the door, I know something has happened. The atmosphere if heavy and full of tension. Ella is talking to Clooney in hushed serious tones. He is frowning back at her, as she bites her lip.

'Oh god. You know already, don't you?' I ask, staring at them both.

Ella stares back at me. 'Know what?'

'Heard that I got sacked. The big scene I caused at Eamon's funeral.'

Clooney runs his hand through his hair.

'Phoebe, I have no idea what you're talking about,' she says, shaking her head slowly.

'Oh. What's wrong then?' I ask, looking between them. My scalp prickles. This is bad. I just know it.

'I...' she starts, her face pale, gulping down panic. 'I... think we've been robbed.'

'WHAT?' I yell, running through the bar and opening the till. What's she talking about? We still have money in here? We haven't even opened up yet. I walk back into the kitchen.

'No, the safe,' she says, her voice soft, treating me carefully like I'm a bomb about to go off.

I run through the kitchen and into the safe cupboard. She's right. The safe door is open and it's empty. All of last week's takings are gone. I collapse onto the floor, staring into the empty hole as a similar one blasts through my heart. Why is it, no matter what we do, everything just turns against us? I don't think I could feel more helpless. Just when I feel we might be okay, something else goes wrong.

Clooney follows me in. I can feel his concern radiating from him.

'Have you searched to see if they're still here?' I ask, suddenly fearful that they could have gone to our living quarters. I could have gone right past them without even realising.

'Shit, no.'

He runs into the sitting room and then I hear him thundering up the stairs, opening and shutting doors. Right now the guy could still be here. He could open the door to murder me with a rusty kitchen knife and I'd just stare at him defeated. Plead with him silently to get it over with quickly. God knows I don't know how much more I can take.

Then I consider Clooney coming across the intruder and having to fight. My stomach drops at the idea of him being injured.

Then he's back, and relief settles over my stomach, reminding me that things could be worse.

'Are you okay?' he asks. His words feel like they're distant. Like my world is closing in on itself.

Ella speaks. 'Pheebs?' She shakes my shoulders lightly. 'Come on, Pheebs; I know it's awful, but you need to pull yourself together.'

'I think she's in shock,' Clooney says, his eyes narrowed on me. I stare off past him, letting my mind wander to happier times. 'We need to get a stiff drink in her.'

I've a vague awareness of them both pulling me under my arms and helping me into the bar. It's as if I'm dreaming, everything seems a bit blurred and distant. I hope I *am* dreaming. That this is all just a terrible nightmare and I'm really back in my flat in London.

I'm placed on a bar stool and then an amber liquid is placed in front of me.

'Drink,' Clooney orders.

I clasp my shaky hands around it and guide it carefully to my mouth. I barely have the strength to lift it. Shit, that burns. I cough into my hand but force myself to take another sip. That one goes down a bit smoother.

I spend the rest of the day pouring whiskey down my throat and wondering what I did in a past life to get such bad luck. Bloody Mum and her reincarnation stories have got in my head. For once I'm glad that we have a slow day with very few customers. I couldn't cope with busy.

'I think it's time for bed,' Clooney says to me around seven p.m.

I giggle girlishly. 'You wish.' I snort a laugh. God, I'm sexy.

He smiles, his eyes full of affection. 'Come on.' He gives me his hand and I clasp onto it like a lifeline. It's all warm and strong. My hand looks so petite in his.

He helps me up the stairs, holding my hand and using his other wrapped round me to steady my waist. I'm a little wobbly on my feet, I'll admit, but I do feel a hell of a lot better than I did earlier. Maybe it's because he's touching me. Damn those hands are large. I remember those fingers inside of me. That feeling of ecstasy. God I want it again.

'Come on, drunko.' He chuckles and guides me into my bedroom. He helps me to sit on my bed and perches his gorgeous butt on the edge of it. Suki jumps off the bed and runs downstairs, clearly sick of my shit. I kick off my converse.

'Are you okay?' he asks with that cute little cocksure smirk of his.

I grin. 'I am now you've plied me with whiskey.' But as I say it, I feel a tear escape from my eye and roll down my cheek. Damn, I didn't see that coming.

He catches it with the pad of his thumb. 'You don't have to put on your tough girl act in front of me.'

Why is he being nice to me? Surely every guy knows the worst thing to do to a vulnerable drunk woman is show kindness. It breaks us open.

I stifle the sob resting in my chest, the tightness almost taking my breath away. The pull towards him has me inching closer.

'Can I just...' I edge closer to him. I need to be in his arms. I don't care how cringy or needy I am. 'Can I just... take some comfort from you and you not hold it against me tomorrow?'

'Of course,' he says without thinking. 'What do you need me to do?'

I scoot forward and place my head into his chest so hard I'm sure, by the thud I hear, I must have hurt him. He instinctively wraps his arms around me, one hand rubbing my back in soothing circles. It reminds me of when we were naked in bed together after I jumped in the lake.

It's here, safe in his arms, I let myself go. I cry. I cry properly for the first time since arriving here. I cry for all of the money I've ploughed into this place. I cry for all of the crushing responsibility I feel. I cry for my great aunt Breda, who I never knew, but somehow feel closer than ever to. I cry because I can hear ghosts I never believed in before. I cry because I want to be back home in England, in the shitty little flat I shared with Valerie. But most of all I cry because I want nothing more than to be right here, in this man's arms, protected from the world, when I know that we can never be.

After a long while my cries start to slow. I test my lungs to see if I can take a full breath again. I inhale his smell of cinnamon, mint and the slightest hint of cigarette smoke. It's become such a comforting scent. It's all I want to smell forever. The thought of moving back to England and never again smelling him breaks my heart.

'You want me to stay here tonight?' he asks, tucking a bit of hair behind my ear.

I lean back and look into those dirty green eyes creased in concern. He has the cutest little wrinkles when he does that look.

'Just until you get to sleep,' he clarifies, shooting down my dreams. I suppose Ella does share the bed with me.

I sniff. 'Am I pathetic if I say yes?'

He smiles lazily. I think it's my favourite of his. 'Of course not. Just stop being the fierce independent woman for just one night, okay?'

'Okay,' I nod on another sniff. In his arms like this I'd probably agree to anything.

He instructs me to lay back down while he shrugs off his boots. He lays down behind me, spooning my back. He sweeps my hair back from my face and places it behind my ear. It's such a gentle gesture. If only I knew I could trust him.

I let the warmth of his body seep into mine, healing all of my gaping wounds. All of my regrets. All of my fears. Calming me, I'm lulled to sleep by the feel of his heartbeat thumping against my back and the sound of his relaxed breathing by my ear.

'Goodnight, Phoebe. Everything will be better in the morning.'

With him here it's so easy to believe.

CHAPTER TWENTY-NINE

<u>Sunday 18th October</u>

*W*hen I wake, I reach for him. My heart sinks as I realise he's not there. Probably had to get away from me. I'm a sleep fidgeter. Ella and Suki aren't even here. I check out the window and it seems I did sleep through until morning, the bright sunshine streaming in.

I stretch my arms to the ceiling. It's weird but I feel better for having a breakdown last night. Today is a fresh day and it's going to be okay. I'm going to focus on the positive. I'm healthy and we are going to turn this place around. I get washed up, dressed and go into the kitchen to make myself a strong coffee. I feel better but I still have a groggy head from all that whiskey.

I hear talking coming from the bar. I look at my watch; it's only ten a.m. We shouldn't be open yet. Who's out there? We're not expecting any deliveries today.

I swing the door open and walk into the bar. I nearly pass out from shock when I see my parents sat with Ella and

Clooney, all having a cuppa as if they're lifelong friends. Suki sits at their feet.

'Mum? Dad?' I gasp. Am I still dreaming? Having some sort of weird whiskey dream? 'What the hell are you doing here?'

'Well, it's very nice to see you, too, Phoebe,' Mum says cheerily, flouncing her long red hair behind her shoulders. She gets up and runs around to hug me.

My parents might drive me mad, hell, I might even resent them massively for robbing me of a normal childhood, but when my Mum takes me in her arms, her scent of rose and wildflowers wafting up my nostrils, it's hard to not hug her back and realise how much I've missed her. She crushes her long dangling crystal necklaces against my chest.

'I'm sorry, I'm just in shock.' I pull back looking into her brown eyes, the same eyes as Ella. I'm always the first to pull back. 'When did you arrive?'

She smiles widely. 'Only about an hour ago. We wanted to surprise you girls. Ella's just been telling me about the robbery. We thought best to let you sleep after all that shock.'

Dad comes up to give me a hug. He's tall at six foot two and crushes me into his embrace, bruising my ribs. He's like a big hairy bear with his beard and long greying hair tied back into a ponytail.

'Jesus, Dad, go easy,' I squeak as my lungs contract with the pressure of my ribs being squeezed.

'Sorry, but I haven't seen my baby girl in so long.' He beams down at me. 'She's always too busy off being sensible.'

I see Clooney smile behind him. Yeah, yeah, another reason for him to rib me; being boring. I can't actually believe he's meeting them. I feel embarrassed that he'll see where we come from. What an obviously looney upbringing we've had. Especially after allowing myself to be so vulnerable in front of him last night.

'We don't actually have a spare bedroom for you,' I admit on a grimace.

'Don't be silly, I'll take the sofa,' Clooney offers.

He can be such a gentleman sometimes.

Mum practically glows back at him. 'Where did you find this lovely young man? He's so charming.'

I look at him puffing out his chest proudly, amusement dancing in his eyes as if to say; *told you so, I'm amazing.*

'Yeah, yeah, he's wonderful,' I snarl, rolling my eyes. 'So were you in Ireland already?' I can't help but ask. I don't believe for a second they've come all this way just for us.

Ella gives a warning look. It says; *this is why they don't visit a lot.*

Well, *sorry* if I like to have my information. Sorry that I don't like to just go with the flow like the rest of them.

'We are due at a protest in Dublin tomorrow, yes,' Mum admits.

'What is it for this time?' I ask, already bored. I knew it. They're always too busy saving the world to give us a second thought.

'We're saving the bees.'

Of course they are.

Mum darts a quick anxious gaze to Dad. 'We also have something we need to discuss.' She wrings her hands together. 'As a family.'

They look to Clooney. This isn't like them. Normally they're so open with everything its crushingly embarrassing. I remember them talking about a healthy sex life with my first boyfriend from a similar protester family. Then suggesting I go on the pill. I nearly died from shame.

'Enough said.' He nods and gets up, picking up his packet of cigarettes. 'I'll leave you to it.' I watch him head straight outside. I really wish he'd have grabbed a jacket. It's freezing out there.

'Sit down, Phoebe,' Dad says, gesturing towards a bar stool.

This is *beyond* weird. He's never asked me to sit down. He's never been serious before. I look to Mum, but she's avoiding my eye line, tapping her foot on the floor.

'Do you know what this is about?' I ask Ella.

She shakes her head, frowning and biting her lip. Okay, so at least it's not just me in the dark.

'So, girls,' Dad starts, twiddling with his fingers. Mum squirms on her seat next to him.

Oh god. That's when it hits me. Dad is ill. He's dying. Of course he is. That's the only reason for him to be this deadly serious. *Deadly* being the word.

'As you know, we don't believe in a lot of traditional values.'

Oh god, he's trying to tell us he's refusing Western medicine. That he doesn't want treatment. He's just going to give up and let it take him. Hope a cup full of Mum's herbs will save him. Stupid bastard.

Ella nods. 'Like why you never bothered to get married.'

Oh poor innocent Ella. This will crush her. She's always been such a Daddy's Girl.

'Yes,' Dad nods at her, his face still grave.

'Although we are married together by the universe,' Mum says expanding her arms out wide. 'Everyone knows it's in mother nature's hands who we are drawn to.'

Jesus. Spare me the rest of this crap. I smile and nod in an attempt to speed things along.

'Well,' Dad continues, clearing his throat. 'One of the reasons we didn't marry was because we don't believe in the conventionality of marriage.'

I look to Ella. 'Sorry, I'm not following.' Why is he going on about marriage? 'Are you ill?'

Mum scoffs. 'Your father isn't ill, Phoebe. He's trying to tell you something very difficult.'

Oh, so he's not dying. What the hell could he be confessing to then?

'Your father doesn't believe in monogamy.'

My mouth drops open. Shit.

'You mean.' Ella swallows. 'That you've had *affairs?*'

Oh my god, my dad is a dirty old cheating bastard. Honestly you think you know someone. Think they're just a boring old fart who talks too much about the environment and then you find out they've been shagging about.

'Not affairs,' Dad clarifies.

Oh thank god, it's just been the one.

He frowns. 'More consensual relationships with other women.'

Oh my fucking God. He *is* a dirty dog.

He takes mums hand. 'Your mother knows all about them and has always supported me in not wanting to limit myself to one person.'

'Jesus fucking Christ, Dad!' I shout, jumping up to standing. 'You came all the way here to tell us that you're a cheater and you don't even feel bad about it?'

'We don't believe in cheating,' Mum says, squeezing Dad's hand in an act of solidarity.

'So what, you're swingers now?' Ella asks.

'Far from it, young lady,' Dad snaps, like *that* idea is ridiculous. 'These were loving relationships.'

God, I feel sick at the very thought of my dad sticking it to other women. Other old women. And now he's saying he was in love with them. That love should be reserved for Mum and us. It's too much.

'Ugh, you're disgusting!' My hands ball into fists. 'Mum, how can you be okay with this?'

'It's our life choice,' Mum nods, like she's reconfirming the fact. 'And it's no-one's business but ours.'

Who is she kidding?

'Fine, but then why bloody bother telling us?' My breathing is heavy enough for us all to hear. 'Do you just want to scar us emotionally for the rest of our lives?'

Like I haven't got enough shit going on.

'Yeah,' Ella agrees. 'Why ruin my childhood memories?' I can tell from the wobble of her throat that she's close to tears.

Unlike me she thinks she had the most picture-perfect childhood, full of travelling, rainbows and lady bugs. That's because she's like them. She believes in Mother Nature, the universe, everything just providing for you. I'm the only one that believes you have to work for it.

They constantly joke that they don't know where they got me from. I used to look at my family and fantasise that they'd mixed me up at the hospital and I actually belonged with a regular, rational family. That both my parents worked, and I went to school in a uniform; had a strict bedtime. Anything normal, that other kids despised. It's funny the things you wish for when you have no rules.

Little did I know I was actually like my great aunt Breda.

'Because...' Dad says, drawing his mouth into a straight

line. 'Some of those relationships resulted in...' he gulps, looking at anything but us, 'children.'

Children? What the hell is he... wait, is he trying to tell us we have siblings?

'You have sisters,' Mum announces, rubbing Dad's back like he should be very proud for sharing. Like he just confessed to eating the last cookie out of the jar, not spreading his seed far and wide.

'Oh my god.' Ella gasps, her breath coming out in pants.

'Sister - s?' I ask. 'As in more than one?'

'Yes.' He nods, assessing us carefully.

I sit back down, the weight of my legs suddenly feeling too much to bear. I have sisters. Other relatives out there that I've never met but am bonded to by blood. It's too much to take in. I just... I can't even begin to fathom it.

'Well how bloody many?' Ella demands. 'How many love children *do* you have darted around?'

He rubs the back of his neck, his forehead covered in a sheen of sweat. 'Six.'

'SIX?' Ella and I scream in unified disbelief

All of the colour has drained from Ella's face and her breathing is getting worse. Ugh, all I need right now is her passing out on me.

'Put your head between your legs,' I instruct. She does. 'So we have six bloody sisters.' I can't stop saying bloody. 'If you've kept it a secret for so bloody long, why tell us now?'

He swallows, his Adams apple bobbing up and down. 'Because some of these young girls have gotten to an age where their mothers have felt they were mature enough to understand.'

I scoff. 'Oh, but you didn't think *we* were mature enough to understand before now? I'm nearly thirty, Dad!'

Mum smiles—the same "humour her" smile she's always given me. 'You're twenty seven, Phoebe. Don't be dramatic.'

Dramatic? She thinks *I'm* being dramatic? God forbid I react at *all* to being told I have *six extra sisters*. How is she so calm?

Ella sticks her head back up straight. 'Did you help raise these girls?' Her eyes dart from mine to his.

I can imagine she's wondering how he's managed to do that while raising us. I don't ever remember him being gone for long periods of times. He was always around.

'No, they're very independent women who ended the relationship once they found out they were pregnant. Your mother always made it clear that you three were my main family.'

I don't know if that's better or worse.

'So you just abandoned all these children?' How could he be so heartless?

He shakes his head. 'No. They wanted to raise the children themselves. If we were in the area we'd pop in for a cuppa.'

'Jesus, sounds very cosy,' I snark.

'What are their names? Ella asks, before pushing her head back down.

Dad smiles. It's sickening. 'Well, because they wouldn't take my surname, *our* surname, I requested that they all have flower names.'

You've got to be kidding me. Just when I think the guy can't get any more ridiculous.

'So there's Posy, Blossom, Fleur, Iris, Marigold, Primrose and Dahlia.'

I count as the names are listed.

'Dad, that's seven. *Please* don't tell me you honestly can't remember how many children you have?'

'Oops, yes you're right,' he chuckles. Actually chuckles, like he's miss counted how many chickens he keeps. Not actual biological children!

Mum starts laughing too. 'I always forget about little Dahlia.'

How can they forget a child? What is this utter madness?

'*Little Dahlia?* How old are these girls?'

I was hoping he'd only shagged round for a few years when we were young.

'Dahlia is thirteen,' Mum says with a sweet smile. 'The others are eighteen and upwards.'

Suppose I can't expect them to remember ages if he can barely remember he has nine daughters!

The information presses down heavy on my chest, suffocating me. I have seven other siblings out there. Seven other parts of me wandering this earth. What if they're like me? What if they want to be a part of my life?

'This is just too much for me.'

I have to get out of here before the walls close in on me. Away from all of these truth bombs. It's too much to process. I was just getting over being robbed and now I find out this.

I run.

CHAPTER THIRTY

$\mathcal{I}$ find myself running out of the pub, needing the fresh air in my lungs. I keep running, needing to rid my body of the anxiety induced tension taking residence in my muscles.

I stop when I'm at the bottom of the pier. Clooney is already sat there, his legs dangling over the edge, sucking from a cigarette, smoke encasing him.

Why is it he looks so bloody sexy smoking? I've never liked smokers. But something about the way he leans over one makes me wish I was that very thing he was sucking from. Jesus, Phoebe, get a grip.

I lean over, pressing my hands to my thighs, trying to breathe in some oxygen to my burning lungs.

'Fuck!' I shout between breaths. It feels good to swear.

He leans back, an amused smirk on his face. 'Went well then?'

I snort a laugh. 'Yeah great. My parents are fucking kooks.'

He smiles, blowing out his smoke. 'I think they're great.'

I cross my arms over my chest. 'You would. Having only

met them for five minutes. You'll never guess what that man just told me.'

He puts his cigarette out on the pier. 'Go on.'

I take a deep breath. 'Brace yourself,' I warn him.

He smirks. 'Consider myself braced.'

'He's been having open relationships for years.' I wait for him to process that. His face remains annoyingly impassive.

'Shit.'

'And not just that,' I rant, pacing back and forth. It feels good letting it all out. Shouting at someone, anyone. 'He's fathered seven bloody children!'

His mouth pops open, his head hanging forward. 'Feck. You've gotta be kidding me.'

'Do I look like I'm kidding you?'

He takes a proper look, surveying over my features. 'No.' He smiles but it's soft, sad almost.. 'You look like your entire world just fell apart.'

It's making my chest burn, making me want to burst into tears again. Dammit, he should know after last night that I can't handle people being nice to me when I'm feeling shitty.

'I'm fine,' I insist, my voice wobbly. I wrap my arms around myself.

He jumps up. 'Come here.' He opens his arms and I practically run into them. I hate that I'm so needy, especially for him.

But this is what I need right now. I need comfort and reassurance. I'm ashamed to admit that it feels better coming from a man. Probably because my own father betrayed me. Oh god, I have Daddy issues. I'm so cliché. This hug is more assuring than a huge from Ella ever has been. It could be a hug from any man.

Oh, who am I kidding?

He strokes the back of my head. 'Tell me what you're most upset about.'

I sigh. 'I guess the most upsetting part of it is that my dad cheated on my mum. Repeatedly. My heart hurts for her. That she wasn't enough for my dad.'

I breathe in through my nose, feeling comforted by the scent of cigarette smoke mixed with soap, cinnamon and mint.

'You said open relationship, so I'm assuming she knew?' he asks, still not breaking his hold on me. I feel so safe in his arms.

'Yes.' My heart breaks for her. 'They're both bloody proud of how open and honest they've been with each other. It's ridiculous.'

He strokes my back with soothing circles. 'Maybe she's honestly okay with it?'

I lean my head back to look up into his honest forest green eyes. 'Can you honestly tell me, as a man, that my father was happy when he decided to sleep with another woman?'

He frowns and looks away, chewing on his lip. 'There's someone you should be talking to about it and it's not me.'

'I don't know if I can talk to either of them right now.'

He smiles down at me. 'Do me a favour and call your parents once the dust has settled a bit. You never know when you're going to lose them, you know?'

Did he lose his Mum? Is that why he's saying that?

'I know it feels like the end of the world now, but if they were taken off this earth tomorrow, you'd feel pretty lousy that you left it on bad terms.'

I mull it over. I know he's right and rational. If my dad

died tomorrow I'd be devastated no matter how angry I am right now.

'It's obvious your family love you. You could do far worse, trust me.'

'Yeah, the only problem is that my dad has so much love to give its spilled over onto other women.' I snort a laugh, trying and failing to diffuse the melancholy atmosphere.

Why did I have to use the words *spilled over*? Now I'm thinking about my dad's sperm. Ugh, gag.

'Still, your mam said she's happy with it right? So why don't you believe her?'

I shrug, already knowing the answer.

'I suppose it's because when I imagine meeting the person I want to spend the rest of my life with, I've always hoped he'd be just as obsessed and deeply in love with me, as I am with him. The thought of the man I love having sex with someone else...' I shudder, memories of Garry darting into my grey matter—not that he was marriage material. 'Well, it would just destroy me.'

He stares at me hard, those eyes assessing me carefully. 'I used to never understand why people stuck to one person, but when you find the right person its easy.'

That has me intrigued. Has he ever had a long relationship? Ever been in love? I just assumed he was a forever playboy.

'Have you never been with anyone and not wanted to sleep with someone else?'

He shrugs, scratching at his chest, his eyes on anything but me. 'There's a lot about me you don't know.'

'What?' I laugh. 'From the man that refuses to tell me anything... Shocking.'

He rubs the back of his neck, as if cautious of my reaction.

'All you need to know is that the ladies love me. I can't help that I was blessed with all of this gorgeousness and a generous personality.'

There's the normal naughty Clooney I know. He's changing the subject, avoiding the question, but for once I don't care.

I laugh, really laugh. He seems to be the only person lately that can really make me. Either that or irrationally angry.

'That's why I could never date a pretty boy that loves himself like you.'

His lips part. 'Pretty boy?' he repeats, affronted. He points over himself. 'I'm no pretty boy.'

I snort a laugh as I look at his broad chest and tattooed arms. 'No, I suppose you're not. What I mean is dating someone prettier than me. Knowing they'd always be searching for a girl better than me.'

Just like Garry did.

'That's not possible,' he mumbles under his breath.

'What?' I blurt before I realise what he's said. I've already heard him though.

'Nothing.' He pulls away, looking instead at the lake.

He thinks I'm pretty? Ugh, I hate that my self-worth these days lies in the hands of this guy.

He turns and glances over my shoulder. 'The person you need to speak to is here.'

He kisses the top of my head and releases me. I turn to see Mum walking towards me. Jesus, the woman has taken off her shoes, her billowy skirt blowing in the wind. We're outside for God's sakes.

Clooney nods at her as he passes.

'I don't get it, Mum. How can you be happy about all of this?'

She sighs and looks to the ground. 'I'll be honest with you. At first I was heartbroken when I realised your father had meant it when he'd said he didn't believe in monogamy. I'd been brought up to believe in marriage or at least faithfulness. Thinking of someone cheating made me think of a lonely, miserable life without him. Instead, I just saw a little less of him.

'What I came to realise was that I loved your father unconditionally. That wherever he went, he always came back to me at the end of the night. He still loved me just as much. His heart is just big enough to love other people too.'

I shake my head. It's crazy. There's no way she can be this rational.

'When the first woman fell pregnant, I was scared I was going to lose him, but still he stayed. Still loved me more than anyone else.'

'But how can you accept that he sleeps with other people? It's gross.'

She shrugs. 'It's happened less and less as he's gotten older. And now we have a huge extended family. More love and light in the world because of your father's heart. How can we be angry at that?'

I scoff. 'Very bloody easily.'

She rests her arm on my shoulder. 'Don't carry hate in your heart, Phoebe. It brings nothing but darkness. We always tried to teach you girls to accept everyone for who they truly are.'

I sigh, pushing her away. 'Yes, well, I didn't think at the time that would include my father dicking around.'

She sighs, her brown eyes boring into me. 'You've always been different to us. I always assumed you were like my mum, but now I know Dad's other daughter's, I realise that it's from his side of the family too.'

'You mean... some of them are like me?' I hate how hopeful I feel. Despise myself for it, but I can't help but finally feel like I might belong somewhere. I wonder if any of them have the *gift* too.

'Yes.' She nods, smiling fondly. 'They've always known about you and the others. Now some of them want to meet you.'

I close my eyes, a tear escaping. Even though I like the thought of being similar to someone, I still don't want to meet them. I want to just pretend like they don't exist. Ella and me have always been so close. This could change that. She could prefer them.

'I can't, Mum. I'm happy you're happy. But I don't want to meet them and bring complete strangers into my life, just because there's some blood link between us.'

She grasps my shoulder softly. 'They're not distant cousins, Phoebe, they're your sisters.'

'Half-sisters,' I correct her.

'Just think about it, hmm?' She smiles, probably already sending a hopeful prayer to the universe fairies for me to change my mind.

I nod begrudgingly. 'I'll try.'

'Now come and say goodbye to your father. We've decided to get on the road early.'

'You're not staying the night?' I can't help but sound disappointed. They might be kooky adulterant weirdos, but they're still my weirdos. Sometimes I'd just like to feel more important than the latest rally.

'Afraid not, love. We've just had a phone call. They've started early.'

I nod and walk back towards the pub, resigned to the fact we'll always be their second priority.

'So, Clooney is a lovely man.'

Here we go.

'Yes, he's nice.'

She smirks. 'Something happening between you two?' She looks so hopeful.

I shrug. 'Why would you say that?'

'Just the way he looks at you.' She smiles dreamily.

'What?' I scoff. 'With arrogance?'

'Like you hung the moon.'

She used to say Dad looked at her like she hung the moon. Now look at them.

I say goodbye to Dad. I hug him, despite wanting to also punch him in the face.

He squeezes me and whispers in my ear, 'Forgive me, Petal. I never meant to hurt you.'

'Well you did,' I whisper back. 'But I still love you.'

He leans back and smiles. 'Thank you.'

He's just getting in the car when he stops and shakes his head.

'I almost forgot.'

'Oh yes,' Mum says, as if also remembering.

Me and Ella exchange an eye roll.

'More illegitimate children you've forgotten about?' Ella asks, hands on her hip.

He chuckles. 'No, it's a better surprise than that, believe it or not.'

I sigh. 'Jesus, spit it out, Dad. I've had just about enough surprises for one day.'

'Well I put some money into a savings scheme when I was eighteen.'

'Right...' Ella and I look to each other in confusion.

'And they contacted me to say it had turned into a healthy ten thousand pounds. I couldn't believe it.'

Oh my god. Only my dad could be that lucky. Unbelievable.

'And because me and your mother don't need that kind of money we've decided to give it to you both. Help you out with the pub.'

Ella grasps my hand and squeals.

'Yay! Thank you, thank you, thank you!' She jumps all over Dad. 'You have no idea what good timing this is.'

I quickly glare warningly at her. I don't want them knowing about the Sky incident. We'll look dumb—which we were, but that's not the point. This is amazing though. We'll have enough to pay the seven thousand euro fine and some left over to help pay the bills. I can't lie, if it equalled my original savings I invested into this place, I'd pack up today and just leave. Unfortunately its nowhere near, so I'll just invest it in the business and hope we get a sale soon.

'Here it is,' Dad says, handing me over a cheque.

'Thank you, Dad. Honestly, I am grateful. Still mad, but grateful.'

CHAPTER THIRTY-ONE

Tuesday 20th October

*T*he most annoying thing about having the pub is that you can never call in sick or cry off. You have to stay open just in case some people decide to come in. Ella's gone for a walk down the lane to try and get some Wi-Fi.

We've got a group of five guards in, finally taking advantage of their fifty percent discount. I'm keeping myself busy by taking all of the glasses from the shelves and cleaning underneath them. It's amazing how grotty it gets.

I can't think too long about my new sisters, I get a headache, so instead I've decided to come up with plans to ruin Clooney's dad's pub. This town isn't big enough for the both of us. It's as simple as that.

'Any other secrets you want to tell me about your dad?' I ask Clooney. 'You know, take my mind off my own ridiculous family?'

'Afraid not.' He grins, drying up a glass. Why do his biceps look so bloody pronounced when he does that? I can sense I might start dribbling so I look away. 'But...' He smiles towards a guy that just walked in. 'I know a man who might.'

I frown at him. What's he up to?

'Hey,

Sean, how are ya?'

The man is about sixty with salt and pepper hair. He's quite trendy, wearing well cut jeans, a polo t-shirt and trainers he definitely didn't buy himself. Something tells me he has grandchildren that keep him trendy.

'I'm good thanks, Clooney. How are you, lad? My first visit to you down here.'

Clooney widens his arms. 'Well, welcome. This is Phoebe Bellerose, the new licensee. Her sister's out.'

'Ah, I did just drive past a little lady holding their phone in the air. Could that be her?'

We both look at each other with secret smiles. I love feeling like we have an inside joke.

'That'll be her.'

'Well, nice to meet ya.' He reaches his hand across and shakes mine. 'Nice to finally have a new boozer.'

New boozer? Why doesn't he like Clooney's dad's place?

'Clooney, I'll have half a bitter please.'

Clooney winks at me while he pumps it out. 'We were actually just talking about me da. He's done so much to try and ruin this business it's unreal.' He hands over his drink.

'Really?' He takes a sip out of his bitter. 'Doesn't surprise me. He's hardly an angel himself.'

'That's what I want to hear,' Clooney says eagerly, leaning on his forearms, his eyebrows wagging ridiculously. 'Give me all the dirt.'

Nobody stands a chance when Clooney turns on the charm. Not even old men.

'Well, where do I start?' He rubs his chin thoughtfully.

I can't believe he's willing to share dirt on him. Who is this guy? And why does he hate Fergus? Everyone else seems to think the sun shines out of his arse.

'Ah, one thing that can get him in trouble for sure.' He leans in, as if about to expose a conspiracy theory. 'Well, as you know, he owns the lease of the pub, not the actual building. So he's supposed to buy all the booze through the brewery or he could lose his license.'

'And you don't think he does?' I ask, leaning in eagerly.

He grins. 'I've seen him at Dublin Costco a few times. Always has a suspiciously large trolley of beer for someone who owns a boozer.'

'He buys it from there?' I ask, wanting to clarify the rule breaking. Why am I not surprised?

'Yeah, if I were you, I'd be contacting the brewery and asking for a stock inspection.'

'Sean, you've saved the day!' I'd kiss him if I wasn't worried I'd scare another customer away.

Later, when he's gone, and after I've chased Suki back into the living room for what feels like the thousandth time, I interrogate Clooney.

'So how do you know that Sean? And why does he hate your dad?'

He sighs, his shoulders tensing. 'It's a long story.'

I look around at the near empty pub. 'Funnily enough, I have time.'

He fidgets, hopping agitatedly from foot to foot. 'Trust me, Phoebe, you're better off not knowing.'

Now he really has me intrigued.

'Why do you say that?'

'Just trust me,' he says, cutting me off from any further questions. 'It's safer for you to not know. The less you know the better.'

Well now I'm left thinking the worst. Damn Clooney and his mysterious secrets. He should have just made something up. Now I'm more intrigued than ever.

'*Hello there.*'

I freeze on the spot. Dammit, just when I was hoping the ghosts had lost me, one appears.

'*I hear you're the lady to come to when I want something passed on, before I... well, pass on.*' The voice laughs.

'I'm just going out back,' I say to Clooney, backing out and rushing through so I won't be called a lunatic.

'Hello?' I ask as soon as I'm in the cellar.

'*Hi, my name is Geraldine and I need your help. I'm told you're the lady.*'

'Right okay. Let's just crack on. What is it you need?'

I already know she's not going to quit. These dead people have nothing but time on their hands.

'*It's a bit of a delicate one,*' she pauses, for dramatic effect, '*you see my daughter is getting married and I wrote her a letter to be given to her on her wedding day. My husband doesn't want to give it to her until after. He's scared it'll upset her.*'

Ah, that's actually really sad. The thought of me getting married without my parents there, however nutty they are, has my heart aching. Crap, will I have to invite my new sisters? Not that I even have a groom yet.

'Okay, when is she getting married?'

'In an hour.'

'What? I have a bloody hour to do this?' Ghosts can be so unreasonable. What kind of person gets married on a Tuesday?

'Afraid so. So are you in?'

'Ugh, fine.'

That's when I hear footsteps and Ella walks round the corner.

'Pheebs, who are you talking to?' She scrunches up her nose, searching around for someone.

Oh crap. Caught in the act.

'Err...' I look around for my phone but I left it in the bar. 'Myself.'

She raises her eyebrows. 'Yourself?' she repeats, her tone unbelieving. 'You were talking to yourself again?'

'Yes, okay,' I snap, already wondering how I can get into town. I don't have time to explain that I'm not insane. I have to find this bride's house.

I'll have to ask Clooney to borrow his car. I walk back into the bar, desperately trying to think of a reasonable excuse.

'Clooney, can I borrow your car?' I smile hopefully, pushing my breasts out. Time is not on my side here. I'll have to resort to desperate measures.

He frowns, his eyes travelling down to my boobs. Gotcha. 'You're not insured on it.'

Dammit, he's right. I didn't think of that.

'What do you need picking up? I can do it for you,' he offers kindly, trying to keep his gaze on my eyes and not my boobs.

'Um, thanks, but it's something I need to do myself.'

He squints his eyes at me. 'Ri... ght. Well you're not

driving the car without insurance. I can take you somewhere if you like.'

It would be quicker than waiting for a taxi. Especially with only three taxi men in town.

'Ugh, fine, then you'll have to. Don't want to hurt your precious car.' I roll my eyes. Boys and their toys.

'Fine.' He grabs his keys and calls to Ella. 'We're just popping out somewhere. You'll have to cover the bar.'

'Where are you going?' Ella questions, appearing from the kitchen. She looks at me with more suspicion by the second. I suppose I do normally tell her everything. This is the first thing I've kept her in the dark about.

'It's just an errand,' I answer vaguely, rushing out of the pub to avoid further questioning.

We get in the car, but Clooney stops and turns to me, his jaw set, brow wrinkled. 'Where are we really going? And why are you acting so weird?'

'*She's going to help me,*' Geraldine says. '*Tell him to put his foot down. Time is ticking away.*'

Damn ghosts, thinking he can hear them. 'Look, I can't explain. Just that we need to get somewhere fast. Can you please just trust me?' I plead with my eyes.

He squints at me, then sighs. 'Fine.'

I rattle off the address Geraldine gives me and try to think of how I'm going to do this. Apparently she's getting ready in the priest's house next to the church. I look at my watch. Less than forty minutes now thanks to Clooney's dawdling.

We finally arrive ten minutes later. Just thirty minutes to persuade a complete stranger to trust me.

'You just stay here. I'll be back soon.'

He sighs and shrugs, resigned to my mystery.

I hop out and head to the priest's house next door to the

gorgeous old-stone Catholic church. I ring the doorbell of the white cottage and wait, hopping from foot to foot. I just hope she's with an understanding friend who will let the random stranger talk to her.

A bridesmaid in a flouncy purple dress opens the door. She looks me up and down.

'Yes?'

'Oh, hi. I'm here to see Nora.'

She assesses me carefully, crossing her arms over her chest. 'You're the English girl. Why do you want to see our Nora?'

I can hear squeals from several girls inside, obviously the bridesmaids enjoying the bubbly.

'Its...' I swallow down the panic. 'It's kind of a long story. But she'll want to meet with me.'

I hope by being confident she'll let me in.

She looks me up and down disapprovingly again. 'Wait here.' She shuts the door in my face. Well, she's friendly, not.

Josephine has always been suspicious.

I check my phone. Minutes tick by. This is torture.

The door is eventually opened back up by Josephine who seems no friendlier.

'She says she doesn't know you and so obviously doesn't want to meet you just before her wedding.'

'But can you please tell her it's really important?' I plead with a desperate smile.

'Look.' She leans closer into my personal space. 'I know you caused that huge scene at Eamon's funeral. I don't know if you're mental or what, but you need to leave. There is no way I'm letting you see Nora.'

She slams the door in my face, barely missing crushing my nose.

'Well, that was rude.' Not that I don't understand. I wouldn't let a mad woman in to see Ella before she got married.

'You have to try again,' Geraldine insists, and I can hear the desperation in her voice.

I scoff a laugh. 'Are you crazy? She's not letting me anywhere near her.' I feel bad, but there's nothing I can do.

'Well, then you'll just have to go sit in the church and get to her that way.'

'Interrupt the wedding? Are you bloody serious?' Disbelief colours my tone.

'I'm very serious, young lady. I want my daughter to read this letter before she gets married and I'm not crossing over until she has.'

I cross my arms over my chest. 'What are you going to do?'

'I'll haunt you for the rest of your life. And I have a few ghost friends that'll gladly come join me. The days are long when you're dead. We've all got nothing better to do than sing Celine Dion at the top of our lungs until sunrise.'

I can't cope with that idea.

Oh my god. I clutch at my forehead. I notice Clooney staring at me from his car. God I hope he hasn't seen me talking to myself. I do a quick wave to reassure him.

I decide to walk back to the car and try to explain away some of the crazy.

'It actually turns out that she's invited me to the wedding.' I hate lying, especially to him, but it's the only way.

'Seriously?' he asks, head tilted to the side. 'I mean, I'd heard she'd invited the whole town, but I didn't think she knew you.'

'Oh, she doesn't, not yet.'

CHAPTER THIRTY-TWO

'So if she doesn't know you why on earth would she invite you to her wedding?'

'Err...' he has a valid point. 'I was just here to wish her well and Josephine insisted.'

'Josephine?' he stares back at me, eyebrows raised. 'And you made me drive you all the way here just to you could wish her, a stranger, well?'

'Yes.' I nod. 'I'm trying to make new friends.'

'Okay...'. He looks stares at me, but then seems to give up trying to understand me. 'Do you think we can leave Ella this long?'

He's right. She might be drunk by now.

'Why don't you go back to the pub and you can collect me after?' That way he won't be nearby when I make a fool of myself. Although I could have done with a getaway car.

He looks to the church and back. 'Nah, I was invited too. I think I'll come with you.'

Yay. Just what I need, another witness to my madness.

'Okay.' I force out through gritted teeth

'*The more the merrier,*' Geraldine says into my ear.

'How exactly am I going to do this?' I whisper hiss to her as he gets out of the car.

'You'll just have to wait until she's in the church.'

Oh my god. The whole town is going to see me being a nutcase. I'll never recover from this. Everyone will be sure to avoid the pub after this.

We walk in, getting disapproving looks from an usher who looks over our everyday attire in disgust. It's beautiful in here. What I'm guessing is original brickwork is painted white with a dark wood cladded roof. Big round windows make it surprisingly light and airy.

We sit near the back, and I'm hoping I can grab her quickly before she walks down the aisle.

'You're acting really weird,' Clooney says, side eyeing me.

'No, I'm not.' I fidget, checking the time every few minutes

Before we know it, the wedding march music starts playing and she's at the end of the aisle in a gorgeous lace ivory princess dress.

'Wow.' Geraldine says into my ear. *'She looks so beautiful.'*

It makes me tear up. You can hear the raw emotion in her voice. I always cry at weddings, apparently when I don't even know them. To think she didn't make it here in the flesh to celebrate it with her is beyond heart breaking. I'm going to ring my mum as soon as I get home.

'Look at you,' Clooney teases, bumping his shoulder with mine. 'I didn't know you could be so soppy.'

I stick my tongue out. I feel like I've done nothing but cry the last few days. I've probably cried more than my whole life.

I try to catch her eye, waving every time she glances

towards our aisle but she can't see me. Damn. This is going to be harder than I thought.

She starts descending the aisle, holding onto her emotional father. I can see why he didn't want to give her the letter. He's already a mess.

'Nora!' I whisper towards her. 'Nora!'

Clooney grabs hold of my shoulder. 'What the hell are you doing?' he hisses into my ear, eyes wide open in shock.

I shrug him off. 'I have something to tell her.'

'Unless it's that her dress is tucked into her knickers, now is definitely *not* the time,' he growls, looking round as if to check no one has seen him with the crazy bird.

By the time I look back at her it's too late and she's already meeting her future husband in front of the priest. Damn. Missed my chance.

'Please,' Geraldine sniffs into my ear. *'It's breaking my heart that she thinks I didn't care enough to write anything for her big day.'*

My heart breaks for her. It's hard enough her missing out on the day. Really this is the least I can do.

I stand up and walk round the side.

'Phoebe!' Clooney calls after me, his voice still barely above a whisper. His face is murderous. 'Get back here.'

I tiptoe towards the front, bent over so I'm hidden from most of the crowd.

'Nora!' I whisper hiss again. 'Nora!'

Josephine spots me from her pew, her eyes widening and her mouth contorting with rage. Uh-oh. She gets up and heads for me, furious. She's clearly going to batter me to death with her bouquet.

'Nora!' I say a bit louder. The whole crowd is starting to turn and stare at me now. Everyone *but* Nora, the one person I need to look my way.

'Not today, nutcase,' Josephine murmurs at me, taking my arm and dragging me backwards. 'No, I have to tell her something. NORA!'

The entire church, including the bride, groom and priest turn to stare at me.

'Hello,' the priest says, adjusting his spectacles. 'Is there something you'd like to say? Would you like to protest this marriage?'

Shocked gasps fill the church. Everyone looks at me as if I'm a monster. Josephine looks like she's about to breathe fire.

'No, I just need to speak to Nora privately before she gets married.'

She looks to her groom, eyes hard. 'Who the hell is she, Graham?'

He puts his palms up to her. 'I swear, I've never seen her before in my life.'

Oh god, she thinks I'm going to tell her a devastating secret about her groom.

'Perhaps we should go into my chambers,' the priest suggests, ushering us towards a side room. Josephine begrudgingly lets go of me, following us into the small yellow room.

'What the hell is going on?' Nora asks as soon as the door is shut.

'Language, please, Nora,' the priest snaps with disapproving eyes.

'Look.' I sigh, hating that I'm ruining her wedding. 'I'm really sorry for causing a scene. I tried to get you when you were getting ready but Josephine wouldn't let me near you.'

Josephine glares at me, clearly looking for any excuse to pounce and beat me to a pulp. I stare back. If she'd have just let me in we could have avoided all this.

'Fine you have me,' Nora says, waving her arms around. 'What on earth do you want?'

'Well...' time to sound crazy, 'I know this is going to sound nuts but I have a message from your mum, Geraldine.'

She gasps. 'My dead mammy. What the hell?'

'Language,' the priest snaps again, tutting and shaking his head.

'I know she's dead,' I confirm with an understanding nod. 'She came to me this morning and she's with us now.'

Might as well go with the truth.

Josephine scoffs and raises her eyes at Nora, as if to say; *this is why I didn't let her in.*

'She wants you to know that she wrote you a letter for you to read before getting married. Apparently your dad thought it would upset you before your big day so held it back, but she wants you to know how she thought about this day.'

She stares back at me, forehead marred in wrinkles. 'I don't believe you.'

I mean, I wouldn't either.

'Tell her I sewed a copy of the letter into her dress hem.'

Ooh, proof. That might help me.

'She says she sewed a copy into the hem of your dress. She had a sneaking suspicion your dad would wimp out.' I reach for a letter opener on the priest's desk. 'Only one way to find out.'

Nora gasps, her mouth opening, eyes wide in horror. 'Get away from my dress, you nutcase!'

Josephine launches herself at me, clutching for the letter opener.

'Calm down, Josephine!' I shout, struggling to keep it. 'I

was just going to hand it to her.' She manages to somehow get me in a head lock.

The door opens and Clooney comes walking in; taking in the scene in front of him with wide eyes.

'Clooney! Will you just tell her to trust me and cut her dress open?'

His eyes nearly pop out of their sockets. 'Phoebe have you lost your fecking mind?' he shouts. I've never heard him raise his voice so high.

'Take her out, Clooney,' Josephine insists. 'Before I kill her.'

'No one is getting killed,' the priest says, hands up between me and Josephine.

He grabs my arm, leading me away. 'So sorry about this.'

I hate that he's apologising for me.

I'm almost at the door when she says, 'Wait.'

We both turn to see Nora mulling it over, chewing her lower lip. She takes the letter opener from Josephine and then feels around the hem of her dress. When she finds a crinkle sound unlike the rest she picks at the hem until it's opened up. Low and behold, there sits a letter.

Nora gasps, looking at me in awe. Thank God it's there and I didn't just destroy a dress for no good reason.

'I told you,' I say proudly, puffing out my chest. Clooney stares at me with a million questions.

She rips open the letter, her hands shaking, and walks to the priests desk to sit down to read it. Her eyes fill with tears. This is probably why her dad wanted to hold it back. Didn't want to ruin her make up.

When she finishes she's got tears down her face but she seems happy.

'Thank you so much.' She clutches the letter to her

chest. 'I don't know how you knew about this, but this means everything to me. Everything. Thank you.'

She launches herself at me, engulfing me into a bear hug. I look over smugly to Josephine.

'Well,' her groom says, clapping his hands together, 'now that's all sorted how do you feel about getting married?' He smiles hopefully.

'Let's do it.'

CHAPTER THIRTY-THREE

<u>Wednesday 21st October</u>

*W*e walked out with a crying bride to loud and unfriendly boos. Everyone obviously thinking I'm an evil cow, but Nora told them all that I'd given her something precious from her mum and we snuck out while everyone cooed over it.

Clooney was full of questions on the drive back home. I had to lie and say that her dad had come into the pub when he wasn't there and confessed everything.

'I can't believe you did that,' he said, looking at me strangely. 'Risked everyone thinking you're mental just so she could have a letter from her mother.'

'Wouldn't you want that if it was your letter?'

His eyes droop downwards. 'Yeah, you're right.'

It makes me wonder about his mum. He never mentions her. I won't ask though. I know by now that Clooney is not a sharer. If he wants to tell me, eventually he will.

This morning he had all of the details laid out for me to call and report his dad for buying stock from Costco, but I still haven't done it yet. Nervous butterflies in my stomach tell me it's not right, and my gut is never wrong.

'I just don't know if it's the right thing to do,' I admit on a sigh later that night.

Clooney rolls his eyes. I secretly love when he does. It's so cute and funny that he finds me so exasperating.

'Jeyses, Phoebe. You're over-thinking this. Just call the number and do it.'

He's so bossy. I bite my lip. 'It's just my moral compass or whatever. It's stopping me. I mean, we could ruin him over this. I've never wanted to cause actual harm to him. Just have a fair chance.'

'And did he stop to think about that before he went after you?' he counters. 'Before the rat in the kitchen? Before reporting you to environmental health?'

He does have a point, I know he does, but... it just still feels wrong. Like I'm sinking to his level. Plus all the other times I've done something back to him it's just come round and smacked me ten times harder in the face. Karma my mum would say. Maybe I should just leave it and see how it plays out.

'Look, I know the guys an arse, but...'

'But what?' he asks, his eyebrows furrowed together.

I can't help but wonder why he hates his dad so much. He really seems to want to harm him.

'But why do you want to see him fail so bad? I mean, he's your dad. What happened between you?'

He looks towards the ceiling, his shoulders slumped. 'To be frank, Phoebe, it's none of your damn business.'

Wow. I can't help but straighten my shoulders, shocked at his sudden change in tone. He can be a real bastard when he wants to be. It scares me how he can go from being so warm to cold so easily.

'Well I'm *sorry* for giving a shit about your relationship.' I fold my arms across my chest. 'It's not my fault you have a lump of coal where your heart *should* be.'

He scoffs, crossing his own arms over his chest.

'Yeah, well not all of us are brought up by hippy parents full of so much love in their hearts it spills out to other women.'

My mouth falls to the floor, my stomach dropping as if taken by surprise on a rollercoaster. Oh no he didn't! Talking about my father's love affairs and using what I told him against me. That's beyond shitty. Whatever crush I previously harboured for him is now dead. RIP my feelings.

'You know what, Clooney?' I snarl, looking over him in disgust. 'Just because you're good looking, it doesn't give you the right to treat people like dirt whenever you fancy it.'

I spin on my heel and storm away from him into the back room. Ella is sat on the sofa watching a movie with Suki settled on her lap. She quickly grabs an invoice and pretends she's scanning through it, doing some sort of work.

'Woah, what blew up your arse?' she asks.

I could punch a wall right now I'm so full of rage. It's the betrayal of trust more than anything. More proof that he's not to be trusted. All the signs were telling me to stay the hell away from him. Why couldn't my body listen?

'Clooney-fucking-Breen!'

Her eyes widen, but she grins, putting her palms up in surrender.

'Calm down. What did he do?'

'I'm just so sick of him,' I start pacing the floor. 'One minute he tricks me by being nice so I think I can trust him, the next minute he's using something I said against me.' Suki's head turns to watch my pacing. 'Being a total arse-hole to me. To *us*, actually.'

Her face scrunches up. 'Huh?'

I know it's stupid and irrational, but I don't want to tell her what he said about Dad. I don't know why I have this tendency to want to protect him. Maybe it's because I have a feeling he has some sort of story. Some reason why he manages to be such a douche-bag. Not that he'll ever open up and tell me. Maybe I'm just coming up with excuses for him. Hoping there's more to him, when actually there isn't.

'Nothing. I just need you to take over for a while. I think I need a nap. I'm cranky.'

She sighs, pausing the Netflix show she's binging. 'Okay, I think you might be right. You go up and I'll wake you if we get busy.'

'I won't hold my breath.'

Ella wakes me up a few hours later and tells me that it's snowed. I walk down expecting just a light dusting but when I look out the front window there must be at least six inches of snow. Wow, Ireland doesn't do weather in halves.

'Yeah.' Ella laughs at my reaction. 'Apparently all weather conditions here are severe.'

'You can say that again.'

I look around. The pub is empty and I can't find Clooney. Not that I want to see the idiot. Unless it's to hit him in the face maybe.

'He's waiting for you out the front.'

I stare back at her, my eyebrows knitted together. Why would he be waiting for me outside? And he expects *me* to go to *him?* That's Clooney all over.

'I'm off to bed,' she announces. 'You guys can lock up

early.' She turns and scutters away before I can argue with her.

'But Ella—' She's already gone.

Great, now I have to face the awkward music with Clooney. Might as well get it over and done with. I just need to remember to keep an emotional distance from him.

Easy.

I take a deep breath, blowing it out slowly, visualising all of the stress leaving my body. It does little to help, but I can't hide away forever. I remember my mum used to cleanse my aura of stress. It never helped but it was still sweet that she cared enough to try.

I grab my coat on the way. When I open the door it's still snowing thick, heavy snowflakes and the icy chill tingles across the skin on my face. I can't see Clooney anywhere.

'Clooney?' I ask into the darkness, the moon light casting a slight glow onto the snow.

It's then that I see it. Someone has carved out *I'm sorry* in the snow and built three snow men. Two have mine and Ella's hats. His one has a carrot as a dick, as well as the nose. I can't believe he did this. I mean, I can believe the dick carrot, but not that he's apologised.

'I am,' Clooney says, appearing from behind me. He speaks to the ground, unable to meet my wide gaze. He looks up for a split second, pain behind his green eyes lit up in the moonlight. 'Sorry, I mean.'

'You did this?' I'm so shocked that he's even bothered to apologise, let alone in such a grand gesture of a way. Part of me wonders if Ella was involved. She loves those romantic comedy movies.

'I shouldn't have said what I did. I was a dick, and I'm sorry.'

I swallow down the lump in my throat. 'It's fine. I shouldn't keep pushing you for information about your life. It's none of my business.'

He takes a step forward, his hands in his pockets. His eyes lock with mine. They're glinting in the moonlight but I see something beneath them. They're deeper and darker than I've ever seen before.

'That's where you're wrong. I want to be your business.'

He does?

'Why?' The desperation in my voice is almost palpable. I look up at him, struggling to keep my emotions under wraps. Why must this beautiful man insist on playing with me?

He shrugs, biting his lip. 'It's just nice for someone to care enough, I guess.'

I smile back at him, but it's small and sad. It breaks my heart to think of no one else caring for him, loving him, putting him first. I think that's where a lot of his mood swings come from. I wonder if he'll ever confide in me. Tell me about his life before I met him, or if he'll always be holding back.

'I'm thinking we should lock up early tonight,' he says with a small hopeful grin.

I snort, glad for the attempt to break the heaviness. 'Yeah, no one is coming out in this snow.' I look across at the frozen lake.

I hear his boots crunching towards the door.

'Oh, but, Phoebe?'.

I turn just in time to get assaulted with a snow ball to the face. Icy shards of snow trickle down the front of my top, stinging my skin.

'Oh my god, you bastard!' I can't believe he just did that. And so soon after apologising.

He doubles over laughing. Well, I'll show that dickhead. I quickly bend down and scoop up a handful, chucking it at him. It breaks up in the air before it even gets close to him. Damn.

He smirks. 'You're gonna have to do better than that, Poodles.'

'Ugh!' I scream. 'I hate when you call me poodles.'

I bend down to collect more snow, but then he's behind me and shoving snow down the back of my jeans.

'Hey, pervert!' I jump up and down on the spot in an attempt to get it down and off me. Goose pimples rise all over my body. So, *so* cold.

I quickly scoop more snow and run over to him. He's still trying to make one so I take the opportunity to throw it close range. I won't take any chances this time.

The snow hits him in the face. His shock is hilarious, only then I realise I'm slipping. I grab onto him to steady myself but just end up bringing him down on top of me.

His chest thuds onto mine like a brick.

'Oooh!' I huff, scrunching my eyes up at the pressure weighing down on me.

'Shit, are you okay?'

I open my eyes to find him staring down at me with such concern in those piercing forest green eyes that my whole body tingles, and not just from the freezing snow.

He looks down at my lips. I wonder if he's thinking the same thing. That he's touched me in intimate places but never actually kissed me on the lips.

I *will* him to kiss me, my chest heaving up and down with the struggle to breathe. I can't seem to do any basic function around him; breathe, talk. It all turns to mush when he's looking at me like that, with the promise of more.

He finally lowers his lips, hesitating for two heart beats

before merging them with mine. My brain screams in celebration. Clooney is kissing me! His lips are welcoming and warm against our cold bodies. He opens our mouths and strokes his tongue against mine.

Jesus. How can this feel more erotic than him finger banging me in the bath? It makes no sense, but damn, this tongue. His dances with mine like we've done this for years, while one of his hands goes into my hair and the other cradles my head, like I'm a delicate flower that needs to be cherished.

He pulls back slowly, almost begrudgingly. The second his lips leave mine I feel bereft. Bereft, cold and awkward.

He smiles down at me, biting his bottom lip. Damn, he's fine. How have I got such a beauty to kiss me?

Quick Phoebe, think of something to say. Anything at all would be good. Just say *something*.

'So... you like to gamble?'

Shit, Phoebe, *really?* That's what you choose to say at this moment?

It's like his walls come crashing down. His face falls and mistrust lights his eyes. Just when I was making some progress.

'Who told you that?' he demands, his jaw rigid.

He removes his hands from me and pushes himself up. So it's true? Why else would he react so badly?

'Err, no-one. I just noticed you were gambling on your phone the other day.' I don't even know why I said that. Verbal diarrhoea is pouring from my mouth right now. Someone get me an Imodium.

'You were going through my phone?' He practically spits in disgust.

I stand up, feeling awful. My gut is telling me to run away and hide. He's furious. How could I have been feeling so good just moments before. Why did I have to go and ruin it again? I wrap my arms around myself, needing the comfort.

'Sorry, I shouldn't have said anything.'

His eyes turn cold. I don't recognise him at all like this. 'No, you shouldn't have. My private life is just that; private. You're way out of line.' He turns and storms into the pub.

'I'm sorry,' I call after him feebly. But it's too late. He's gone and the damage has been done.

Well done, Phoebe.

CHAPTER THIRTY-FOUR

<u>Thursday 22nd October</u>

*B*y the next evening we're crazy busy. So busy it has me wondering if Clooney went ahead and reported his dad himself. He wouldn't do that, right?

Clooney not talking to me has put me completely on edge. I've caught myself chewing my nails a few times. I haven't done that in years. I still can't believe I went from forgiving him, to kissing him and then upsetting him, all in about three minutes.

But the more I think about it, its him I should be mad at. He can't go around kissing me and then telling me I'm none of his business. The two are kind of inclusive of each other.

'Talk about going zero to ninety miles an hour,' Ella complains next to me, us both pumping out different bitters, most of it spilling into the overflow tray. I'll never get used to its consistency. It has a life of its own.

'Why are you being so weird?' Ella asks, looking curiously over at me as she serves the man his bitter.

'I'm not,' I shrug. Maybe I shouldn't have had that third coffee.

'*Please.*' She gives the man his change. 'You're all jumpy. Have you fallen out with Clooney *again*? He's been acting sulky all day too.'

As I hand over the bitter and take payment, I quickly check he's not within ear shot. 'Okay, I kind of said the wrong thing last night and upset him.'

'Ooh, really.' Her eyes light up. She's always loved a bit of gossip. I suppose without the internet there's not much else to do around here.

I sigh, needing to tell someone. Lighten the load of the burden and all that.

'Yeah, I asked him if he was a gambler.'

She huffs out a shocked breath. 'Well, yeah, that'll piss anyone off.'

'And...' I cringe, ashamed of myself. 'I'd looked on his phone to find a gambling app open.'

She shakes her head. 'Jesus, Pheebs. You'd go mental if someone went through your phone.'

I nod with a grimace. 'I know, I know. But look at the evidence. A gambling app open on his phone, him putting on a bet on a horse, he was playing poker with his mates. I mean, that's all proof. And he reacted so badly, there *has* to be something there.'

She gives me a pointed stare. 'Or you're just reading too much into things.'

The other niggling thought is one I'm really ashamed to admit out loud.

'And something his dad said just keeps circling round in my head. He said he can put on the charm, but he's nothing but a bad-un. That scares me.'

She sighs and looks at me sympathetically. 'He's probably just trying to stir up more trouble. Either way, you need to apologise.'

I hate how she's always on his side. The nagging idea that her and Clooney would probably be better suited hangs over me. He doesn't need a control freak like me poking into his business.

I tried to apologise this morning at breakfast, hoping that his mood would have disappeared like the snow, but he just glared at me and walked off.

'I have, but he won't listen.' I hate bad blood with anyone, but with Clooney, I feel sick to my stomach.

'I don't blame him.' I hate even more that she's right and not automatically on my side. Surely that's what sisters are for? She rests her hand on my shoulder. 'Just give him time.'

She's so laid back. She wouldn't be pressuring him to tell her everything about his past. She'd make the perfect girlfriend.

'Yeah.. Easy to say when we work and live together.'

'I heard he's had his licence suspended,' I overhear one man say and it catches my attention.

Damn that man Clooney. Has he reported his dad to spite me for upsetting him last night?

I didn't bother telling Ella mine and Clooney's plan to report Fergus. Didn't want her to be an accomplice in case it ever came back to bite us in the arse. Ever the older sister. I'd confront Clooney if he wasn't being such an arse. I'll avoid it until I absolutely have to.

We're busy all the way up to closing time. The time, which normally drags, the graveyard hour, flies by.

'I can't believe that was just a Monday night,' I say with a heavy sigh, massaging my tight neck. 'I'm shattered.'

'Ella,' Clooney says as he dries a glass. 'Why don't you go up to bed and I'll help Phoebe lock up?'

She shrugs, looking to me. 'Okay.' She gives me a quick wink before escaping.

Why is he trying to get me on my own? Is he going to have another go at me? Tell me to butt out of his business again? Tell me he's moving out? Just the thought has my chest constricting in pain. How have I become so attached to this man in such a short space of time?

'So it worked then?' he says, wiping down a table, not actually looking at me.

Ah, so he *did* report his dad. He really does have no shame.

'I can't believe you did it without checking with me first.'

He has no idea the repercussions that could come from this. He had a right to be pissed at me, but that doesn't excuse this.

He shrugs. 'I knew you weren't going to do it.'

Jeez, thanks for the faith in me.

'Don't you feel even a tiny bit bad?' I can't help but ask.

I mean, he's linked to this guy by blood. But then I suppose my seven extra sisters are too. They're invading my thoughts more and more lately.

He grins, looking at me endearingly, as if we didn't fight at all last night.

'No, but I can tell you do.'

I nod, hating that his smile lights up my evening. My cheeks burn. It bothers me that he can throw his dad to the dogs like that. It doesn't give me confidence in trusting him if he doesn't even have loyalty for his own father. Alarm bells are ringing, reminding me of how humiliated I felt after being taken for a mug by Garry.

'I can't help it. I mean, this is serious. We could have just taken your *father's* livelihood away from him.'

He scoffs, shooting me an exasperated look. 'Phoebe, he's the one who started this. He's been the one keeping everyone away from this place.'

I chew my lip, an uneasy feeling settling in my stomach. 'Still.'

He grins. 'You're such a rule follower, aren't you?'

Oh God, this again. My parents always complained that I accepted the limits society put upon me. It's their fault for always getting me to see everyone's good sides. See the potential beauty in them. Not that I expect to find much in Fergus.

'I can't help it. It's just who I am.' I fold my arms across my chest. If he doesn't like me, tough. I'm not changing myself for him, or anyone.

'It's even weirder after meeting your parents,' he continues, wiping down another table. 'It's not like you had a strict upbringing or anything.'

As he loves to remind me.

'Yeah, but they also taught me to be a good person.'

I'm wondering if his dad ever bothered with that life lesson. I can't imagine someone as ruthless as Fergus teaching morality lessons to his son.

He raises one eyebrow. 'I'm sorry I said that about your dad. I think your parents are great. It's just strange how different you are to them.'

I sigh, knowing he's right. People always joked I was adopted. I'd laugh, but it hurt to be so openly different to my family. It would have been easier if I *were* adopted.

'Yeah, well I'm sure a shrink would say I developed coping methods and gave myself boundaries to feel safe, seen as I was raised by such hippy, eco warriors.'

He laughs as he stacks the chairs on top of the table. 'So you have thought about it then?'

I sigh, my fatigued muscles begging for this day to be over. 'Can we please not talk about my parents?'

Hell, if he can take personal topics off the table so can I, God damn it.

'Fine.'

I still need to apologise for last night. Regardless of whether he's trying to gloss over it.

'Look I'm really sorry for what I said last night,' I blurt. 'It was out of order and it really was none of my business.'

'You're right.' He nods, his face suddenly serious.

Shit, he's not going to make this any easier for me.

'But...' He looks at me expectantly. Obviously wanting me to ask him to continue.

I sigh and throw my cleaning cloth on the table. 'But what?' I ask, quickly losing my patience.

He smiles, but his eyes are dull, without their usual sparkle of mischief.

'But... I do want to tell you something.'

'Oh?' I don't move, for fear I'll scare him away like an animal in the wild.

He takes a deep breath, raking his hand through his hair. It messes it up, just like how he looks first thing in the morning. Delicious. I let a pleased little sigh escape.

'Well, I want you to know that my dad's always treated me like a screw up. Like a nuisance.'

Ah, he's starting to explain why he hates his dad so much. I'll greedily take any little titbit he wants to throw my way.

'After a while you start believing you *are* the loser he thinks you are.'

The overwhelming urge to go to him and throw my arms around him, to comfort him and tell him everything is okay, well, its unbelievably strong. I fight myself. I don't want him to get the wrong end of the stick.

'Did something happen for him to start treating you like that?' I can't help but ask. It's rare he's so open and honest with me. I have to take advantage while I can.

He leans against the bar. 'The only thing I've ever been able to think of is that I remind him of Mum. I lost her when I was nine.'

Shit, I had no idea she'd died so young.

I imagine a small Clooney having to cope with the loss of his mother. Raised by that pig Fergus. Poor baby.

'I do look like her.' He smiles briefly, as if from a memory. 'After she died he was more angry than upset.'

I try to imagine a female version of Clooney. She'd be stunning, all long black hair with those unusual bright eyes.

'Do you have a picture of her?' I ask hopefully, wanting as much as he's willing to share.

'I do.' He takes his phone out of his back pocket and scrolls through it for a while. 'Here we go.'

He hands the phone to me. I zoom in to see a woman cuddling a young cute Clooney. Just as predicted she has the exact same jet black hair and dirty green eyes as him. I can see why his dad might have been hurt seeing him grow up to be more like her, but that's no excuse to take it out on a young boy. To break him and his confidence down to nothing.

'She was beautiful.' I smile sadly, handing it back to him. 'And yes, you're the spitting image of her.' I never did think he looked like his pig of a dad.

He smiles, it not meeting his eyes. It does explain why he feels such contempt towards him.

'Look, I feel like shit for upsetting you last night and I

hate this atmosphere between us. Tell me what to do so we can go back to being friends?'

That grabs his attention. His head whips round to stare at me like I just called him the C word. Wow, one eighty degree mood change.

'Is that what we are?' he snaps. *'Friends?'* He says it like it's a dirty word.

I frown back at him. 'I mean... yeah. I thought we were?'

Could it be that he doesn't even want me as a friend anymore?

He blows out a heavy breath. 'Fine, Phoebe. If that's what you want we'll be just that. *Friends.'*

I open my mouth to say something; anything to try and understand him. To try and stop him being so angry. But it's too late. He's already turning and storming out into the kitchen, slamming the heavy door behind him.

Well what the hell was that all about? I sit down onto one of the chairs and try to replay the conversation in my head. Is he angry because I said we were friends? Did he think we were something more? Does he *want* something more? God, I'm more bewildered than ever.

I don't think I'll ever understand that man. He goes from happy to angry in what feels like seconds. Maybe I'm better off not knowing inside that fucked up head. Better to see him as a work colleague and roommate. Distance myself from him. All I seem to get around him is muddled and upset. Nobody has time for that, especially me.

Yet the thought of not having him in my life scares me more than anything. Could it be that I'd prefer to be completely head fucked than the worse alternative; without him?

CHAPTER THIRTY-FIVE

<u>Friday 23rd October</u>

*B*anging on the door wakes me up with a start, my legs and arms flailing. Ugh. It took ages for me to get to sleep last night after Clooney's confession. My mind was coming up with reasons why it's not such a terrible idea being involved with him. Someone banging the door down is the last thing I need first thing in the morning.

'What the hell is that?' I ask Ella, wiping at my sore eyes.

'Ugh, shut up,' she mumbles, rolling over and putting her pillow over her head. She's never been good in the mornings, bless her.

Now that I'm awake there's no chance I'll be able to go back to sleep again. I huff as I swing my legs out of the bed, my back creaking like a lady twice my age. Thankfully Ella sleeps closest to the window as I'm normally first up.

I grab my dressing gown and put on my fluffy unicorn slippers. A cup of tea; that's what I need. I head downstairs flicking on lights as I go. It's a bit creepy this early in the morning by myself. Since we were robbed, I only really feel safe when Clooney is around me. That can't be healthy.

Oh well, I push through the heavy fire door into the kitchen, ignoring Suki who seems intent on getting in. I jump when I notice the light is already on. Clooney is sat on a stool sipping from a cup and scrolling on his phone. He looks delicious in just his black boxer shorts and a tight white t-shirt. His dark hair is in disarray, stubble on his perfect jaw. Damn. It's like looking at a Calvin Klein ad.

'Morning,' he says through a yawn.

'Morning.' I smile, flicking the kettle on. I check my watch. It's six a.m. 'What are you doing up so early? Did you hear someone banging on the door?' I quickly rub my eyes, hoping that any unsightly crusty sleep comes out.

'No,' he answers briefly.

He fidgets with his phone, his lips pressing together in a slight grimace. Must be reading the news with a face like that.

'That bad, huh?' I laugh, hoping he's not going to hold a grudge from last night. I still don't get how he can be so pissed at me for calling us friends.

He doesn't laugh back. Now I'm worried.

I turn to face him fully. 'Clooney, what is it?' My stomach starts doing nervous somersaults.

He sighs, his shoulders loosening for a second only for them to tense again immediately.

'Promise you won't get mad?' he asks, scrunching his face into a grimace.

'Oh god.' This isn't good at all. A sick feeling settles in my stomach.

He quickly jumps up and pulls me by the waist so I'm

sat on his stool. Apparently I need to be sat down too. My skin whimpers when his hands leave my body.

'Just tell me, please.' The anticipation is probably worse than the actual news.

'Okay.' He takes a deep breath, running his hand through his hair. 'So it looks like my dad's leaked that we dobbed him in for alleged improper conduct to the local newspaper. Basically it reads that we've gone after him, unprovoked.'

He hands me his phone. I quickly skim through the article posted from the local newspaper. It's pretty bloody damming. Makes us out to be heartless monsters intent on ruining him, the man that was born and raised in this town.

I close the article and see the link on their Facebook page. There's already seventy five comments. I scroll through them. None of them are good.

These girls need to go back home to England, where they belong!

These lasses should be ashamed of themselves.

Snitches get stitches.

My stomach rolls at the hate pointed towards us. All because Clooney wanted some sort of revenge on his dad. I knew nothing good would come from this.

'Oh my god.' I clutch my forehead, an instant headache forming.

'I know.' I look up to see the skin around his eyes bunched into fine crinkles. 'I'm so sorry, Phoebe. I should have listened to you and just left it.'

Bless him, he feels responsible. I mean, he *is*, but at least he feels bad about it. I sigh, letting my head fall down onto the table.

'You know what? Don't worry about it.'

He narrows his eyes at me. 'How can you be so calm about this?'

I sigh. I feel like all I do these days is sigh. I'm strangely numb about yet more bad news.

'It just means we're back to square one.' I shrug my shoulders. 'Luckily I didn't raise my hopes in the first place. It's just another sign that we should give up, cut our losses and move back home.'

'Don't say that.' His voice low and full of melancholy.

I smile sadly. 'As my mother would say, it's what the universe is telling us.'

'Well I say the universe is talking bullshit,' he says with conviction, losing his temper as he bangs the worktop.

I burst out laughing. It's strange. Him feeling so passionate makes me giggly.

He claps his hands in front of him. 'That's it. We're going out.'

'Huh?' I go to the boiling kettle and start to make my tea. It is still *far* too early for all of this.

He follows me. 'We're going out. Today.'

'Where?' I yawn. I don't know if I can be bothered. I fancy bringing this tea back to bed.

'Somewhere to take our minds off this. It'll be my surprise. Go get dressed into something comfy.'

'Comfy?' I narrow my eyes at him. 'Why? Where are you taking me?'

He grabs my shoulders, his eyes resolute. 'Phoebe, stop trying to control the situation. Just have some breakfast, go upstairs, get dressed and let me take you somewhere.'

He tucks a strand of my crazy morning hair behind my ear. It makes me shiver. He notices and does that delicious naughty smirk. Bastard knows he has me hanging on by a string.

Half an hour later I'm ready, dressed in jeans, a loose tank top and an oversized snuggly jumper. He's wearing his usual jeans, tight black t-shirt and leather jacket. The guy thinks he's Danny Zuko from Grease. The worst thing is that he almost is.

'Listen...' I start, ready to give him an out. He might have thought about it and changed his mind.

He puts his palms up. 'I know what you're gonna say. You're worried about leaving Ella alone today. I've already asked my mate Roairy to work. He can help out.'

'But I don't have the money to pay him.'

He shakes his head. 'He owes me a favour. He's doing it for free.' He warns me with his eyes to stop listing excuses.

'O...kay.' I search around for another reason, but he seems eager to take me out. Maybe he's right, I should just go with it.

'Just relax.' He grins and it lights up my heart. 'Today is a day of fun.'

He takes my hand and leads me out. I can't help but feel that it's a very 'date' like thing to do. I could almost close my eyes and pretend I'm his girlfriend. God, see what I mean? I turn into a teenager girl with a humongous crush around him. Rational thoughts disappear.

'Ah, there you are,' a female voice says just as I'm getting into Clooney's car.

'Did you hear that?' I ask Clooney and look around us.

'Huh?' He looks around, puzzled.

Okay so it's clear he didn't.

'I was trying to knock on the door earlier but you mustn't have heard me.' She sounds young and cheery.

Oh god. Not now. Not a dead person when I'm trying to have a nice day.

'Don't worry, I'll come with you.' Her voice is suddenly behind me in the car. *'Where are we going?'*

I grit my teeth. Today is going to be *long* if this girl is following us.

CHAPTER THIRTY-SIX

'So where are we of to?' I ask Clooney. Hopefully if I ignore her she'll think I can't hear her and go away.

'And who is this hunk? Oh, it's Clooney. Of course it is.'

He licks his lips, his delicious grin exciting me in inappropriate places. 'Just wait and see would you. God, you're shit with surprises.'

I laugh. 'Yeah, my worst nightmare would be a surprise party.'

'So I see you're ignoring me, but I know you're the one. Breda's great niece. The one that can help me. They told me at the funeral home.'

Jesus, she's really not going to leave me alone.

I try to talk over a cough. 'What,' *cough,* 'do you' *cough,* 'want?'

Clooney looks at me, eyebrows raised. Obviously realising I'm a grade A weirdo.

'Did you say something?'

'Nope.' I shake my head.

'Well, I'm wanting to tell my mammy not to chuck out a

dress of mine. I promised it to my niece. She said she'd like to make a pillow out of the fabric. You know, to remind her of me.' I nod discreetly. *'Only the crazy old bint has put it in the charity shop bag. If we don't get there today it could end up god knows where.'*

I get my phone out and pretend someone has called me.

'Oh hi. Yeah I'm so sorry but I'm not going to be able to do that today. But I can get right on it as soon as I get home?'

'Oh really? I hate to have to wait. What if she decides to go early? It could be gone forever.'

'Sorry, but you won't get anywhere with me until then,' I insist, standing my ground.

I hear her sigh. *'Fine. I suppose I'll have to wait.'*

'Thank you.' I pretend to hang up the phone.

'Who was that?' Clooney asks as we take a turn down a country lane I've never noticed before.

'Oh just... the brewery,' I lie. 'Anyway, how much longer?' I quickly ask, hoping to change the subject.

'We're actually here.'

He pulls into a small deserted parking lot. I look up at the sun bleached sign.

'Paint balling? We're going paint balling?' I ask in disbelief.

Is he insane? What part of being belted with paint balls did he think I'd enjoy? I thought this was supposed to cheer me up?

He laughs and leans back in his seat. 'We are indeed.' He snorts. 'Don't look so terrified.'

I get out of the car, already regretting agreeing to this. See, this is why I hate surprises. They're never good.

'Sorry, but... you want to fire me with balls made of paint? Kind of hard not to be offended about that.'

He smirks. 'There I was thinking that I annoy you so much you'd revel in getting to hammer *me* with them.'

He takes my hand and leads me through the gates. God, I love when he holds my hand. I have to stop myself from rubbing his fingers with my still deformed looking thumb.

'Don't get me wrong. I've thought about it,' I admit with an easy laugh.

He chats to a guy, I'm assuming another friend of his, and introduces me as the new landlady of the Cock and Bull pub. Luckily the guy doesn't balk or get out his pitch fork. Obviously hasn't read the article yet. He has a quick look around for his manager before letting us in for free.

'Do you know *everyone* in this town?'

Clooney grins, his eyes warm. 'It's a small place.' He leads me into an area full of dark blue boiler suits. 'Don't panic though, it's a slow day by the looks of things and we're not going for the guns.'

'We're not?' How the hell am I expected to shoot him without a gun?

'No, we'll just both get a bag of them and we chase each other round, smashing it into each other.' He leans into my personal space, so close I can smell his cinnamon, mint and cigarette smoke scent, and waggles his eyebrows. 'Far more up close and personal.'

Just smelling him has me wet. I need to get a damn grip.

We put our overalls on over our clothes. Thank god I wore a tank top underneath my jumper. I'd have sweated to death in my jumper.

His mate hands us both goggles and a sort of satchel full of what looks like little water balloons.

'Okay, Poodles, try and catch me,' he shouts, already running ahead.

I chase after him. 'Do *not* call me poodles!' I reach into my bag, grab a ball and throw it at him. I miss, dammit.

'Ha ha! You're a shit aim.' He laughs, slowing down to gloat and point his finger.

I quickly get another one out, aim, throw and this time it hits him on his stomach. It explodes into red paint. Quite satisfying actually.

'Ha! You cocky shit.' I laugh. 'Got you!'

'Oh, you're gonna be sorry,' he warns with a grin, getting three balls out at once.

Oh crap. I run, as if running for my life. I hear him gaining on me. Three balls hit me; one in the leg, one on my lower back and one on my left arm. It doesn't hurt *that* bad, but I still think I'll bruise like a peach.

I take a ball out and turn round smashing it into his neck. His mouth pops open in shock. Ha ha, he didn't expect that one. I run again. Except this time I don't hear him running after me. I turn round but I can't see him. It's eerily quiet.

'Clooney?' I whisper, peering around bales of hay. Oh my god, I just know he's going to jump out and attack me any moment. I can't bear the suspense, my pulse going crazy at the base of my neck, almost nauseating.

That's when I feel the splat on the top of my head. I screech as yellow paints drips down the side of my goggles.

I spin to find him doubled over wetting himself laughing.

'My hair! You absolute *bastard!*' I run after him, but he's too quick, those athletic legs carrying him at twice the speed of mine. I see a short cut through the hay bales to where he's running. Aha!

I run towards it, getting two balls out of my bag. I collide straight into him, taking us both down to the floor. I land on top of him, legs around his waist; he's broken my fall.

'Oops.'

He laughs. Proper throws his head back and does a belly laugh. It's rare for him to laugh so hard and naturally. I feel special that I can make him, even if he is laughing *at* me.

'Oh, Poodles. What am I going to do with you?' He looks up at me, his gaze quickly turning from amusement to dark pools of lust.

My chest heaves up and down. I hope he thinks it's from all of the running and not me perving all over him. I clench my legs together, trying to ease the tingling between them. It only pulls his groin up towards me.

He reaches his hand up and clasps my cheek. I melt like a puddle into it. He leans up at the same time as I lower myself. We meet in the middle, our mouths crashing together like we're starving for oxygen and each other provides the only chance of survival.

Our tongues dance like they were created just for each other. My heart starts to ache when he runs his hands through my sticky yellow smeared hair.

What am I doing? This guy doesn't do relationships and not only that, but I'm planning on leaving. Packing up and moving back to England as soon as we manage to sell. Nothing can ever be between us.

I put my hand on his chest and begrudgingly push him away.

He looks up at me, his brows knitted together. 'What's wrong?'

'We shouldn't be doing this.' Even though I want nothing more.

'Why not?' He pouts, cutest thing ever.

I sigh sadly. 'Because I'm a relationship girl and you're not a relationship guy. I just think its best we stop this now, before one of us gets hurt.' I won't let him know I'm bound to be the one. I can't risk injuring my heart again. Not after Garry. I already know I have far stronger feelings for Clooney, so it would sting twice as hard.

'But... we have something between us, right?' He takes my jaw in his hands. 'Why deny ourselves?'

He's clearly never denied himself anything before, especially pleasure.

'Because we'd never work,' I admit, my chest tight at having to voice our sad reality. 'There's no point getting involved physically if we can't ever be together. I just think its best we stay as friends.'

He sighs, sitting up. 'I suppose you're right.'

'I am.' I nod, sitting back onto my heels. Doesn't mean it doesn't suck.

'But...'

'But what?' I ask far too eagerly. Does he have a plan? Is he willing to commit? To follow me back to England?

He splats a paintball into my cheek. 'Sorry, Poodles, but you deserved that one.'

CHAPTER THIRTY-SEVEN

The minute I get back in the car dead girl starts again. I'd actually forgotten about her.

'Finally! If you could just stop kissing Clooney for five minutes, we might actually get somewhere.'

The bloody cheek of her! Spying on me. Then I think of all of the potential ghosts watching us at any given time. Eww, do they watch me in the bath? Gross. What if there is such a thing as ghost perverts? What if they saw what me and Clooney did in the bath? My cheeks heat just at the idea.

'She lives just down Drum Road.'

'Straight home?' Clooney asks as he straps in his seat belt, half dried paint still in his hair. Oh how I'd love to get him in the shower and scrub him clean.

'Erm, yeah.' How do I word this? 'Actually I have to run an errand.'

'Really? Where?'

'Oh, just down Drum Road,' I answer vaguely looking out of the window. 'I'll get a cab when I get back.'

'Well that's on our way home. I'll come with you.'

'*Great news!*' Ghost lady cheers in delight.

Not great news. I don't want him knowing what a freak I am. It was close enough at that wedding.

'No, honestly,' I insist with a polite smile. 'I'll just take a taxi. I think its best I just do it on my own.'

He frowns at me, quirking one eyebrow. 'Why?'

I grimace. Quickly Phoebe, think of something you have to do by yourself. It's a residential house, nowhere near a shop, so buying something isn't an option.

'What is it exactly that you need to do?' He presses, each minute passing taking us closer to Drum Road.

'Um... I...'. I literally can't think of *anything*. Why am I such a shit liar? Being raised around rainbows and butterflies did nothing for this very vital life skill.

'What, Phoebe? Why all the secrecy?' His eyebrows bunch together, his jaw tense.

'*Oh, just tell him,*' ghost lady says. '*Clooney's got an open mind. He might believe you.*'

'No way,' I accidentally blurt out.

'No way what?' he asks desperately, looking at me every few seconds.

'*Go on,*' she cheers. '*Tell him, tell him.*'

'Just shut up will you!' I snap at her.

'Jesus,' Clooney says, hurt clouding his eyes. 'There's no need for that, Phoebe. I thought we'd had a nice day today.'

'No, sorry, I wasn't speaking to you.' Ugh, my head hurts.

He frowns back at me. 'And who, may I ask, are you talking to?'

Oh god. 'You wouldn't believe me if I told you, okay? So just drop it.'

We pull into Drum Road and Clooney parks up. He turns in his seat to face me, his gaze serious.

'Phoebe, you said you trust me. You either do or you don't, so which is it?'

Ugh, I am not going to get out of this and at least this way someone will know. I haven't even told Ella for fear of her having me locked up. It's a big burden to bear on your own.

'Okay, but swear you won't laugh?' I warn, already second guessing whether this is a good idea.

'I can't promise anything of the sort,' he says with a light grin. His eyes scan over my face, looking for answers.

I take a deep breath and try to swallow down the discomfort of doubting him. I suppose I have nothing to lose.

'Okay, well... wait, promise you won't try and have me committed?'

'Oh Jeyses, Phoebe.' He taps his fingers on the steering wheel. 'You're driving me mad. Just spit it out.'

'I hear voices,' I blurt out, trying and failing at being funny.

He frowns back at me. Oh, those were definitely the wrong words. He'll obviously think I'm crazy with that one.

'I mean, not like in my head,' I try to explain. 'But, well I hear ghosts speak to me.'

He stares at me, not moving one muscle on his face. I wait for this reaction, sick with terror.

'Is this a joke?'

I snort a laugh. 'Yeah I thought it would be really funny to tell you I'm a nutcase.'

He strokes his stubbled jaw. 'I mean, I heard the rumours that Breda spoke to the dead, but I just assumed it was a load of bull.'

Ah, so it was common knowledge in town by the time she died. I suppose it's something that eventually catches up with you. The thought of anyone finding out about it fills me with dread.

'I found her hidden diaries and turns out she had the *gift* too.'

'Right, so....' he rubs at his forehead. 'Have you always heard them?'

I shake my head. 'No, it started when I was working at the funeral home.'

Recognition meets his face. 'So that's why you were doing all the crazy stuff that got you fired.'

'Yes,' I nod. It's nice to explain it to someone. 'They just won't shut up until I do what they ask.'

'Pfft, how rude!' ghost girl says.

'And how you knew Nora's letter from her mam was in her dress at the wedding.'

I nod.

'You're sure about this?' he presses, chewing on his bottom lip.

'Yes. Trust me, I wish I were wrong. I have one here right now that wants me to go tell her mum something.'

He looks up at the houses. 'Wait, Helen? You have Helen here right now?'

'That's me!' she shouts.

'Apparently.' I shrug. Then I get an idea. 'Helen, you knew Clooney. Tell me something about him that I wouldn't know.'

Clooney's shoulders become rigid. What's he so worried about?

'Let me think. Oh, I know, his last girlfriend was Orla.'

'Orla?' I repeat, staring at him. 'Who is Orla?'

The colour drains from his face.

'No one.' He looks away, avoiding my gaze, his playful mood abruptly over.

He just lied to my face. It's so obvious.

'She says it was your last girlfriend. I thought you didn't do girlfriends?'

'*Oops, awkward,*' ghost girl says, having no idea how much she's just landed Clooney in it.

He shrugs, no warmer. 'I don't. It was just Orla.'

Damn that hurts. What was so special about Orla? What did she have that I clearly don't?

'And where is Orla now? I haven't met her, have I?'

I think back to all his fan girls at the pub. I didn't think any of them were particularly special. Don't get me wrong, they're all beautiful, and I'm definitely no outstanding stunner myself, but something tells me this Orla was model worthy stunning.

'No.' He shakes his head, looking out of the window. 'She moved to England.'

My head is reeling. Clooney had a girlfriend. A girl-friend named Orla and now she lives in England?

'Why did you break up?'

I know I have no right to ask. I'm just the girl who was snogging him less than half an hour ago, but I *need* to know. It's another puzzle piece in the mystery that is Clooney Breen.

His face hardens. 'That's none of your business, Phoebe.'

I shake my head. Shutting me out again. I'm so sick of him telling me his life is none of my business, but then expecting me to get involved with him, even if he is just offering sex.

'I thought you trusted me? Or is that only when you feel like it?'

He ignores me so I open the car door. 'See, this right here.' I point between us both. 'Is why there can never be anything between us. Because I'm the only one willing to put myself on the line.' I slam the door behind me.

'*You go, girl,*' Helen says. If she could click I'm guessing she would.

~

After a long and rather exhausting talk with Helen's mum I finally convinced her that I knew what I was talking about. She's taken the dress out of the bag and has promised to get it made into a cushion for her grand-daughter.

'*Thank you so much,*' ghost girl says as we walk out.

I expect Clooney's car to have gone, but the bastard has stayed. I don't know if I'm happy or sad about it.

'You're welcome.'

'*Listen, I was friends with Orla. I know why they broke up, if you want to know?*'

Oh my god. Could it really be that easy? No, I shake my head. I don't want to know. It wouldn't be right finding out like this.

'I'm good, thanks.'

'*It's such a shame. You guys seem good together.*'

I look at him through the car window, brooding sexily.

'Yeah, well unfortunately that doesn't guarantee that it can work between two people and all the signs are telling me that it won't.'

'*Still... don't give up on him. He's just his own worst enemy.*'

'What do you mean by that?' I listen out for a response. 'Helen?'

Oh, of course. *Now* she's decided to cross over.

CHAPTER THIRTY-EIGHT

Monday 26th October

*W*e drove home in awkward silence and haven't really talked since. Its beyond awkward, but it just confirms to me that he's a man child. He should have apologised. Even if he didn't want to tell me the story he could have apologised. Yet instead he ruined a perfect day.

It's harder to avoid him with it being so painfully quiet. We seem to have even less customers now that article has exposed us as underhand hacks. Just the few people from the looney bin and few old men that live close by.

I see the postman pull up and go to collect the post. Any excuse to get out from that awful tension. In amongst the normal bills is a leaflet.

BALLYKIELTY DEVELOPMENT PLANS

Find out more at the

COUNCIL MEETING
Sunday 8th November – 7.30 pm
The Scout Hut

Verity Development's plan could lead to huge parts of our town being bought up to build a supermarket, risking many local businesses and lively hoods.

If you don't agree with the proposed development options join us and object.

Wow, a huge supermarket. Things like that could really ruin a small town.

'Have you seen this?' I ask Ella as she's wiping down the bar.

'What?' she asks.

'They're asking people to attend a town meeting this Sunday. They want to stop a big developer buying up the town and turning it into a supermarket.'

Clooney walks into the bar and takes the leaflet from the side.

'Jesus, it's getting worse then,' he says with a shake of his head.

It's his only direct speech towards me in days.

'Has it been going on for long?' I ask, quick to take my chance to bury the hatchet and engage in friendly conversation.

'Yep,' he nods, 'that Sean you met, he had his home forced from him.'

'Forced from him?' I repeat like a parrot. 'How can they even do that?'

He leans over the bar and nods. 'They start playing nicely with a reasonable offer. Try and throw a bit more money at first, then they start making things difficult for you. Court cases, threatening phone calls, being followed; he had it all.'

'Oh my god! How can that be legal?'

He scoffs. 'It's not, but they have so much money and clout, they can get away with it.'

Poor Sean. Hang on a minute. A crazy idea whirls around my head. I have to know the answer immediately.

'You,' I point at Clooney, 'follow me.' I grab his arm, giving him no choice, as I drag him through the kitchen and into the back room, ignoring Ella's confused stares.

'What the hell's up with ya?' he asks as soon as I release my grip. Suki looks up at us from the sofa. She stretches out, as if to show what an inconvenience being woken up is.

I swallow, feeling sick at even asking this. I just hope I'm wrong.

'You said that happened to Sean, right?' I'm shaking and I haven't even asked the question yet.

He nods, his eyes narrowed in suspicion.

'And you said that he hated your dad, but you couldn't tell me why.'

He nods cautiously, chewing on his cheek.

I take a deep breath, steeling my nerve. 'Is your dad in with the developers?'

I hope for him to burst out laughing. To tell me what a ridiculous drama queen I am for even suspecting this, but instead he puts his hands in his pockets and looks to the floor, his shoulders hunched.

'Please tell me I'm wrong.'

Hooded eyes look up at me. 'You're not wrong.'

'Oh my god.' I sit down on the sofa, needing some support for my jellied legs. 'Why doesn't everyone know?'

Surely if they did they'd all boycott his pub.

'Because Sean was made to sign a non-disclosure agreement. If it got out he'd be liable to pay back his settlement. He might hate him for it, but he has to protect himself. He wants to leave some money for his grandkids.'

I suppose I can understand that.

'But why have *you* kept it quiet? I thought you hated your dad?'

'I never said I hated him, Phoebe,' he snaps. He runs his hand through his hair. 'Hate is a strong word. I just...'. His face is tortured.

'You still feel loyalty towards him, don't you?'

He inhales and exhales a breath full of regret. 'I realise how stupid that is.'

I actually kind of get it, an overwhelming sense of relief settles over me. He does have loyalty to him. He *can* be trusted.

'It's not stupid. He's still your dad.'

He moves to look out the window, arms crossed against his chest. 'I just... I'm ashamed to tell people that my father would do that. Buy up and destroy the town he was born in.'

I nod in understanding. 'I get it. Guilty by association.'

'Plus, I don't think my dad is really evil or anything. It's just that he was brought up with nothing. He's always been mad about money. When the developers approached him about getting on board and giving them inside intel, well he jumped at the chance. Running the pub you can imagine the secrets he knows at any given moment.'

I nod, even though he's not looking at me.

'I actually...' He runs his hands through his wayward

hair. 'I actually have a secret of my own I want to share with you.'

'Really?' I can't help but sound super pleased and desperately hopeful.

He nods. 'You shared a huge secret with me, so it's only fair, right?' He smiles, but it doesn't meet his eyes. 'Something I'm sure my dad will revel in telling you. I wanted to be the one to break it to you.' He rubs the back of his neck.

'Right...' He's scaring me now.

What the hell has he done? Is this the reason him and his dad fell out? And how many more revelations in my life can I take before I completely lose it?

CHAPTER THIRTY-NINE

'Only, well.' He closes his eyes, taking a calming breath. 'My dad might be a bit of a bastard, but he's bailed me out a few fair times. Money wise.'

His eyes flick to mine, holding me, imploring with me to understand.

'Oh.' He was in debt? This must be what his dad was warning me about.

'Because... well.' He takes another deep breath, licking his lips. 'You were right as it turns out. I'm a recovering gambler.'

My stomach nearly falls out of my knickers. I knew it! I was right. I've never wanted to be more wrong.

'Shit, really?' I blurt out. Must fix that brain to mouth filter.

He nods, chewing on his cheek. 'You know how I disappear every Tuesday evening? Well that's my support group.'

Okay, so at least he's getting help. But then hang on, I caught him gambling on his phone just the other day. It might have only been a card game with friends, but I thought you were supposed to go cold turkey.

'But you're still gambling,' I utter, thinking aloud. 'I saw it on your phone that day.' Oops, probably shouldn't have brought up going through his phone again.

'I was only looking that day.' His voice loses its power. 'I managed to resist, but some days are harder than others.' I can tell he's ashamed with himself by the way his eyes are downcast and his shoulders slump. I just want to wrap him in a cuddle and tell him everything will be okay.

'And you put that bet on the horse the other day.' I remember him on the phone in the morning and being in such a bad mood by the evening.

'You heard that?' he asks, looking down at the floor, chewing on his bottom lip.

'Yep.' I nod with a grimace, wishing I hadn't brought it up.

He squeezes his eyes shut. 'Well, I didn't really get to put it on. All the local bookies have blacklisted me, thanks to Da.'

Now it all makes sense.

'That's why you were in such a god awful mood that night?' He hadn't lost a bet, he'd found out he was blacklisted.

'Yeah,' he admits, biting his lip so hard I'm sure he's going to draw blood any minute. 'You're quite the perceptive detective.'

Then I remember his poker game.

'But wait, you play poker here with your friends. Do they not know?'

He grimaces. 'They do. We only play for cents now. I've found going totally cold turkey is almost impossible. Being able to still gamble, but not be in the chance of losing any real money, well, it just works better for me.

'I see.' Unconventional but if it's working who am I to judge? I bet that's why he doesn't mind us not paying him. No money to lose.

He nods, his eyes guarded. 'So, now you know. Now you can see why I'm not such an eligible bachelor. How I'm actually a screw up not worth wasting your time on.'

It breaks my heart that he thinks so little of himself. He puts on this big show about loving himself, but really he's as insecure as anyone. He's so much more than he realises.

'You're not a screw up,' I snap back, as if he's insulted me not himself. 'You've fucked up,' I shrug, 'we all have, but it's how we put things right that matters.'

He looks up and smiles at me, his puppy dog eyes doing something to my heart. No matter how many times he bruises it, it still welcomes him back. It's like it just expands to allow all of his mistakes.

Another question I just have to ask sits on my tongue.

'You said your mates and the bookies know about your gambling. Is it common knowledge, or is your dad holding that over your head too?'

It would make sense as to why he hasn't spilled the beans.

He turns to face me, his face tortured. 'Yeah. That's what led me to move in here. He threatened to expose it to the whole town. I just... I can't have everyone know how weak and pathetic I am.'

'Hey.' I move quickly, wrapping my arms around him. He flinches at first, but as I push my face into his chest he accepts my embrace and squeezes me to him so hard that I struggle to breathe. He needs this hug more than he'd ever admit.

'You're not weak and pathetic.' I inhale his scent, letting

it settle over my frayed nerves. I hate bad blood between us. 'Your dad should never have threatened you with that. No matter how scared he was of being exposed.' I rub his back soothingly.

God, how I want to belong here, in his arms, but I don't. We'll never be and its better like that. We'd never work, I know now. I could never be with a gambler. I thrive on order and control. Gambling is reckless. I could never trust him.

'Thanks, Phoebe.' He starts rubbing my back too, his large hands taking up almost all of my lower back. I curl into his touch, wishing things were different. 'And sorry for being such a shit the last few days.'

'It's fine.' I shrug, looking up at him. 'You don't have to tell me anything you don't want to. Its only because I want to know you, the *real* you. Not the Clooney the whole town thinks they know.'

He looks genuinely scared. 'Will you promise to keep my secret? Even from Ella? If this gets out...'

'Of course,' I promise, nodding my head without hesitation. 'I'll keep your secret, as long as you keep mine.'

He frowns. 'Oh, you mean the chatting to ghosts thing?' His lip quirks with amusement.

'Although I'm sure it wouldn't make my reputation any worse than it already is.' I snort a laugh.

He takes my chin and lifts it to face him. 'Phoebe, I know I'm selfishly asking a lot of you right now. It's my fault the town is against you. I'm the one that took it too far and reported him. I should stand up and take responsibility for it.'

For some reason I have an overpowering urge to protect him. God knows he's got such a sensitive heart underneath all that bravado. In a way he's still the little boy that lost his mum.

'It's honestly fine. I'm happy to just take it.'

He shakes his head. 'It's not fair.'

I take his giant hand in both of mine. 'Just let me do this for you, okay?'

I see him wrestle with it internally, those eyes clouded with a million emotions.

Despite everything, I trust him. I never thought I'd be able to trust anyone after Garry and here I am trusting him, despite a million red flags.

'Thanks for trusting me with your secret.'

He smiles, his eyes honest. 'I trust you, Phoebe.'

My heart dances in delight. 'I trust you too.' I don't even have to think about it, I just do.

And that's why I'm in serious trouble.

'What's going on in here, then?' Ella asks, appearing from nowhere, looking accusingly at us.

We spring apart. Way to ruin a moment, Ella.

Clooney clears his throat. 'We were just saying that we should go to the town meeting. Explain that my dad has been going after you for a long time and that if you're forced to sell it will just be another space for these develops to snatch up.'

That's actually a good idea. He's good at thinking on his feet. I can't help but be worried he's such a convincing liar.

She nods along. 'Good idea. I was also thinking that we should have a Halloween party.'

I scoff. 'Ella, everyone is avoiding the pub right now. I think we should skip the party and keep our head down.'

She huffs like someone half her age.

'No, Phoebe.' She stands her ground, a steely determination on her face. 'I've taken a lot of shit lately. All I'm asking for is a Halloween party.' She pouts, giving me the full effect of her brown puppy eyes.

I sigh, quickly relenting. 'Fine.'

She grins, jumps up and down like an excitable puppy and then swiftly leaves, no doubt to order herself an outfit.

'Nice to know where her priorities are,' Clooney says.

We lock eyes and both barrel over laughing.

CHAPTER FORTY

Tuesday 27ᵗʰ October

*I*t's been so nice to get back to normal with Clooney. Honestly it hurts my soul so bad when there's friction between us. He makes me happy—is that so bad? Now his tattoo with the cards on fire makes all the more sense. His gambling habit got him burnt.

Around six p.m. Clooney seems to disappear. I keep asking Ella if she's seen him but she's, as usual, oblivious. Then I remember his support group is Tuesday nights. I'm glad to see he's still going, committed to getting better.

She answers her phone at just past seven thirty, looks at me, laughs and then hangs up.

'Clooney has said for you to meet him at the end of the pier.'

I frown back at her. 'Are you serious?' Nervous bubbles of excitement dance around my stomach.

She laughs. 'Apparently so.'

I grab my coat and walk towards the pier. The sun is

setting, creating a gorgeous amber glow over everything. When I spot him my heart melts into a puddle on the floor.

He's stood up, waiting for me, at the end of the pier next to a picnic blanket spread out with a basket hamper. The sun bounces off the river, lighting him up like a magical fairy tale character.

'What's all this?' I ask when I reach him.

He puts his hands in his pockets, rocking on his feet. 'It's a picnic, duh.' He has that boyish charm, his sweet and slightly shy smile gracing those beautiful lips.

'I got that,' I retort. 'I mean, what's the occasion?'

Then I notice the double sleeping bag behind him. Oh, so he's looking for a bunk up.

'I thought you needed a proper apology and a little treat.'

I point to the sleeping bag. 'And then what do you think is going to happen?'

He rolls his eyes, his cheeks actually reddening. 'I thought we could sleep under the stars.'

'Hmm, what part of me doesn't believe it's so innocent?' I rub my chin dramatically.

He holds out his hand for me to take. 'Do you want the food or not?'

I take it and let him lead me to the red and white checked picnic blanket.

'When have I ever refused food?'

'Exactly.' He grins and reaches into a picnic basket, handing me a can of vodka, lime and soda. I'm pleased to see its chilled; nice.

He gets himself a bottle of Peroni. Then he takes out two takeaway bags.

'You got a takeaway?' I ask on a laugh.

'I had to go to my support group first so I picked this up

after. Figured we deserved a feast.' He grins, taking out a burger and chips for us each.

I grab the burger and munch into it eagerly. 'Oh my god, it's SO good!'

I haven't had a greasy burger in years.

He raises his eyebrows. 'Alright there, lady. I didn't realise how much you loved hamburgers.'

I laugh, covering my mouth so he can't see what a big greedy pig I am.

'I just haven't had any kind of takeaway in so long.' He smiles at me like I'm adorable. 'Did I ever tell you our parents raised us vegans?'

He snorts a laugh, covering it with his mouth. 'No! Jesus.'

'Yep,' I nod, 'obviously we rebelled when we were teenagers. The first time Ella ate beef she chucked up everywhere.'

He points to the burger. 'Eating here.'

'Sorry.' I grimace.

'So you didn't want to carry it on?' he asks, seeming genuinely interested.

I chew my burger more so I can talk. 'The sad truth is, that once I had a taste of dairy and meat there was no going back. And I mean, I shouldn't be eating them at all. I was brought up going to rally's and protests against them.'

'All the while sneaking off for a yoghurt, you rebel.' He chuckles.

'Exactly. See, I can be the crazy one,' I joke. 'Ella is still vegetarian. Well, except when she's ridiculously drunk. If she smells bacon when she's inebriated she's eating it, no matter how much you try and pull it off her.'

He snorts a laugh. 'You know I don't eat pork?'

'Really? Why?' I don't think I know any meat eaters that don't like the taste of bacon.

He shrugs. 'My mum was actually Jewish. Not orthodox or anything, especially since she married my dad, but it's one thing I've kept up. To sort of honour her. I know that sounds weird.'

I shake my head. 'It really doesn't. In fact, someone refusing something as tasty as bacon is a real testament to their love.'

He does that weird smile again. Like he thinks I'm cute. Or ridiculous, who knows.

'That's why you have the Jewish star tattoo,' I muse out loud. He nods. 'Kind of ironic, seen as Jews aren't supposed to have tats.'

'I'm nothing if not full of contradictions.' He grins. 'That's also why I have the butterfly.' He looks down at it fondly. 'My ma used to always tell me that people who had passed came back to visit their loved ones as butterflies.'

I smile. He's so cute.

'I know that sounds stupid, but remember I was young.'

I shake my head. 'It doesn't sound stupid at all. Remember who you're talking to here. Reincarnation is not a surprising thing to believe in.'

He scoots closer. 'If you look really closely at the wings there's a little D in there.'

I look closely and finally find it hidden away.

'Her name was Deborah.' I look up to see him smiling shyly. God he can be adorable.

I need to change the subject. Things have gotten too serious.

'But what about the sausages you cooked us?' I blurt out.

'They're Quorn. I knew you wouldn't be able to tell the difference.'

I laugh. 'Suki sure did though.'

We laugh together, finishing the food in no time. Especially with me shovelling it down my throat like a heifer. Way to appear sexy.

'Well, to think I thought you were a lady.' He snorts, balling up the fast food wrappers and throwing them into the picnic hamper.

I try not to smile. 'Yeah, yeah. You just caught me when I was hungry.'

'Didn't realise you hadn't eaten in twelve years.' He chuckles.

I throw my empty can at him. He gets another one out for me.

'Trying to get me drunk?' I joke. There's that nervous excited bubbling in my stomach again.

'Maybe.' His eyes light up with that mischief I've come to love so much. Dammit, there I go with the love word. I am *not* going to fall in love with Clooney.

I take a large sip. 'So, can I tell you why I was so upset with you the other day?'

It's been eating away at me. He rolls his eyes. 'Oh god, we're going to re-hash this again are we?'

I smile to let him know I'm not in a mood. 'Unlike you, I like to *talk* about things. Not let them fester.'

He looks up at the sky. 'Go on then.'

'If I'm honest, it wasn't even that you wouldn't tell me how you broke up with Orla. It was that you'd had a relationship at all. You basically, in so many words, told me that Orla was different. She was special to you.'

'She was.' He nods, as if not understanding why this would upset me.

'So to me, that kind of felt like you were saying I'm *not* special. I'm just another regular girl you'd like to hit it and quit it with. It doesn't exactly make a girl feel special.'

He frowns. 'Phoebe, that's not it at all. You *are* special. It's just that I don't have a heart to give to you. It already got shattered a long time ago.'

Okay, so she definitely broke his heart. Noted. This got heavy really quick. I blame the vodka. It's always given me a loose tongue.

'I don't want to get into it,' he continues, 'but it taught me one thing; relationships are not worth it.'

I sigh. 'Yeah, see, in girl language it's like you're telling me *I'm* not worth it.'

He sighs, as if the weight of the world is on his shoulders. 'That's why I've been so at war about us,' he admits. 'We're a bad idea.'

'Obviously.' I grin, wanting to bring things back to light.

'But...' He locks his eyes with mine. They are brimming over with sincerity. 'That doesn't stop me wanting to make the mistake.'

'Seriously, stop referring to me as a mistake,' I snap. 'And it's not like you've talked me into *anything*, Clooney.'

He tilts his head, smirking adorably. 'You know we're good together. We've got amazing sexual chemistry.'

I nod. I can't deny it. 'Half of me wonders whether it'll calm down once we've done it.' Shit, did I really just say that out loud? Damn vodka.

He snorts. 'Clearly never had sex with Clooney Breen. I'm addictive, baby.'

I roll my eyes, but I'm actually considering it. I mean, it's not like I want a relationship anyway. As soon as I can sell up we'll be going back to England. Could it really hurt that bad to scratch the itch? This way we both go into it with our eyes wide open.

He leans in to me, taking a lock of my hair in his fingers. 'Just give in to it, Phoebe.' He kisses my cheek slowly, the heat of his lips leaving my skin searing. 'Let yourself go.' He places his lips on my neck and I shamelessly throw my head back and groan.

He chuckles into my neck. 'But if you don't want to, that's okay too.'

I grab his face. 'For once, Clooney, just shut up.' I thrust my lips onto his.

CHAPTER FORTY-ONE

*H*e parts our lips, his tongue immediately in my mouth. Normally I don't like guys who are tongue happy, but Clooney is such a sexual being, it just gets me worked up and panting. His hand travels from cradling my jaw to my breast. I arch my back to push my boob into his palm. He grins against my lips.

I reach out my shaky hands to grab at his t-shirt. I can already feel the heat of his body through it. I have no idea how he runs so hot when it's so freezing over here.

He runs his fingertips under my fleecy jumper and to my bare breast. Thankful that I didn't bother with a bra today. That's the benefit of jumpers, they hide cold erect nipples.

'You're so soft,' he whispers gruffly in my ear.

I groan again, lifting his t-shirt and running my hands greedily over his taut chest. I count his six pack, one by one, and then come to his delicious V. Down to the start of his jeans and the beginning of coarse hair. God, I've never been so excited to see a penis.

He lifts my fleecy jumper off me. I shiver, my body

goosepimply from the cold. It's a relatively mild evening here, but that still means its freezing by normal standards.

'I think it's time to get in the sleeping bag,' he suggests, his voice breathless as he steals more kisses. We crawl towards it. It's then that I realise once we're in it'll be a nightmare to get my jeans off.

So I do what any horny gal would. I kick my boots off and then shimmy myself out of my jeans, leaving me in just my knickers and tank top. He watches me, eyes alight with lust.

'Fuck, you're hot,' he says, while shedding himself of his leather jacket and own jeans.

I jump in the sleeping bag, every bone in my body freezing cold. Are we seriously going to be able to do this out here? Should we just go inside? But then I'm worried that if I leave this pier right now I'll lose my nerve.

He crawls in, not smiling, but looking at me with hunger in his eyes. I shamelessly cling to him, the warmth of his body forcing back the cold. My last shred of resistance melts with it.

He grins and starts kissing me again with his hands delving into my hair, pulling and grasping urgently. I gyrate against him, grasping at his shoulders, my nails digging greedily into his skin.

He peels off my vest top and gazes down adoringly at my breasts.

'You have no idea how many dreams I've had about these.' He sucks one into his mouth.

'Jesus,' I croak, unable to form any kind of sentence.

He plays with the other one, pebbling my nipple underneath his teasing fingers. His tongue flicks it, before his juicy tongue laves around it, warming me through to my bones.

I reach down and dare to grab his erection through his boxer shorts. It's been poking me in to the stomach and my *god*, he's bigger than I assumed. A thrill of fear goes through me. Maybe it'll hurt. God, do I want it to hurt? With him, *most definitely*. Who have I become?

I reach inside his boxers and palm his smooth velvety skin. He moans around my breast, the vibration travelling all the way down to my toes. He takes my hand and removes it.

I look up at him, suddenly overcome with self-conscious doubts.

'Did I do something wrong?'

I mean, I know I'm not overly experienced with sex, but surely there's only so many ways you can grab a dick?

He smiles, unleashing the full, devastating power of his eyes on me, as if trying to communicate something crucial.

'No, but if you start playing with my dick right now I think I'll last about two seconds.'

'Oh.' I chuckle, reassured. I can't believe he's so turned on by little old me. Garry was never overly excited to have sex with me. It's always made me doubt my sexual ability.

'Just lie back and let me take care of you.'

And take care he does. One hand goes down to grab roughly at my arse cheek, bringing my core closer to him. I shamelessly rub it against his erection. Another groan from him. He makes me feel powerful when I can get those sounds from him.

He dips his hand into my lacy knickers and circles my clit ever so softly. God that feels amazing. I push against his hand, needing more friction.

He grins against my lips again before slipping one finger effortlessly inside me. I tense around it, revelling in the feeling.

'God, you're soaked.'

All I can do is nod manically as I push his boxer shorts down with my feet.

He adds another finger in, circling until my eyes are rolling back in my head, blood pumping round my body so fast I worry he'll hear it.

'Jesus, Clooney, just fuck me already.'

He grins. 'So bossy.' He reaches for his jeans, extracts a condom out of the pocket and puts it on, all the while keeping his eyes locked on mine. Then he's back kissing my neck, his length nudging at my entrance.

'You're sure about this?' He checks one last time.

'Shut up.' I wrap my legs around his arse and pull him into me.

He grits his teeth, like he's in pain. I revel in the full-ness. So deliciously full.

'Clooney? Are you okay?'

'Yep,' he says through his gritted teeth. He slowly pushes all the way inside me, so high I think he's going to come out of my mouth any moment. Damn.

'Just give me a minute.' He strokes my hair back away from my face, his eyes pinning me in place.

I pant underneath him, greedy for more.

'Clooney, I swear, if you don't—

He covers my mouth with one hand while he grips my hip with the other. Then he's pulling back and thundering back into me, causing a scream to escape my throat.

He fucks me like that; angrily, with his hand over my mouth, like he hates me. And I fucking love it.

Within what feels like minutes I start to feel like I'm going to be sick. No, not sick, but maybe like I'm sea sick. I'm sweaty, my pulse rapid as my head goes dizzy. I squeeze my eyes shut as an overwhelming weight seems to weigh on my body before its released. My eyes fling open and it's like I can taste the early stars that have come out to watch us. Every muscle in my body rejoices as a calming balm soothes over me, making me moan so loud I worry cows in a distant field will hear me.

He tenses soon after, biting my neck as he finds his release.

We pant like that together in the beautiful after glow for what feels like hours. He eventually lifts his head, his eyes finding mine. I feel like he can see every thought I've ever had in my head. Like I'm laid bare for him, which I suppose in one way or another, I am.

'That was amazing,' he says, kissing me chastely on the lips.

'U-huh.' It's all I can manage. I can still feel his teeth biting into my shoulder. Every caress.

I shiver, as he gets off me to remove the condom.

'Don't throw it in the river,' I mumble. Dammit, I shouldn't be thinking of the environment right now.

He chuckles. 'I wasn't going to.' He comes back and leans over me. 'Do you think you can walk?'

I shake my head. Definitely not. He chuckles again. I've decided it's my favourite sound in the world. He gets dressed and throws my clothes inside the sleeping bag. Then he scoops me up, still inside it, and carries me all the way back. Luckily there's no one in the pub. Not that I think I'd have cared anyway. Right now, in his arms, is exactly where I want to be.

CHAPTER FORTY-TWO

Friday 30th October

*W*e've spent the last few days in Clooney's bed having the most amazing mind blowing sex. We seem to venture between pure animalistic bitey sex to the more lazy, delicious, soul baring love making. I can't work out which is my favourite.

All previous doubts of my own sexual ability have been erased.

I'm completely sated. I mean, the man is an orgasm machine. Ella is disgusted, but I know she's secretly pleased for me with her hidden smiles. I keep waiting for her to tell me to be careful, to protect my heart from him, but I keep forgetting she's not the sort. She's normally the one *making* the terrible decisions about guys, not judging others. It's one of the things I finally understand about her. It might be a mistake, but it sure is fun making it.

Clooney's just gone out to the wholesalers to buy some crisps. I'm ashamed to say that we've eaten most of them ourselves. I bloody love the Tayto crisps they have over here.

Plus Clooney got me to try red lemonade. Oh my God, total game changer. And I *have* always loved potatoes. Maybe that small Irish streak in me is stronger than I originally thought.

I hear the door swing open so I plaster on my customer smile. Professional, friendly and polite.

'Hi, what can I -' I stop when I realise its Clooney's dad that's just walked in. 'Oh.'

He stalks up to the bar, nostrils flaring. A dart of apprehension shoots through me. God I hate this guy.

'I came in to tell you and your pathetic sister that your little stint didn't last long. I'm back up and running, and you are going to *seriously* regret crossing me.'

'Is...' I steel my spine, attempting to look unafraid. 'Is that a threat?'

He slams his fist down on the bar so hard I jump. 'You bet your arse it is.'

'Well then I suggest.' My voice pitches high and wobbly. 'You leave before I'm forced to call the guards.'

He sneers at me. 'My son's done a real number on you, hasn't he? I can see it in your face.'

I look away from him. 'I don't know what you're talking about.'

Do not let him get in your head. I hate his poisonous lies.

'He's charmed you, I can tell. But I can tell you now that you don't know everything about Clooney.'

Oh here we go. I roll my eyes.

'What, like his gambling problem?' I ask, hand on my hip.

His jaw falls open. I wish I could take a picture of him right now, because he is seriously stumped. There's no way he thought I knew that.

'Oh, so he's told you.' He scratches his protruding belly.

'Well.' He raises his eyebrows. 'If you want to take on his thirty grand debt, be my guest.'

Jesus, thirty grand? I assumed ten grand tops. How wrong was I? Still, I school my features and try to look unaffected.

'We have no secrets between us.' I sound more confident with that fact than I am.

He leans in, resting his forearms on the bar, a sick glint in his eye.

'Ah, but I bet he never told you the *reason* he started gambling, did he?' He smirks and I want to punch his smug face.

He has me there. I never thought to actually ask him *why* he'd started. I'd just assumed that he started doing it socially and it spiralled, eventually going out of control. I didn't think he'd had some sort of issue which led him to it. Well, apart from his dad resenting him his whole life.

Some depressive event maybe? Maybe it was breaking up with Orla, who I'm quickly believing was the love of Clooney's life. Her moving to England could have been the event that turned his world upside down.

I really wish he'd talk to me about it. For some crazy reason I thought that with us sleeping together now he might open up a bit more. But no, he seems to be able to compartmentalise everything pretty neatly.

I know he's still hiding things from me. I feel it whenever I try to ask him something remotely personal. His muscles tense up. I don't get how bad it could have been. I mean, yeah his heart was obviously broken by her, but how? Did she cheat?

'Well, maybe you should ask my lad what happened just before he developed this gambling habit. That's if you have the guts.'

'Oh, piss off.'

I really wish I had a better come back than that, but the guy puts me on such an edge. I try and see the good in all people. Normally everyone has some redeeming feature that I cling onto, even if they are being a major thorn in my side, but I just can't find one with him. What is his bloody problem?

He scoffs. 'Let me know when you're ready to give in and sell this ramshackle of a pub to me. My price stands, but the longer time goes on the lower it will drop.'

I steel my jaw. 'I know exactly why you want to buy this pub,' I snarl through gritted teeth. 'You'll have to prise the deeds out of my dead cold hands.'

He sniggers. 'That can be arranged.' He turns and strops out of the pub.

Did he just threaten my life? It was just a joke, right? God, with him who knows.

Ella comes out of the toilet just as the door slams after him.

'Are you alright, Pheebs?' She takes my arm. 'You look like you've just seen a ghost.'

I laugh, but it sounds fake even to my own ears. She hasn't noticed when I'm *actually* talking to one. I only realise now that I'm shaking.

'No I'm fine. I just...' I choke on a sob that appeared from nowhere.

'Shit, sit down.' She leads me to a chair. 'What just happened?'

'It's just Clooney's dad again.' My tongue is trembling, making talking a challenge.

She balls her hands into little fists. 'Ugh, that man is just vile! We should call the guards.'

I shake my head. 'No, I'm fine.' I don't want to add to

the drama and turn this into something bigger than it needs to be. That's probably what he wants me to do.

Clooney walks in and I know he's seen his dad by the way his shoulders are bunched up by his ears. Now I look closer as his eyes search around for me, I can see that his cheeks are flushed. His shoulders visibly relax when he spots me.

'Phoebe.' He rushes over, kneeling in front of me, taking my hands in his. 'What did he do? What did he say?' The worry etched all over his face makes me want to cry harder.

'Nothing.' I shake my head, feeling stupid for over-reacting. 'I don't even know why I'm crying. I'm fine.'

'She's obviously shaken up,' Ella says, as if I'm unable to speak for myself.

'Phoebe,' he pleads, eyes desperate. 'Please talk to me.'

Oh how ironic. He wants *me* to talk to *him*. For me to open up. I've been nothing but an open book with him since day one. Its him with all of the secrets. His secrets I'll never learn. It makes my heart harden just enough to realise I need time on my own to gather my thoughts.

'I'm fine, honestly. He was just trying to scare me.' I wipe my tears away. 'But you know what, I'm just gonna go for a lie down if that's okay with you two? You know, just relax a bit.'

'Of course,' Clooney says, helping me to stand, as if I'm suddenly incapable.

'I'll be fine.' I push past them both and head for the bedroom. I just need to wallow for a while under the duvet.

CHAPTER FORTY-THREE

I hear someone walking up the stairs as I enter the bedroom. I turn, ready to insist to Clooney I'm fine again. Instead it's Ella.

She smiles sweetly, almost cautiously. 'It's just me. You don't have to bullshit. What's going on?'

I sigh, sitting on the bed cross legged. My eyes start to well up again. Why am I so bloody emotional all of a sudden?

'I don't know what's wrong with me.' I sob, the back of my throat threatening to close. 'I must be due on or something.'

She sits down next to me patting my leg. 'It's obvious for me to see. You thought you could just screw Clooney, but now you've caught feelings.'

How can someone as oblivious as Ella be so perceptive?

'You make it sound like a disease,' I snort, a snot bubble appearing from my nose.

She smiles, eyes drooped in sympathy. She takes a tissue out of her pocket and hands it over to me. 'So, is it just that you want more and you're scared he doesn't?'

I sigh, dabbing at my eyes. 'Oh, if only it were that simple.' I blow my nose nosily.

'Explain,' she demands.

Where to begin? I'm emotionally drained from it all.

'He's basically told me he doesn't want more. He's been messed around or something in the past. Doesn't think relationships are worth it.'

She grimaces. 'That's madness. You guys are great together.' She shakes her head. 'And from the screaming coming from his room I'd say you have no problems there.' She winks, grinning.

Oh god, I hate that she hears us, but these walls are very thin. You'd think the ugly, thick bobbled wallpaper we couldn't get off would provide some sound proofing.

'Yeah, but that's just how it is.' I shrug. 'Just sex.' I pull my legs up to my chest.

'So what spooked you today so bad it brought the tears on? Did Fergus say something particularly nasty?' I've never heard her so gentle and soothing before. She must think I've really lost it.

'Okay, but first, promise you won't repeat this. I'm breaking Clooney's trust by saying this.' I already hate myself for it, but I need to confide in someone.

She raises her eyebrows. 'Cross my heart, hope to die, flick a -'

God, she's like a pre-schooler sometimes.

'Yeah, fine,' I interrupt. I lower my voice to a whisper. I really shouldn't be telling her this, but there's no way to explain and leave it out. 'So he actually has a gambling problem. His dad has bailed him out for a lot of money.'

Her eyes widen. 'Shit, you were right after all.' She scoots closer so our knees are touching. 'Sounds like that's a reason not to fall in love with him.'

I scoff a laugh. 'I'm not falling in love with him.' As soon as it leaves my mouth, I know it's a lie.

She barks a laugh. 'Please, Phoebe, you fall in love with everyone.'

'No, I don't!' What the hell is she talking about? I'm not some hopeless romantic that falls for every guy I meet. That sounds more like her.

'Oh come *on*.' She crosses her arms over her chest. 'Even when we were kids you'd fall in love with a lady bug and insist on naming it, putting it in a jar and bringing it with us. You used to cry so hard when Mum made you put it back out into the wild.'

'Maybe I just wanted a pet,' I reason with a shrug. I forgot about my lady bug phase. That doesn't mean she's right though.

She nudges me on the shoulder. 'And what about the homeless man near your flat?'

'Lenny?' Ah, I miss seeing Lenny. 'I'd love to call him, but he doesn't believe in mobile phones, the eclectic love-able weirdo.'

'Most people would just give him some change, maybe a sandwich, but not you. No, you talked to him and found out his story. Then you brought him home cooked food every day.'

'It was hardly home cooked. Most of the time it was just cheap microwave meals or KFC.'

'Regardless,' she snaps, clearly losing her patience with me. 'You didn't stop until you'd registered him with that charity. Until he had temporary housing and then a council flat. Then a job. And even now we've moved to a new country you still wish you could call him to check in.'

'I'd just like to catch up, check everything is still going smoothly.' I don't think that's unreasonable.

She sighs. 'It's not a bad thing, Pheebs. Your big heart is one of the reasons I love you so much. What I'm saying here, is that you get attached to people. When you let people in you give them your whole heart. Even that dickhead Garry.'

Oh god, she's right. Not that it makes any of this easier. No matter how I've tried to rationalise with my heart, its gone and fallen for him. I have no control over it.

I shake my head. 'Well I know I can't get attached to Clooney. It's not like we're planning on staying here. It's just sex,' I lie to myself. 'As soon as we build the business up again we'll sell and move back to England.'

A floor board creaks, alerting me to someone outside the door. I look up to see Clooney's wide green eyes staring back at me. Shit. I relay the last few sentences in my head. Well they don't sound good. I never told him we planned on moving back to England regardless of whether the business picked up or not.

'Oh, is that how it is?' he asks, his head shaking, hurt shadowing his eyes. His shoulders drop as he backs out, running down the stairs.

'Shit.' I feel sick to my stomach. If he just heard the last bit of the conversation it could sound like I'm the one using him.

Ella grins, raising her eyebrows knowingly. 'For a guy just fucking someone, he's acting pretty upset.'

I stand. 'Shut up, Ella. Not helpful.'

I run after him. Yes I might be pissed off that he's a closed book to me, but I never wanted to hurt him. This whole time I've been worrying that he'll hurt me, but instead it was my secret that got out. I've hurt him.

I find him out the front of the pub smoking a cigarette.

He looks all the more sexy for being so brooding right now, encased in a cloud of smoke. His arms and shoulders are tense; It looks like his hurt has evolved quickly to anger.

I stand in front of him chewing my bottom lip, unsure what to say now that I've tracked him down.

'I'm sorry.' Best to just keep it simple and go from there.

'Sorry for what?' he asks, his chin high, eyes cold, anger radiating from him, tangible pulses that make me squirm. 'Why should you be sorry?'

'Because that sounded bad back there. Like we were just fucking and—'

He looks me dead in the eye. So hard a shiver escapes down my spine. 'We *are* just fucking, Phoebe.'

Ouch. That stings. My heart squeezes in my chest. I'm losing him.

'I know that,' I say, my voice wobbly. I *do* know that, so why am I acting like I'm his girlfriend? Why do I feel like I'm going to burst into tears again?

'So whether you choose to stay here, or fuck off back to England, it's completely up to you.' He throws his cigarette on the floor, stamping it out with far more gusto than usual.

He goes to walk past me, but I grab his shoulder. 'Please, Clooney,' I beg. I can hardly breathe at just the thought of not being with him. 'I can tell you're upset. Just talk to me.'

'About what, Phoebe?' A vein on his forehead twitches. 'What do you want to talk about?'

I sigh. 'Look, I never told you because I felt bad that you were helping us out here for free. Then I thought it wouldn't be a big deal, seen as you don't want a relationship.'

'Yeah, but you were the one making out that *I'm* the problem. I'm the reason why we could never be. Then I find out you were never planning on sticking around anyway.' He laughs but it has a cruel edge to it. 'Yet you had no problem trying to push me to be honest with you about everything. While holding back your own little secret.'

Well, when he puts it like that, I sound like a dick.

'Look, I'm sorry, okay. I didn't mean to hold anything from you.'

I walk closer to him, urging him with my desperate eyes to calm down and forgive me. To hold me, stroke my hair and tell me everything is going to be okay.

He sighs heavily, rubbing at his forehead. 'I don't know why I'm getting so upset anyway.'

I take another cautious step towards him. Could it be he feels more invested in us than he first let on?

'Can't we just go back to how we were?'

I make the last step and curl my body into his chest. I press my cheek into him, begging silently for him to accept me. To forgive me.

I wait for what feels like forever, until finally I feel his arms around me. He cuddles me to him and smells my hair. My heart starts to unclench.

'Sorry I'm acting so crazy,' he says, letting out another sigh, his voice kinder. 'I just... I saw my dad driving away and I was just so panicked about what he'd said to you. Then I saw you upset and... it was just a lot in a short space of time.'

'It's okay.' I should be asking him what he's afraid his dad might have told me. What he's still keeping from me, but right now, in his arms, I don't want to risk being out of them again.

The fear I felt the last few minutes is enough for me to realise that Ella is right. I've fallen head over heels for the guy. The guy that doesn't do relationships. The guy that won't open up, that has secrets, but that also smells my hair, cradles my face and looks deep within my soul when we make love. I can't help but hope that he changes his mind at some point. Either that or we manage to sell up and move back home before my heart is completely broken beyond repair.

CHAPTER FORTY-FOUR

<u>Saturday 31st October</u>

$\mathcal{W}$e've been decorating all day for this stupid Halloween party Ella insisted on, the sad part is that we don't even know if people are going to come. Clooney says he's spread the word to all his mates that he's DJ-ing and that should bring in a small crowd. Now that we're sort of together, or well, more realistically, sleeping together, I feel shy seeing his friends.

They'll all be watching us and judging me. Everyone already thinks I'm a monster for reporting his dad. He tried to explain to his mates that it was him, but they all just thought he was taking the blame for me. *Pussy whipped* some of his mates apparently said.

'Don't be so nervous,' Clooney says, sliding up behind me, wrapping his hands around my waist. 'Did I mention that you look fucking phenomenal?'

I giggle. Actually giggle. I'm not a giggler.

'You did, a few times.'

I stupidly let Ella order our costumes from the local

fancy dress shop. She's made me a slutty nun. It was better than her outfit, a slutty nurse. I don't understand why every Halloween outfit for a woman has to be the slutty version. I'm sure even if I tried to be a pumpkin it would be with some knee high tights and stripper heels.

Although right now, with Clooney lusting on me, I'm kind of pleased. He's dressed as Freddy Kruger. Basically just jeans, a white and red stripy t-shirt and he's drawn some stupid scars all over his face. I told him it's not very sensitive to acid victims. He just laughed and told me I was very PC. Apparently they don't do that crap here in Ireland. Well, *sorry* for being sensitive.

It's annoying that he still looks hot, fake face scars and all. I look around the pub as people start to arrive, my tummy dancing with nerves. We've got cobwebs all over the place that actually remind me of the first time we saw inside. Between that, most of the lights being out due to the epic disco lights he borrowed, and the danger tape, it looks pretty awesome.

An hour later I'm shocked to see that Clooney did well and we've actually attracted a large young crowd. The place is packed. Every young person in the town must be here tonight. That and a few of the local old men who grumble about the loud music and young'uns acting rowdy.

I wait until there is a slight lull before I allow myself a wee in the toilet. God it's been crazy, but I can't complain. We need the money in that till.

The door swings open and I hear someone enter whilst I sit on the loo.

'Okay, I'll admit I'm shocked,' a woman says.

'I told you it was true. I was shocked too,' another gossips.

Ooh, toilet gossip. Who doesn't love a bit of that?

'But it's not like he's ever going to be anything more to her than a fuck buddy. You know what he's been like since Orla left.'

Oh shit. The toilet gossip is about me. I gasp but quickly cover my mouth with my hand. I can't be heard.

'Yeah.' She snorts a laugh. 'It's sad though. I've seen the way she looks at him. I think she really thinks she stands a chance.'

My stomach dips as my bitter reality is discussed.

'Poor cow,' the other one says, while having a wee in the cubicle next to me.

They giggle uncontrollably before eventually leaving. I wash my hands, trying desperately to push the sad melancholy in my chest down. I can do this. I haven't learned anything I didn't already know. This shouldn't be some sort of revelation to me.

But then why do I suddenly feel embarrassed? So humiliated that I want to run upstairs and hide away from everyone. The fact they're all laughing at me behind my back. They've known Clooney a hell of a lot longer than me, and they know, without a doubt, that he won't commit to me or anyone. Orla must have done a real number on him.

Maybe I should ask one of them what happened? But then that would be cheating. I want him to feel like he can confide in me, if he doesn't what's the point?

I'm just pulling one of the old men a pint of bitter when Clooney starts pouring a coke beside me.

'I've told Ella we're locking up tonight.' He leans into my ear to whisper, 'I plan on fucking you from behind, over this bar.'

My whole body heats up at the very idea, tingles running up and down my spine. I look at him, his eyes meeting mine with such promise. Dammit, I'm already hot for him. There is no foreplay needed. How can I be upset when the man is a walking sex god who insists on pleasuring me with intense orgasms?

He kisses me on the cheek. I wish he would stop being so sweet, it's like giving me a hint of what it would be like to truly have him. It hurts more, my heart aching so much it feels like pieces of it are breaking off and filling my lungs, making breathing steadily impossible.

I make a promise to myself. I'll enjoy it all tonight, but in the morning I'm asking him about Orla. I'm going to be brave and ask him one final time to confide in me. If he chooses not to that's fine. He'll have chosen his past instead of his future.

I'll just have to accept whatever his answer is. Because I know if I let it go on any longer than this I am going to be broken by this man. And I can't risk that. Not even for Clooney Breen.

CHAPTER FORTY-FIVE

Sunday 1ˢᵗ November

I wake up dreaming of Clooney pounding into me over the bar. When I feel him grabbing at my boob and feel the tenderness down below I realise it wasn't a dream. It was a delicious reality.

Except today I'm going to ruin it. Do I really want to do this? I know I don't, not *really*, but I need to know. Its long enough of us being together that I think I can ask this of him. I need to know if he's in this for real or if he's just along for the ride. Literally.

'Morning,' he croaks into my ear. Even his voice sets my body on fire.

I wiggle round in his arms to face him, running my hand down his cheek. I want to commit his beautiful face to memory. After asking him this he might run for the hills. I mean, I hope he doesn't but I have to be realistic.

I take in those beautiful forest eyes, his strong stubbled jawline, those prominent cheek bones. He really is sex on a stick. Remind me why I want to do this again? Oh, that's right. Protect my heart. It's already breaking in anticipation.

He kisses me and it feels delicious yet so bittersweet, I decide I can't wait any longer.

'What's wrong?' he asks as he pulls away, stroking my hair off my forehead, his eyes narrowed with concern.

'I'm sorry. It's just...' I swallow down the panic. 'I need to know.'

He frowns. 'Need to know what?'

I blow out a breath. Be brave. 'I need to know what happened between you and Orla.'

His eyes widen to nearly twice the size as he sits up, already pulling away from me.

'What? Orla? What are you going on about?' He swings his legs off the bed, running his hands through his hair.

Normally I'd change the subject, but not this time. I deserve more.

'I'm sorry, but your dad said something about it when he came in.'

'My dad?'

I suppose he has just woken up. Maybe I should have asked him this when he was more wide awake. After a coffee.

'Yes,' I nod, 'and I know that he was just trying to stir up stuff between us, but he mentioned that it's the reason you started gambling in the first place.'

'So what if it is?' he snaps, glaring at me, all previous warmth gone. 'It's nobody's business but mine.'

I know underneath that anger is vulnerability. It doesn't stop his words biting.

I sigh, my chin wobbling. 'That's just it, Clooney. It's made me realise that I can't do this. I can't be physical with you, but then have you push me away whenever I try to connect with you on a deeper level.'

He stands up, letting out a frustrated growl. 'Why do you need to know the most painful thing that's ever happened to me? You know me, plenty.'

I look sadly down at my hands. This is it. I can feel it. It's over.

'Because it'll make me understand why you developed the problem with gambling.'

'Just be honest with yourself, Phoebe.' He turns to face me, his eyes guarded. 'This isn't about Orla. It's about the gambling. You can't trust me because of it.'

'No.' I shake my head. 'It's not that. I just... I need more.'

He sighs, banging his head back against the wall. 'I always knew you would, but I tried to convince myself that this could be enough for you.'

I feel my throat start to clog up with emotion. 'I *so* wish it was. But I need all of you.' A tear escapes from my eye, running down my cheek.

'So it's all or nothing?' he asks, kneeling down and grabbing my chin, forcing me to look up at him through the blur of my tears. I see the little boy who lost his mother, begging to be understood and cared for.

I so want, more than anything in my life, for it to be enough. For me to be able to just accept Clooney for all that he can give me. Live in hope that he'll eventually open up to me, share all of his scars. But my aching heart knows the answer already. I have to put myself first. I have to stop this before I fall even deeper in love with him.

'Yes. I'm so sorry, but yes. It's all or nothing.'

He hangs his head, his forehead resting against mine. 'I'm sorry too.'

Another tear escapes. He catches it with his thumb.

'Give me a few days and I'll move out.'

The thought of losing him forever is terrifying. I need him in my life, in whatever capacity I can.

'No, you don't have to do that.'

He shakes his head. 'I do, Phoebe. I'll try and still work here, but there's no way I can live with you knowing we can't be together.'

He smiles sadly, stands up and walks out of my room, and possibly my life, forever.

CHAPTER FORTY-SIX

Monday 2ⁿᵈ November

*Y*esterday and today have been pure torture. Clooney decided he'd move out straight away. Seeing him packing up his stuff and moving out yesterday was painful, like someone was trying to cut off my air supply. I knew deep down that it was for the best. That he was doing it, not because he wanted to hurt me, but because he knew it would hurt less in the long run. It still sucks though. It doesn't stop my heart breaking bit by bit.

Suki has also sunk into a deep depression. She's hardly eating and I swear she keeps looking at me as if to say; *this is all your fault*.

He insisted on still coming into work today even though now he's not getting accommodation as part of the deal. I decided to make myself scarce. The thought of seeing him again has my heart racing and my neck sweaty.

At first I spent the time cleaning out his bedroom and moving my stuff back in there. At least I don't have to sleep with Ella anymore. Then I did a deep clean of the kitchen.

307

Around five p.m. it suddenly feels stifling in here, like I can't bear to breathe the same air as him. I need to escape.

So I grab my trainers, coat and hat, and decide to go for a walk. I don't know how long I walk for, alone with my thoughts. Just that its almost dark by the time I'm walking back. It turns out your thoughts can be a lot scarier than you realise.

It's given me a lot of time to think about what I really want now that Clooney is out of the equation. Soon he'll find a new job and then we won't have a chef or a bar manager anymore. So that's going to affect the already shocking business. I dread having to change a barrel on my own.

I've had to think if I want to make a go of this business, really beg, plead and steal to get it going again. Or if I want to just cut my losses and go back home.

It's funny how I think of England as my home. That little pokey shared flat with Valerie. Really I grew up like a traveller, my home a camper van.

I have to consider what I want out of life. God knows I've never had a career, just relying on temp jobs to pay the bills. My parents' home schooling meant I never got any proper qualifications. They preferred the 'school of life' as they called it.

It's hard to judge whether I want to stay here, when we haven't really been given a real chance at it. Just a lot of false starts. I wonder what it would have been like without Fergus out to get us.

As I head back into the warm and toasty pub, strangely the feeling of home settles over me. Am I meant to be here? To make my home in Ireland?

Ella is nowhere to be seen. Clooney is sat with his mates. Just seeing his beautiful face has pain radiating through my heart. How can I even consider staying here without being able to have Clooney? If he asked me to move to the moon with him I would.

I frown, noticing they're playing poker again. He knows I didn't want him playing poker here. It wouldn't be my problem if it wasn't on my premises. Will he just disregard all previous things I've asked of him?

An old man comes to the bar so I run round to serve him. As I'm getting his change I notice the notes in the till. We normally keep one hundred euros in the till, but this doesn't look that much.

I give the man his change and then open the till again. I quickly and discreetly count up the notes and then the change. We're definitely fifty euros short. That's weird.

I look over to Clooney playing with his mates. He said he only played for cents, but what if he's used it to bet big tonight?

'Clooney.' He looks up at me. It breaks my heart every time I look into his eyes and see my hurt mirrored back. 'Did you take some money from the till for your game?'

His jaw physically drops. That's when I realise I've made a huge mistake. A life altering, humungous mistake. My stomach drops as he stares back at me, his eyes full of betrayal.

He excuses himself quickly from the game, walking towards me, his shoulders tensed up to his ears.

'I'm sorry,' he says, his voice a ferocious whisper. 'Did you honestly just ask me if I took money from the till to gamble with?'

I sigh, leaning on one hip. Why the hell did I have to say that out loud?

'Sorry, it's just that it's short.' I already know there's nothing I can say to try and take it back.

'And you just straight away assumed that Clooney, the dumbass gambler, must have stolen the money?' His tone might sound angry, but his eyes portray his real emotion; betrayal.

'I'm sorry.' My voice wobbles, my throat thickening with unshed tears. 'I just —'

'Yeah.' He nods, pushing away from the bar. 'You just assumed. Well I'm sorry, Phoebe, but you've just made this decision really easy for the both of us. I quit.'

No! He might as well have shot me straight in the heart.

He grabs his jacket, gives me one more scathing look and storms out, slamming the door behind him. His friends turn to stare at me with frowned faces, obviously wondering what the hell happened.

God, I feel sick. Why was my first thought that he had taken it? I know he's a gambler but I also know he's not a thief. He's a good person. I'm the worst. The damage I've just done will never be undone. I could apologise a million times but I know I've fucked up. Used his biggest weakness against him. A secret he'd trusted me with.

Ella appears, carrying some glasses. 'Hey, what's wrong?'

I sigh, my entire body aching from my loss, from my own stupidity.

'Long story.'

She nods. 'Oh, before I forget. I took fifty quid out of the till to pay the cleaner.'

Of course she did. I'm the world's biggest idiot.

CHAPTER FORTY-SEVEN

<u>Sunday 8th November</u>

*N*ot having Clooney around is pure torment. It feels like my heart has been ripped out of my body and in its place just a hard, black coal. Like I'm still going through the motions of life, but not actively living it. It's like Clooney injected colour into my life and now I've been left with drab grey.

Suki now sleeps next to the fire door, as if expecting Clooney to walk through from the kitchen any moment.

By seven p.m. we're considering whether to lock up. Not one soul is in the pub. Everyone will be at that town meeting discussing the developers.

'You know what we *could* do?' Ella asks, a mischievous glint in her eyes.

'What?' I even *sound* bored and hopeless.

'We could gate-crash the council meeting. That's where everyone is right now.'

I sigh. 'And why would we do that? Everyone hates us, remember?' I miss optimistic Phoebe. I think back to a few months ago. I used to be so determined, so full of life. Now look at me.

'For exactly that reason. We need a chance to clear our name.'

She still has faith in this all working out.

I shake my head. 'There's no way we can clear our name without throwing Clooney to the dogs, and I refuse to do that. I've hurt him enough.'

She pats my shoulder. 'Hey, don't make out he's some angel. If he'd just have opened up to you there wouldn't have been all of those doubts in your head.'

I suppose she's right. Not that it matters. Being right isn't going to help my broken heart.

'Maybe we should go,' I muse, sounding less than convinced. Do I have the energy to try again? 'Give ourselves one last chance.'

'That's the spirit!' she cheers, grabbing my shoulders and shaking them. 'Come on, we have a council meeting to ruin.'

We lock up and walk in dark to the local scouts hut, where the meeting is taking place. There's already nearly every car in town parked outside.

The big heavy doors creak open, so by the time we manage to open them all the way, the entire town has turned in their chairs to stare at us.

The speaker at the front looks down at us. 'Come in please, late comers.'

I gulp, suddenly feeling like I'm having a nightmare. I mean, just take my clothes off and this is exactly like a reoccurring nightmare of mine. Everyone starts whispering, clearly about us. Discreet people, *real* discreet.

We look around for a spare seat, but they're all taken,

every member of town squashed in. Instead we stand awkwardly at the back, grimacing.

'Actually, perhaps the sisters would like to come up and take the stand? Tell us what you think of the developers?' the speaker asks with a hopeful smile.

Ella looks terrified, eyes wide like a rabbit in headlights, all her enthusiasm she had in the pub has disappeared with our arrival. Looks like this is up to me. What else is new?

I steel my shoulders and walk to the front, Ella following on behind like a terrified lamb about to go for the slaughter. What have we got to lose?

The male speaker smiles at me. I gulp but take the stand, staring back at the sea of unimpressed faces.

'Hi everyone,' I croak. I clear my throat. *Pull yourself together, Phoebe.* 'I'm sure you all know who we are. We just actually want to take this opportunity to apologise.'

Shocked gasps fill the hall followed by gossipy whispers.

'Although our rival, Fergus, did start the war, we eventually went too far. It got out of control. But we want the support of this town. We think it's big enough for the both of us.'

Everyone starts muttering louder to themselves. I need to win them over.

'Look, my great aunt loved this town. Her diary is full of entries of the mischief she got up to in her youth and we've learnt to love it too. We'd like a fresh start and a fair chance. So who's in?'

There's rumbles of chatter as people ponder if they really do want to forgive us. I look around the faces, noticing that Fergus is missing. I need to give them another reason to help us. I look at the planned supermarket plans on the easel. That's it! Just what Clooney had suggested.

'And if you don't want this huge supermarket built by

the developers then we need a business. If we don't we'll be forced to sell to them too.'

Ella raises her eyes at me, as if to say *get you!*

A grey haired man stands up. 'Most of our loyalty understandably stand with Fergus.'

I scoff a laugh. 'He's the last person your loyalties should stand with,' I mutter.

Confused eyes meet mine.

Frank's wife, Colleen, stands up. 'Why is that, Phoebe?' she asks with a kind smile. She's trying to help me. I smile back.

'Because...' I remember my promise to Clooney. I can't tell them Fergus is in with the developers. 'Well, I can't really tell you,' I admit lamely.

'How convenient,' someone mutters loudly.

'Look, just listen to me,' I plead. 'He is *not* to be trusted. And look around, he's not here, is he? Ever wondered why?'

'He has to work, obviously,' a red haired woman says with an eye roll.

I roll my own eyes. 'Let's just say, I doubt he'd be shedding any tears if more property got bought up to build that supermarket.' Oh god, why am I still talking? I'm breaking Clooney's promise.

More murmuring.

'Are you saying he's involved with these property developers?' an old lady asks.

I shrug my shoulders. At least this way I'm not *actually* telling them it. More letting them decide for themselves.

Sean stands up. 'The girls aren't wrong.' He turns to face everyone. 'You all need to open your eyes to what's happening right under your noses.'

I smile at him, mouthing, *"Thank you."*

Kathleen, the lady I got Suki from, stands up. 'I say we

give these girls a chance. God knows Breda would have wanted us to welcome them into town. It's their birth right to live here.'

'I agree.' It's Nora, the bride who's wedding I ruined. 'Phoebe went out of her way to return something to me. A letter from my mammy.' She smiles knowingly at me. 'She deserves a fair chance.'

Ciara, Eamon's wife stands up. 'Well she told me my husband had cheated on me! Hardly a stand up neighbour in my opinion.'

Seamus and Niall try to sink into their seats.

'I have said I'm sorry for that,' I mumble into the microphone. 'I didn't want to tell you, but...'

Ella jumps in. 'But she felt morally obligated to tell a fellow female the truth about her husband. If anything she should be rewarded for that.'

'I can't explain it, but this place feels like home. I've been searching my whole life for that feeling. I'm not going to give up now. We're here to stay. We're just asking for your support.'

A few people smile back.

'On that note I think we'll leave and I hope to see you all in the pub soon.'

I grab Ella and walk out, before the tide turns against us again.

We're just opening the back door when I feel someone behind me. Clooney appears, as if from nowhere, grabs my elbow and pulls me to one side.

'Clooney,' I say, suddenly breathless. He looks just as good as always, although he has dark circles under his eyes.

'What the hell was that, Phoebe?' he snarls, his stance wide, chest pushed out.

I frown, attempting to play dumb while I think. Seeing him has thrown me off. 'What do you mean?'

'I *mean* that I told you that in confidence. Now you've told the whole town? That really is low.' He looks at me with such an intense fevered stare I know I've just added another nail in my own coffin. He'll never forgive me for this.

'They deserved to know.' I feel awful for hurting him, but I know I'm doing the right thing for this town.

'And what about me? Huh?' That vein in his forehead bulges, but his eyes are raw with vulnerability. 'I've got to move back in to live with that man. How am I going to do that now?'

'I thought you had somewhere to go?' I want him to move back in. For me to take care of him. To heal all of his emotional wounds.

He scoffs. 'Sofa surfing is not the same as having a proper place to live.'

I wish he'd have told me that. I touch his arm, but he shakes me off. It stings.

'Clooney, you know you can come back to live in the pub.'

He shakes his head. 'I don't want your sympathy. First you think I'm taking money from you and now you're outing my father. Any trust I ever had in you, no, in *us*, is over.'

CHAPTER FORTY-EIGHT

Two weeks later

<u>Monday 23rd November</u>

*I*t's been a painful couple of weeks. It's strange how I can be happy about the pub finally having enough customers to pay the bills, while also feeling such extraordinary pain. The fact I caused harm to Clooney, the last person who deserves that kind of treatment, breaks the last piece of my surviving heart. I haven't seen him since that night and I doubt I will again.

I don't have the guts to ask any of my customers if they've heard from him, or if they know what's going on. I just know I'm going through the motions of living. Getting up, getting ready, stocking the bar and putting on a smile for the customers.

'Phew,' Ella says, the second we have a slight lull in customers. 'This being busy lark is tiring as hell.'

I laugh. It sounds fake even to my ears. 'Tell me about it.'

She starts fidgeting, playing with her jeans pocket. 'Look, I've been trying to find a good time to tell you this, but there's never a good time to deliver shitty news.'

'Oh god, what is it?'

Just what I need right now. Another blow. I don't know if I can take much more.

She takes a deep breath. 'Don't hate me, okay?' She stares up at me, her brown puppy eyes already begging for forgiveness.

'I could never hate you. Just hit me with it.' I brace myself. Whatever it is I can deal with it. Nothing can be worse than how I feel right now.

'I'm leaving.'

Well shit, I didn't expect *that*. Maybe it *can* get worse.

She grimaces. 'I'm so sorry, Phoebe, but I've got to find our sisters.'

'Our sisters? You mean Dad's love children?'

'Yes.' Her face contorts apologetically. 'I just can't carry on, knowing that there's parts of us dotted around the country. I have to find them and get to know them.'

Well, shit. I'd almost succeeded in imagining they didn't exist, but apparently Ella has other ideas.

'I mean,' I sigh, 'I don't blame you. Part of me has been wondering whether we should sell up soon, now that business is booming again.'

She smiles hopefully. 'Well then come with me. We can do it together?'

I bite my lip. I know it's stupid but I don't feel like I can leave yet. Being here, although painful, still makes me feel like I have some sort of connection with Clooney. Moving to another country, well it would just feel so final. Strangely Ireland is home now. It would feel unnatural to leave.

'But you want to stay for Clooney,' she says, reading me like a book.

I smile sadly. 'I know it's stupid.'

Her face lights up, a devilish grin on his lips. 'Well, would you look who just walked in.'

I turn round to follow her line of vision to see Clooney walking up to the bar. He looks as gorgeous as ever, but those shadows under his eyes are still there.

'Phoebe,' he says quietly, hands in his pockets, his broad shoulders rounded over. 'Can I speak with you please?'

'Err... yeah...' I swallow, my mouth suddenly dry.

I can't believe he's here. Is he asking for his old job back? Maybe things with his dad have turned sour again.

He walks hurriedly round the bar, takes my hand, as if no time at all has passed between us, and leads me to the kitchen. Just feeling his warm skin on mine again lights my entire body up with a desperate yearning. The door slams behind us, the echoing sound the only one in the quiet kitchen. He lets go of my hand. I look down at it, mourning the loss of his touch.

'Hi,' I say with an awkward wave.

He smiles, like all of his worries have now been lifted from his shoulders. 'Hi.'

'So...' God, he really needs to say something before I lose my mind. Right now, in this silence, all I can do is inhale his signature scent and pray he's not here with more harsh words. I don't think I can take it.

'Right, sorry.' He shakes his head as if to clear his thoughts. 'Phoebe, I want to apologise for how I behaved. Both at you mistakenly accusing me of taking the money and outing my dad. But say what you want about the man, he's paid for me to have CBT and talking therapy these last few weeks. I wanted to finish my course before I came to see you.'

Oh, I see. It's like one of those twelve steps. Apologise to people you've wronged. He's just saying he's sorry so he can move on with the rest of his life.

'It's fine, Clooney.' I shrug. 'I deserved it.'

He shakes his head. 'No, you didn't. I only acted so angrily because I was annoyed that we couldn't be together. I wanted you, without fully letting you in and I'm sorry for that.'

'Again, it's fine.' I nod. I need him to leave before I beg him to stay. I'm so weak around him. 'It's your own business.' I shove my hands in my jeans pocket to stop reaching out for him.

'No, I want you to know.' He starts to pace, his hands in his hair. 'I was with Orla for about a year. We were naturally coming to the end when she found out she was pregnant.'

My mouth drops open. He got her pregnant? Shit.

He stops to blow out a breath. 'I shocked myself by being over the moon. We were going to be a little family and I couldn't believe my luck. After all those years of being resented by my own da I was excited to become one.'

I nod, trying to look understanding, hoping he won't stop. Like fearing moving in front of a skittish animal.

He slumps over, hands on his face. 'She miscarried at eleven weeks.'

My heart stops beating. Oh my god. My poor Clooney.

'The day it happened I was working in the pub. Orla rang and spoke to my da. Asked him to get me to call her urgently. It was a busy day and apparently he *forgot*.'

Oh my god. So this is the real reason he hates his dad so much. Why he feels so much resentment towards him.

His eyes turn glassy, tortured, as he relives the agony. 'She went through all of that alone. Losing our baby.'

I reach out to take his hand in mine. He looks down and rubs the dove on his hand.

'Is that... for the baby?' I ask. I'm sure doves are a symbol of death or grief.

He nods.

'Obviously we were heart broken.' His chin wobbles. He blows out a slow breath, trying to compose himself. 'But Orla was particularly bad and I blame myself for not being there. She got depressed and I tried to help her, I did, but she just... She tried to take her own life.'

'Oh my god.' I step closer, the overwhelming need to comfort him. No wonder he didn't want to tell me this. I see him cut open in front of me, exposing his biggest and most painful wound.

'Luckily I found her just in time. Her family didn't want anyone knowing anything about it so I've kept it from everyone for years. When she got better she decided she needed a fresh start. Away from me. She said every time she looked at me I reminded her of all she'd lost.'

That is heart breaking.

'Clooney, I'm so sorry.' I step into his chest, wrapping my arms around his waist.

Here I've been thinking he's been holding back, but really it wasn't all of his secret to tell. He was protecting Orla. Orla and their unborn baby.

He scoffs a laugh, his chest vibrating under me. 'I've spent my life being resented by my dad because I look like my mum and then the woman I loved said she couldn't look at me anymore.'

'None of that was your fault.' I press my face into his

chest, praying he believes my words. 'You realise that, right?'

He shrugs. 'Anyway, I suppose I went into a type of depression too. I just went kind of numb. When I placed my first bet I felt the first bit of life coming back into my body. Feeling alive again was addictive, and I didn't want to lose it. Not like we lost our baby.'

He wraps his arms around me hugging me back, squeezing so hard I struggle to take a breath.

'I'm so sorry I forced this out of you, Clooney. I should have been more understanding.'

He leans back to look down at me, his green eyes imploring mine. 'No, you were right. You needed to know. I *want* you to know.'

I look down at his forearms. 'Will you tell me what your other tattoos mean?'

He smiles. 'Actually one of them is pretty special. You see these mountains and lake?'

I nod. 'Yeah, it looks like our lake.'

'It is our lake. I didn't tell anyone but whenever I felt ridiculously down I'd come here, sit on the pier and think things through. Breda found me once. She was a great listener.'

'You knew her?'

He nods. 'After that whenever I needed to think she'd find me down there.'

I smile, loving how she helped him through a difficult time in his life.

'In a way I think she brought you to me.' He shakes his head. 'Anyway, sometimes just looking at this tattoo brings me back that peace. I never knew that it would also come to mean more to me because of you.'

'Really?'

'Look... I know you contemplating any kind of relationship with me is a major risk, but the truth is that you're my new addiction.'

I sigh. 'Clooney, you can't replace gambling with me.'

He smiles. 'I know that and I still haven't gambled in a hell of a long time. But I can imagine life without gambling. I can't imagine it without you. You're it for me, Phoebe. I know I'm far from a catch. I'm jobless and in debt. And, well, I know it's really selfish of me, but I've still got to ask.'

'Ask what?' I look into his eyes, immediately knowing this pub isn't my home. He is. Wherever he goes I'll follow.

He bites his bottom lip. 'Will you take a gamble on me? On us?'

I wrap my arms around his neck, my smile so big it hurts my mouth. I crush my lips to his, finally feeling at home.

'I've always been all in, baby.'

EPILOGUE

Four Years Later

I clutch onto my dad's arm as I walk down the aisle to *"Blackbird"* by the *Beatles*. We decided to get married on the pier at the lake. It means so much to both of us, it just felt right. It's early evening, dusk just setting around us, an added glow from the string lights overhead. The lake looks beautiful, all the more for the light fog settled around us.

I smile back at my sisters as we pass them. Yes all seven extra ones. Ella didn't only find them, but integrated them into our family. It's weird, but I couldn't imagine life without them now. It's nice to belong to a big blended family.

I smile at Clooney dressed in a dark grey suit his dad had made for him. Yeah, we're kind of on okay terms with Fergus now. I know, I wouldn't have believed that four years ago, but little by little we've come to some sort of unspoken agreement where we're civil for Clooney's sake.

It helped that he wrote off his thirty grand debt, on the

condition that Clooney still attends his support group every Tuesday night, and encouraged people to visit our pub. We seem to attract a younger crowd to Cock & Bull while he's kept the over fifties at The Dog and Duck. It's a fair compromise that found us fairly naturally.

It's funny to think there was a time when Clooney wouldn't even tell me about his tattoos. There's no secrets between us anymore. I know every little detail about his life, not because I've forced it out of him, but because he chooses to share it with me.

I know that the rose tattoo and the dove is to signify his and Orla's lost baby. They'd talked about calling their baby Rose, had she been a girl.

I know that the song verse on his arm, *'And in the end the love you take is equal to the love you make,'* is the last lyric in the last song of the last Beatles album. Yep, who knew he was a Beatles fan? He's even converted me, hence the music playing.

Ella takes my bouquet at the end of the pier smiling proudly. I turn to face the gorgeousness that is Clooney Breen. He takes my hand, his butterfly tattoo now having a tiny *P* on the other wing. He winks at me, and I swear, I still go weak at the knees.

'You look stunning,' he whispers into my ear under the rustic arch covered in greenery.

I beam back at him, never feeling more beautiful. Not because I'm wearing the most beautiful champagne and gold gown, unlike any other bridal style I've seen. I could be wearing sweat pants around him and I'd still feel the most stunning girl in the room. That's just how Clooney's love makes you feel. Like you're on top of the world.

Two layers of buttery, stretch silk skims over my hips like a second skin, cascading into a flared hem and train.

Over it I wear a cape and gown overlay. Two tiers of rich 3D floral hand embroidered gold and champagne tulle cascades over my shoulder and ties at my waist, falling down into a stunning train. My hair falls in loose waves, parts taken from my face and tied into plaits along with wildflowers Mum picked.

Mum is officiating the ceremony, dressed in a floaty orange dress that blows in the breeze and of course, she's barefoot. She got ordained online and insisted on *blessing our union.*

'I believe in the universe,' she begins.

Oh Jesus, here we go.

'But as a little girl Phoebe didn't believe in most things. She was always very practical, but she's finally found something to believe in; true love.'

Clooney and I grin at each other like idiots.

'The fate gods had a hand in putting her and Clooney together. She might laugh and roll her eyes over that, but deep down she knows it's true. His soul was bound to hers as soon as they were born.

But it's not just love that makes marriage, or even a long lasting relationship, work. It's time, effort and understanding.' She looks lovingly at my dad. 'It's compromise and hard work. Tough times and tears. But through it, if you can find that love and laughter, it will see you through it all.'

She rambles on for a bit longer before we say our traditional vows, albeit the promise to obey him, and exchange the plain white gold rings.

'I now pronounce you husband and wife.'

Clooney grins at me before smashing the glass in the bag on the ground. A little nod to his Jewish heritage. The crowd cheers raucously as he leans down and kisses me like he hasn't seen me for years, instead of hours.

We turn, raising our joined hands victoriously, to the applaud of the entire town. Then we walk down the pier, past our immediate family and into the green land where the rest of the town claps for our union.

It's crazy to think how they've now welcomed me into their community. It helped that we decided to host some free community events in the pub to bring in more of a crowd.

The scout hut got bought up by the developers, but luckily everyone else is staying firm about not selling to them. For now, all development is frozen. We now host all the kids after school clubs, which means the parents have a drink while they wait and then most of them treat their little ones to our kids dinner deal.

We get hugged and kissed by almost every member of town as we pass through them. We lead everyone back to the pub garden which now no longer resembles a jungle. The same string lighting that the town helped us set up down at the lake hangs over us. We decided we wanted a fun festival vibe for our reception. We're calling it Cloobe. Clooney tried to make it Cloodles, but I told him I didn't want to explain the Poodles nickname to everyone.

Everyone arrives, taking a glass of prosecco, cramming in, over spilling into the car park and lake.

Clooney dings his glass. 'We're not bothering with speeches, because who wants to listen to a load of bollocks?' Everyone laughs. 'I just want to thank everyone for coming and for helping set this up. I also want to thank my beautiful wife, Phoebe.' He looks down at me adoringly, his eyes filled with warmth that I can feel deep in my bones. Everyone cheers. He wraps his arm round my waist. 'I'm nothing without you, Poodles,' he says quietly, so only I can hear. He turns back to the crowd. 'Now let's dance!'

He leads me into the centre of the grass which is our make shift dance floor, surrounded by hay bales for seating. *"Til There Was You"* by *The Beatles* blasts out of the speakers. He grabs me round the waist while I wrap my arms around his neck.

He takes my hand and holds it to his chest as he sways us. He mouths the words *'til there was you,'* every time its sung. Goosepimples rise all over my body. This moment right now, in his arms, wearing his wedding ring, surrounded by my friends and family is what I'll remember about this day. The amazing intense feeling of happiness and contentment.

"Took you long enough..." I start at the voice in my head, whirling us both around. Clooney's soft gaze drifts over my face.

"What's wrong?"

I shake me head. "I thought I heard something."

He continues humming, moving us in time to the beat.

"I think I can leave now, my pub is in the right hands."

"Breda?" I breathe her name. But she's gone, and I never knew she was there. Clooney gives me the most beautiful smile and I know she's right, her pub is in the right hands. Clooney's and mine.

I know that together we can go through anything and find the other side. My whole life I've been looking for a place to call my true home. Now I have it, my heart bound to this man and this town.

Turns out Great Aunt Breda had a master plan all along.

The End

ACKNOWLEDGMENTS

Thank you so much for taking the time to read my book.
Reviews mean so much to us indie authors, so I'd really
appreciate a quick review on Amazon/Goodreads.

Thank you first of all to my family for their continued
support. That means me being a sleep deprived zombie
mum, unable to form a complete sentence and having to
take naps to keep up with my crazy writing hours. It can't be
easy living with that!

Thank you to Anna Bloom for her insightful input and
editing skills. Her suggestions made the book all it could be.

Tammy Clarke pulled another one out of the bag with this
beautiful cover. I just love it!

Thank you to all the readers and bloggers who take time out
of their crazy schedules to share my posts and help spread
the word. Without you I'd be nothing.

Thank you to Nicola Cassells, my cousin in Ireland, who helped research so much for me. If it wasn't for her my characters would probably sound Scottish not Irish!

Special thanks to my Indie author friends that are constantly there for me when I need a rant/share/funny message. You guys rock.

ALSO BY LAURA BARNARD

The Debt & the Doormat Series

The Debt & the Doormat

The Baby & the Bride

Porn Money & Wannabe Mummy

One Month Til I Do Series

Adventurous Proposal

Marrying Mr Valentine

Babes of Brighton Series

Excess Baggage

Love Uncovered

Bagging Alice

Standalones

Tequila & Tea Bags

Dopey Women

Road Trip

Once Upon a Wish-mas

Heath, Cliffs & Wandering Hearts

Sex, Snow & Mistletoe (short story)